Zombies!
Book 3

"Violence Solves Everything"

R S Merritt

This book is dedicated to my beautiful (extremely patient and understanding) wife and family.

Cover Design By:
Harry Lamb

Table of Contents

Chapter 1: The Laughter of Children

Eric recognized he was completely paranoid at this point. His ulcers probably had ulcers. He pushed his aching body up from the floor where they were playing chutes and ladders and excused himself to make a quick round of the house. The board game had the girls all excited and laughing. Eric loved to see them being children for once. Especially in light of how recently they'd lost Brenda and how close they'd all come to being taken away to some sort of concentration camp setup by the apocalyptic red necks running this part of the world.

Knees creaking and back kinking up Eric walked slowly around the inside of the house. He stopped to peer out into the darkness that had settled over them like a thick dark comforter. He was looking for anything that might give away enemies moving in on them. They'd chosen this house pretty much at random. He was hoping the men who'd tried to take the girls had all died back at the other house they'd abandoned. The last time he'd seen the house it'd looked like the Zombies had completely surrounded it. Most of the time once that happened the occupants had a high probability of becoming Zombie chow. Especially with all the noise they'd made in that final shoot out. They must've attracted Zombies from half the county.

Not seeing anything when he peeked out the windows Eric quietly padded up the stairs to the loft. He tried to avoid breathing when he got to the musty, mold-covered room at the top of the stairs. A window had broken in the loft and enough rain had poured in sideways during the frequent Florida afternoon thunderstorms to gradually soak the floor of the entire room.

The aftermath was a squishy, moldy mess that had him wondering again about the health hazards of inhaling mold spores. He walked across the waterlogged carpet to where the window was on the far side of the loft. They'd pulled the curtains tight on the window earlier when they'd cleared the house. It was standard practice to make sure no Zombies were sitting around waiting to surprise them. It only took a Zombie sitting up in the shower beside you the first time you were trying to relieve yourself in a dark bathroom to get you in the habit of checking houses thoroughly before relaxing in them. Eric was trying to avoid creaky spots in the floor but with all the water damage that was pretty much impossible. Cussing under his breath at the amount of noise the floor was making Eric posted up by the window. Standing there as quietly as possible he looked out into the front yard and over at the two-lane road in front of the house.

He looked around for about a minute. When he still didn't see anything, he began to back away from the window. The top of the hedges down by the road twitched momentarily. It happened so fast Eric wasn't positive he'd even seen anything happen. If something had happened then most likely it was a squirrel, an errant draft of wind or even a lone Zombie stuck in the shrubbery. Eric stared hard for another minute at the spot he thought he'd seen the motion but nothing else happened. Wracked with indecision he took the stairs down to the ground level as quickly as he could without making a lot of noise.

When he walked into the living room the look on his face must've tipped the girls off. He watched as the laughter died down and the smiles melted from their faces. He walked to the front of the room and ducked down to take a look out of that window to see if he saw anything. From this lower angle he could barely tell where he thought the hedge had moved before. He didn't see anything that looked out of place, but he couldn't get over that little movement he'd picked up on. He motioned for Caitlyn and Myriah to crawl over to where he was.

"I thought I saw something when I was upstairs. I think you should take the girls and fade back a few hundred feet into the woods while I go and check. If you hear gunshots make a run for the lake house." Eric whispered out his plan. The only rendezvous point he could think of being the one they'd decided to leave in the messages to their parents in the letters to be dropped off at their old house.

"Why don't you just come with us?" Caitlyn asked.

"I need to be here to slow them down and give you time to get away." Eric answered.

"No! We just lost our grandma. There's no reason why you can't just slip out the back with us. There might not even be anyone out there." Caitlyn wasn't giving in. She was horrified of the idea of going out alone with the kids. The idea of having to wait in some other moldy house to see if Eric showed up or not. The idea of that responsibility falling on her shoulders was just too much.

"There may be people moving in on this house right now. If we all go out the back they're just going to come through and come right after us. I need you to get the kids and get a few minutes head start. I'll come right behind you. I can move faster than you can with the kids in tow. The sooner you get out of here the sooner I can get out of here. Make sense?" Eric finished up emphatically. He felt like time was getting short.

Caitlyn must've felt the same. She started to try again to get him to come with them but then gave up and just started gathering the kids together. They all knew enough to keep their supplies in a manner that they could gather it up and be out of a house within minutes. In this case they'd started gathering their stuff as soon as Eric started talking to Caitlyn. They were all standing there now waiting for Caitlyn to gather her belongings so they could get rolling. Caitlyn angrily shoved her stuff in her bag. She was shaking with emotion. Her eyes were shiny with unshed tears.

Eric questioned himself. He looked over at the discarded chutes and ladders game. Had he really seen anything moving in the hedges? It'd happened so fast it really might not be anything. Did he want to make these kids troop out into the forest in the middle of the night? There were Zombies in the woods. They knew that for a fact. Did he send them out there while he stayed behind? Should he go try to see if it really was someone standing in the hedges that he'd seen. Looking at the kids he knew he couldn't risk it. If his gut told him there was danger, he had to roll with it.

"You guys listen to Cait ok? I'll be right behind you. We're going to go head for that nice house on the pond you told me about. The one you used to go to with your mom and swim in the pool. I love you guys. Go ahead and get going. I'll be right behind you." Eric was smiling as he ushered them out the sliding glass doors. He watched as they skirted the green pool in the back and disappeared through the plastic fence into the wooded area behind the home.

He let his smile fade from his face. He replaced it with his game face as he hoisted his own pack up on his back and made sure the magazine was slammed home in his rifle. With the ammunition he'd found on the Zombie he'd killed out in the woods he had enough to hold the house against a decently armed group of attackers for a few minutes at least. He really hoped he was wrong about someone being out there.

He quickly moved up the stairs in the house and back into the loft. His focus on the window drowning out any random concerns about mold spores this time. He moved low and fast over to the window to look out. He was praying he wouldn't see anything. His plan was to stand his post in the loft for another minute and then head out to catch up to the girls. He was hoping to join up with them with no issues and then spend the night trekking over to the lake house they'd told him about. It'd be a miserable night spent stumbling through briars and muck but at the end of it they'd hopefully be in a safer location. Hopefully they could use it as a base for a little while. He'd just have to take a side mission to drop off the info at their parent's old house like he'd promised.

Letting his eyes adjust to the ambient light in the room he gazed out the loft window down on the street below. The soft moonlight revealed a two-lane blacktop covered with the standard road litter of the apocalypse. Eric was on the verge of getting up and leaving when a party of men came riding down the road on bikes. In the dark from this distance he couldn't tell much about them. The men were moving quietly. When they got close enough, they dismounted the bikes and dispersed quickly to approach the house. Eric lined up a shot and squeezed the trigger. The sound of the shot shattered the quiet like the first peal of thunder from an afternoon thunderstorm.

Not bothering to look to see if he'd hit his target Eric pulled the trigger twice more before turning and sprinting down the stairs. He smashed into the hallway wall opposite the bottom of the stairs and bounced off like a pinball being struck by one of the paddles. Careening down the hallway he slid into a firing position in front of the down stairs window. He fired off two random shots in rapid succession from the window before turning and hauling ass out the open sliding glass door leading into the backyard.

The sounds of shots fired kicked off behind him as the attackers went from stealth mode to attack mode. Eric was hoping the attackers would think at least two people were set up to shoot at them. One shooter on the top floor in the loft and one downstairs by the window he'd fired out of. He was hoping they'd shoot at the house for a few minutes before deciding to rush in. He planned on being long gone by the time the attackers had moved into the house and cleared it.

He ran out the open sliding glass doors so fast he almost ended up in the pool. Catching his balance before toppling into the nasty green water he spun to his right to run around the pool and out the fence for the woods. A man wearing camouflage stepped out from around the side of the house. He was sweeping a rifle barrel across the back porch. The barrel passed right over Eric without the man pulling the trigger. Eric and the man both realized what was going on at the same time. The man jerking his weapon back to aim at Eric while Eric pulled the trigger several times on his rifle. He had the weapon pointed in the general direction of the camouflage wearing attacker.

Eric stumbled backwards and almost fell into the pool again when a bullet caught him in the wrist. It felt like someone had swung a hammer and hit him dead on right at the top of his left hand. He held on to his M-16 and grimaced through the pain. He knew he needed to keep moving or he was going to get caught and then his wrist would be the least of his worries. Holding the rifle in his right hand he pointed it in the direction of the man who'd just shot him. He didn't see the guy standing there anymore so assumed he'd either shot him or the guy had ducked back around the side of the house.

Trying to avoid being shot Eric went the opposite way around the pool as fast as he could. Reaching the edge of the yard he ducked through the missing section of the fence to get to the woods. He stopped for a few seconds on the other side of the fence and waited to see if the pursuers would come barreling around the sides of the house. A flashlight beam cut through the darkness on the opposite side that he'd run around. Ignoring the pain in his wrist Eric waited to see if the man would be dumb enough to stick his head around and take a look. A second later the man with the flashlight stuck his head around to take a look.

Eric peeled off two fast shots in semi-automatic mode then turned and ran into the woods to catch up with the girls. The gunfire had died down enough that the screams of the Zombies were now clearly audible in the cool night air. The loud noises had woken them from whatever hole they'd dug themselves into to nest for the night. Now they'd be running full force towards the sound of the gunfire. Eric was hoping that'd force the men who'd just attacked them to take their ball and go home. To continue to attack at this point would just bring more Zombies and increase the likelihood of dying.

Eric ran another thirty yards in the general direction of the lake house. It wasn't easy running through the briars and weeds at night. Every step seemed to include inhaling spider webs and stomping in a puddle. Briars and weeds tore at his clothes. It was a journey made even more miserable by his inability to use his left arm to move obstacles out of the way as he ran. After he'd made it deeper into the woods he turned and sat down. He tried pulling off his pack with the intent of bandaging up his wrist but the pain from his wrist was so bad he wasn't able to get his pack pulled off. He knew he'd never be able to sit there and tighten a bandage around it.

Giving up on administering his own first aid he scrambled back to his feet and turned to continue to move in the direction of the lake house. His big hope now was to catch the girls. They were going to need him to defend them from the Zombies that were bound to be moving through the forest towards the sound of the gunshots. He needed the girls to help him get his wrist bandaged up. He took a look back the way he'd come but didn't see any signs of pursuit. He was hopeful the rednecks would finally learn their lesson and just leave them alone. Hopeful but realizing that so far, their pursuers hadn't shown a lot of common sense so he found he couldn't be too optimistic. The best course of action was going to be to find the girls and get the hell out of Dodge.

He had run about ten more yards into the woods when he heard a different tone to the screeching coming from his left. Not really knowing why he was doing it he turned and ran in the direction of the Zombie cries that seemed different to him. Two steps into switching directions his instincts were validated when he heard the scream of a young girl in terror intermingled with the cries of the Zombies. He couldn't tell who it was crying out, but he poured on the speed with a gigantic burst of energy fueled by his fear for the girls.

He burst through a wall of briars and forward rolled into a quarter inch of disgusting water covering an open muddy section of the woods. His tumble forward brought down a skinny, dirt covered Zombie who'd been howling at the girls. Eric grabbed the things head and shoved it under the water. He saw two more of the Zombies had turned from where they'd been fixated on the girls and were coming towards him now. Not having time to properly drown the demon he'd managed to accidentally take down Eric jumped to his feet in the mud and brought the stock of the M-16 hard down on the things head. That Zombie dropped back down into the water and didn't seem to be a threat any longer.

Eric turned to face the two he'd seen coming at him when a third Zombie came out of nowhere and tackled him to the ground from behind. Eric twisted in the air and landed hard on his back on a root. His left wrist was screaming in pain. His back joined his left wrist in screaming in pain from the collision with the hard root. He brought up his right hand to grab the Zombie on top of him by the neck. Face to face he could see the youth in the face of the maddened demon trying to snap at him. He had no clue where his rifle had gone. He was hoping he hadn't broken it bringing the stock down so hard on that other Zombies skull.

He pushed up as hard as he could and tried to roll but the Zombie on top of him was moving along with his motions. The other Zombie would be on top of him any second now and it'd be all over anyway. From somewhere behind him he heard Caitlyn screaming at him, but he couldn't tell what she was saying. Bracing himself for the onslaught of teeth and nails he waited for the other Zombies to fall on him and start ripping him apart. He was screaming now as loud as he could for the girls to run. He was hoping that if the Zombies were focused on eating him alive, they'd miss the girls making a quick exit.

Bullets ripped through the Zombie on top of Eric sending it sliding lifelessly into the swampy water beside him. More shots rang out in the small clearing. The shots were answered by the screams of the damned all around them. Eric struggled to his feet alternating between fighting off the blackout that kept trying to pull him back to the ground and the massive pain from his wrist that kept rearing up to bite him. He finally got to a standing position and saw that Myriah was helping the little kids down from a large tree while Caitlyn was standing in the middle of the clearing turning in a circle holding the M-16. The ground was littered with the bodies of the Zombie's she'd killed. The problem was that within minutes there were probably going to be hundreds of Zombies storming through the woods hunting for the source of the gunfire. Any Zombie within earshot would be headed this way. Any Zombie within earshot of a Zombie that was within earshot and decided to screech out loud would head this way as well.

Completely disoriented Eric limped over to Caitlyn. She went to hand the gun back to him and he shook his head. He handed her the extra magazine he had in his pocket.

"You hang on to that. My wrist is all messed up. We need to get the hell out of here right now and no more talking. You remember the way we need to go to get to the lake? Take us that way but deviate if you need to. I'll bring up the rear and watch the little kids. Now go. We've got zero time to screw around."

Caitlyn nodded at him then took a second to check the number of bullets left in the magazine. Satisfied with that she turned and led them through the hole in the briars Eric had made when he'd barreled into the clearing. Eric watched her proudly as he helped Myriah shepherd the younger girls along behind Caitlyn. He loved how naturally Caitlyn had checked the ammunition left in the weapon before moving into the woods. He'd tried drilling that into his young charges every chance he got but it was nice seeing it had actually sunk in. Even with all the pressure she was under she'd remembered that small but critical lesson.

Myriah had to do most of the work with Doreen, Ali and Zoey to get them moving in the correct direction. Eric was pretty busy just trying to stay upright. With the adrenaline starting to fade the blood loss and water soaking his clothes were taking their toll on him. Normally he'd have picked up Doreen and carried her but now that was left to Myriah. Ali, his niece, and Zoey were picking their way carefully along the trail Myriah and Caitlyn were breaking for them. All around them they could hear the cries of the Zombies as they converged on the clearing they'd just vacated. Caitlyn had the rifle in her hands and knew how to use it. She also knew pulling the trigger would make all the Zombies currently heading towards the spot behind them adjust and head straight towards them again.

Muddy and miserable the six of them tried to move as quickly and quietly as they could through the woods. It was a race now to see if they'd stumble on a random Zombie before they were able to get far enough away from the scene of the shooting to be safe. A nearby screech encouraged Eric to summon the strength to force himself to take a more active role. He took Doreen from Myriah and put the tired, terrified little girl over his shoulder. This let Myriah focus more on helping the other two little girls move through the woods.

Ready to drop Doreen to the ground and attempt to pull a knife to attack any Zombies who decided to pop out of the woods Eric gamely continued stumbling forward. At this point it had turned into nothing more than a test of will power. How long could each of them continue to put one foot in front of the other. How long could a couple of pre-tweens, a toddler, a couple of teens and a beat to hell middle aged man evade a horde of Zombies in the middle of a swamp? Eric knew they were at lottery winning odds to still be alive as it was. If they survived the night, they'd definitely hit the power ball.

Hoping they'd be able to make it into the woods and find the lake without running into any additional threats Eric kept them moving. He was stepping over a stump and trying to brush a bunch of spider webs off a squirming Doreen when a Zombie stepped out of the weeds right in front of him. The Zombie stared at him for a second like it was just as surprised as he was. Eric let go of Doreen who clawed at his body the entire way to the ground. Ignoring all that Eric fumbled his knife out of the sheath he had on his shoulder and punched the knife forward as hard as he could. No skill or aim or much of anything other than just a tired man putting everything he had into killing the damned thing that'd gotten in his way.

His bladed haymaker ripped about half the Zombies neck off. It toppled over gurgling with blood shooting out the side of its neck like a plastic bottle of catsup getting stepped on by an elephant. Scooping up Doreen after he'd shoved the bloody knife back into its sheath Eric continued on the night time march through hell. He was determined to do his best to keep them all alive. No matter what it took from him. If Brenda was looking down and watching them from above, he felt like she'd approve.

Chapter 2: Long is the Road and Short is the Life

Kyler stared over at Chief Presley. He was anxiously waiting for the command to run for their lives. No way they'd be able to stay here. Zombies were everywhere and the man in the ditch beside him was missing the top half of his head. Kyler could see the man's brains. This was the same man he'd been trading your momma jokes with less than eight hours ago. Like Zombies weren't bad enough someone was taking shots at them with a high-powered rifle. Someone who was a good shot and had a damn nice rifle. Looking at the bugs walking across the exposed brains of his comrade in arms Kyler idly wondered if there was a way to get issued a helmet. Hell, he decided he'd go ahead and find himself a military surplus store and get one if he made it out of there alive. He leaned back as the ground exploded around him and the screeching of the Zombies grew closer.

Flashing back twenty-four hours they'd been notified that they were needed to go investigate a mayday call at a settlement about twenty miles from the one they'd been resting at. Chief Presley had woken them up and given them ten minutes to assemble and be ready to ride. Still mostly asleep they'd ridden mountain bikes a few miles up the road to a staged vehicle. This one was an old station wagon so at least it had plenty of room in it. They'd put it in neutral to push it up the ditch while the chief went to find the concealed battery and red jug of gas they'd need. Kyler remembered sitting in the backseat of that station wagon as the calm before the storm.

Prior to that it'd been a couple of weeks of settlement hopping. He'd been given booklets to study to learn more about the roving patrol roles and responsibilities as well as regular sit-down sessions with the chief. One thing he had going for him was most of the other guys were newly recruited as well. So, at least he wasn't the new guy on the block like he'd been when they enlisted him in the salvaging crew back at the settlement. On the other hand, it was kind of scary that they were all learning on the fly. As the chief explained it, they were the men responsible for providing a safety net to the settlements. The men who were thrown at danger wherever it popped up.

The core values of the patrols were military. Military doctrine was heavy in the training, but no one was prepared for this. You figured maybe five percent of the military had actually seen action in the last few years before all of this started. The special operations teams from the various branches of the military would be familiar with sneaking around surrounded by the enemy. They were even experienced at keeping different villages supplied with weapons, but did that experience really translate directly into surviving an America overrun with Zombies? The skills they had as far as survival and fighting absolutely translated well in this new world. As far as building out a successful post-apocalyptic community everyone was playing it by ear. A very few had specific training in that sort of thing, but even that training was suspect as it was based on a lot on theory and brainstorming by military think tanks. None of whom had really been considering an actual Zombie Apocalypse.

The training had been pretty rudimentary up to this point. The chief assured them once they did a circuit and make it back to headquarters, they'd have more time for formal training. A lot of that training was around why they did things the way they were doing them with an emphasis on making suggestions if you saw a better way. The chief was tight-lipped with details around the location of headquarters. About all they'd gotten out of him so far was to confirm it existed and that it was called central command by most of the patrols. The chief had also kept silent about how everyone else in his patrol had died and he'd managed to survive.

None of this really mattered right now to Kyler. Other than to retrace his steps to how he'd managed to end up pinned down in a ditch next to his headless companion with a bunch of over-excited Zombies headed his way. It's not like he had much else to do other than focus on not lifting his head above the edge of the ditch where the sniper would blow it off. He had no desire to sport the same haircut as his dead ditch buddy. Trying not to piss himself as bullets slammed into the ground around him and the screeching of the Zombies kept getting closer Kyler kept his eyes glued to the chief. The chief was evidently waiting for some sign from above that it was time to haul ass out of there.

Chief Presley finally waved his hand in a circle and stood up and started firing towards the enemy. The rest of them all got up and hauled ass for the tree line on the other side of the road. Kyler ran for all that he was worth even as the man a step or two in front of him stumbled and fell forward. Kyler had seen the puff of red coming out of the back of the guy's jacket before he had even heard the sound of the shot. The sniper must be hanging out a long way from them if there was that much distance between the shot hitting and the sound of the shot hitting. Kyler poured everything he had into running as fast as he could. He tried to snap his head from side to side as he ran to make himself a harder target. He knew he was only alive because the sniper had randomly decided to shoot the guy next to him instead of him.

He hit the wood line. The bark of the tree directly beside his head exploded showering him with splinters and pieces of bark. He dove forward into the woods trying to get as deep into the cover provided as possible. A few more bullets pierced the woods leaving trails of destroyed branches. Then the shots stopped and all they had to fear was the Zombies sprinting into the woods to try to kill them. The chief was nowhere in sight. Kyler moved towards the one guy he'd seen make it into the woods. He'd recognized him as one of the men in the patrol he'd connected with on the long hikes between the settlements. Guy's name was Sean and he'd done some time in the USMC. He hadn't been Force Recon or anything like that, but he'd done basic training and he knew how to march and shoot.

That training was showing now as Kyler's reward for going to check on him was getting a rifle barrel shoved in his face until Sean recognized him. Kyler had his hands in the air wondering if Sean was going to shoot him when Sean suddenly shoved his rifle barrel up onto Kyler's shoulder. Sean rested the rifle on Kyler's shoulder and blasted away at a group of Zombies who'd gotten into the woods behind them.

"Let's go!" Sean yelled after possibly causing permanent hearing damage to Kyler's right ear. Not able to hear a damn thing but getting the gist of the communication Kyler fell in behind Sean. They started tearing through the woods and weeds towards the rendezvous point.

One thing the training and common sense dictated in this brave new world was to always have a fallback spot. Operations went south so often that the chief was fond of saying every time something worked out the way it was supposed to, he was completely surprised. In this case they'd been ordered to go check out a settlement that'd sent in a cryptic mayday saying Zombies were surging on them and they were taking incoming fire. If ever a statement sounded like it required a fallback site that was it.

They'd made it into the settlement easily enough. Moving slowly and stealthily through the night they'd gone under the wires and made their way in to see what was going on. As quickly and easily as they'd gotten in, they'd turned around to leave. Zombies had been everywhere. Some of them still chewing on what was left of the people of the settlement. Some of the Zombies wandering around had that fresh new look of a recently turned human. Dead bodies were scattered around. Some of the ones they'd been able to check out before being forced to leave had been killed by bullets versus the teeth of the Zombies.

What'd forced them to eventually leave had been the sniper fire they'd started taking. It'd riled up all the Zombies who'd nested in the area. It'd also led to them having to carry two of their teammates out. That had required dragging them through mud to get them under the barbed wire. The guy Kyler had helped drag left a good bit of his skin on that barbed wire. That sacrifice had been nothing compared to the big chunk of skull and brain he'd lost in the ditch later that night. The recruits in the patrol with no military experience had been extremely freaked out. They were the lucky ones. The ones with military experience knew that for snipers to be making those kinds of shots they were well armed, and they had this site dialed in. Infrared and night vision had to have been in play as well since the light from the moon was basically non-existent.

In the end Kyler and Sean made it back to the rendezvous point and didn't see anyone else for almost two hours. They'd just about given up on anyone else showing and been making plans of where to go the next day when Presley limped up to the house. After helping him inside and getting him settled on the couch with a warm bottle of tequila and a full can of cheese whiz they found in the cupboard they asked him what they should do now.

"We keep fighting. I know I haven't told you guys a lot about central command or what we're trying to do but basically, it's just that. We're just a bunch of good guys who are trying to keep the fight going. We're trying to fight for people to live. We want to drive out all the infected and get the land ready for everyone to live again. That's it on our side but there's a lot of other groups out there trying to take control. People who see this as a message from God that their ideology is right. I can only imagine how crazy it is in some of the middle eastern and third world countries but even here in the US it's gotten nuts."

"What do you mean by nuts?" Sean asked. Kyler listening intently as well despite his muffled yawns. They hadn't slept in over a day now.

"You guys were recruited to be in the patrols that go between the settlements. There're other patrols that get sent out to see what the rest of the world is doing and to gather supplies from strategic locations or whatever. A lot of that stuff is 'need to know' and we don't necessarily need to know it. What you do need to know is that the crazies have come out in force. Down south there's a bunch of guys trying to start a modified third Reich or just a new confederate states of America depending on who you ask. Out west there's groups who've gone back to the Indian days. There're groups running around who look like they just escaped from the Renaissance Faire. Which makes sense when you think about having your body covered in armor and not making a lot of noise by shooting guns. Just all kinds of crazy all over the place."

"So, what do we do?" Kyler asked the question again.

"The same thing. We keep fighting. We keep putting one foot in front of the other and we keep fighting for what we think is right. I can tell you right now there's a ton of people who've got your back. Worse case we hold the territory we have. Best case we're able to expand before these people with the weird ideologies take over too much land and infect it with their crazy. It sucks that with actual Zombies roaming the earth we have to worry about fighting one another but there it is."

"How often do settlements get shot up like that?" Sean asked.

"Not that much. We tell people the rule that you can only have forty people per settlement is to keep the noise levels down, but I think another part of it is so that we only lose forty people at a time to these attacks. As far as I know we don't even know who's doing the attacking. Just that they seem to move in the same way each time. Snipers and Zombies and it's over before we can get protection to the settlement."

With that the chief volunteered Kyler for the first watch and him and Sean racked out. Kyler stood up for the watch since he was sure he'd fall asleep if he sat down. He walked the house waiting for his turn to sleep. His mind haunted by the faces of the newly turned he'd seen earlier that night. The vision of the guy's head beside him exploding in the ditch kept playing in a loop too. Kyler decided he'd make a difference. He dedicated himself to serving something larger than himself that night. Not because he felt like it but because if he didn't focus on something besides himself, he was afraid he wouldn't be able to hold it together much longer.

Chapter 3: It's Electric!

"Accuracy is going to be on you guys, but I think you know enough to be dangerous." Randy said after the third day of instructing the old rich people how to shoot and loot. He was getting really tired of references to clay pigeons and cousins who'd graduated from West Point. If only one of these geezers had graduated from West Point maybe they could've just handed over half the guns and been on their way to the airport.

Kelly was fuming at the delay. She figured the training should've taken about twenty minutes and then they should have been on their way. Randy hadn't been that optimistic but even to him three days seemed pretty excessive. Tony had a decent amount of knowledge but none of them were gun experts. These people just kept asking questions. They wanted to know what the world was like outside their fence. They wanted to know every detail about how him and Kelly and Tony had managed to survive for this long.

It didn't help that most of them were raging alcoholics. That included the guy who was supposed to fly them to Florida. Tony was happy enough to jump in and sample the really good bourbons they had. His behavior really irritated Kelly since she was trying to prod everyone along and Tony was busy getting drunk with them. That irritation didn't stop Kelly from enjoying select bottles out of the extensive wine collection. These people had the good stuff. Randy and Kelly had always stuck within the twenty to thirty-dollar range for a nice bottle of wine. The stuff they were drinking at night from the wine cellars here would have been price prohibitive back in the days when money still mattered.

On the third day Kelly finally told Gordon, the man who'd professed to being able to fly a plane, that it was go time. She felt like they were just waffling to keep them there as long as they could. After a spirited conversation it was decided they'd head for the airport in the morning.

"You really felt the need to tell him you'd shove his plane up his ass and launch him to the moon if he didn't get off his ass and take us to Florida? There wasn't a nicer way to put it?" An amused Randy asked Kelly as they headed for their room with a couple of bottles of reserve reds. Tony had immediately headed down to the card room to get hammered with his new found geriatric poker buddies following the tense confrontation. They wouldn't be seeing him again for a while.

"The old bastard was going to have us sitting here explaining how to line up the sight picture on a rifle until he died of old age. I had to say something. What else did they think they were going to possibly learn from us. Hell, we don't really know that much."

"I know this is the kind of wine we never would've bought back in the old days. I know the ceiling fan actually works in our room. I know this may be our last night with any kind of privacy for a while." Randy winked at Kelly and moved in for a kiss. She slid neatly out of the way.

"I'm thinking you go heat up a tub of water and bring it up here so I can take a nice long hot bath and really enjoy this expensive wine."

"Your wish is my command and such." Randy said with a bow and some twirls of his arm. The he set off to go get the water heated up for her. One of the wonders of the modern world was that the solar cells on the roof of this house actually gave them the ability to utilize the appliances in the house to heat up water for bathing. The house was even old enough to have its own cistern to collect fresh rain water for them to use.

The lights were cutoff as was the air conditioning. Basically, they'd pulled the breakers out on anything that made any noise that may attract the Zombies. That still left plenty of modern conveniences for them though. Tony had been like a little kid when someone had shown him there was indeed a working ice maker available in the house. It was amazing how used to things like icemakers everyone had gotten. Take them away and life sucked. Randy lugged the hot tub of boiling water upstairs where Kelly had the tub about a third of the way filled up with the cistern water. He added the first big bucket of hot water and set off to get another one after soliciting her promise that she'd make it worth his while.

The next morning Randy woke up with a bit of a headache and some confused memories of the night before. He smiled and kissed Kelly as the pleasant memories solidified a bit more for him. She woke up after the second kiss and sent him to go get breakfast while she got ready for the day. The way the old house had been plumbed there was even the ability to flush the toilets. Talk about an extravagance!

Randy went down to the large kitchen and began looking around for something to heat up for breakfast. Gordon was already in the kitchen opening a giant can of kidney beans. Randy guessed that meant it was kidney beans for breakfast for everyone. Randy had no desire to see Kelly's mood change. She'd been happy last night as the date had finally been set for them to get moving towards Florida again.

"You ready to fly out today?" Randy asked Gordon after helping himself to a bowl of the kidney beans.

"Just as soon as we go gather some supplies." Gordon responded.

"We're leaving the weapons. You guys should be able to go raid some of the houses along the bay here and gather plenty of supplies." Randy said in exasperation. He was damned if they were going to be delayed another few days collecting cans of beans for these geezers.

"I can't just fly away from here without making sure this place is fully stocked. You agreed to help us gather supplies." Gordon said. His voice rising with indignation as he spoke.

"My kids are down in Florida right now waiting for their daddy to come save them. Your people are just going to have to go find their own canned food and liquor. We're driving you to the airport today and then you're flying us down to Florida. Once you drop us off in the land of sunshine and palm trees, I don't really give a shit what you do but that's what's happening today. Are we cool?" Randy felt like getting in Gordons face and screaming at him, but he held himself back. He held himself back until Gordon continued to just stand there not saying anything.

Randy grabbed Gordon by the front of his shirt and yanked him, so they were face to face. "I asked you if we're cool asshole. I suggest you say yes and go pack your toothbrush and some extra boxers for the trip. We head for the airport in an hour. You have a problem with that?"

"Nope. I'll be happy to fly you to Florida and leave you there." Gordon responded dryly as he turned on his heel and pulled his dignity back around him to go pack a bag.

Randy took a few deep breaths to calm down then went to grab Kelly and Tony. Kelly was easy as she was already up and moving. She looked like she was going to be auditioning for one of those female assassin movies. She was strapping weapons to every conceivable place on her body she could get a strap to stay attached to. Randy figured he'd end up carrying her bag for her since it was probably too full of ammunition for her to actually pick up. God help anyone who got in between Kelly and the kids once they landed.

After making sure his stuff was ready to go Randy went down the hallway to Tony's room. It was empty so he went to check out the game room. The game room was the last place he'd seen Tony headed. He went down the stairs and flicked on the light switch after staring into the dark room for a minute. It was weird how quickly he'd forgotten the old habit of reaching for the light switch as soon as he walked into a dark room. He was actually fumbling for his flashlight before realizing that he should be able to just flip on the light switch.

The miracle of light coming on in a room at the flick of a switch was slightly ruined by the sight of Tony passed out on a pool table. He was holding a bottle of rum in one hand that'd spilled all over the top of the table. It was a good thing they were leaving soon. After looking around the room and sniffing a few times Randy got the idea that Tony probably wouldn't be allowed back in the game room anytime soon. He walked over and poked Tony softly in the shoulder. When that failed to wake him up, he smacked him in the face.

For a hungover guy who'd been passed out on a pool table Tony moved really fast. Randy jumped back out of the way narrowly dodging the thrust-out knife Tony had pulled from somewhere. Tony jumped off the table and pulled a pistol before finally recognizing Randy through his bloodshot eyes.

"Good morning." Tony mumbled as he put away the pistol. Once he'd snapped the pistol back in its holster, he started looking around for the knife he'd dropped to free up his hands to pull the pistol.

"Morning man. Looks like you tore it up pretty good last night. You happen to forget they have flushable toilets in this house?" Randy asked.

"Oh man. If that was me, I'm so sorry. I honestly don't remember too much after that one guy with the messed-up toupee asked me if I needed a sippy cup for my bourbon."

"No worries. Let's get upstairs. I just had a talk with our host and he's going to be flying us to Florida in an hour. Gather whatever gear you want to bring and meet us in the living room in about twenty."

"Cool. When you say you had a talk with the guy…"?
Tony trailed off looking sharply at Randy.

"Exactly. I wasn't spending another day here with
them trying to pull more information out of us on how to
survive. I'm definitely not trying to go gather groceries and
crap for them. We need to be in Florida by this afternoon to
start looking for the kids. We'll leave them whatever weapons
we can't easily carry. Don't bring any bourbon."

"I don't really ever want to see another bottle of
bourbon again. I'll meet you in twenty in the living room by
the front door. Living room, foyer, family room, ball room or
whatever the hell they call it in this big ass house."

Tony and Randy headed up the stairs then spilt up so
Randy could go hurry Kelly along and Tony could get packed.
They all had the weapons and other supplies they wanted to
take with them already loaded up and organized. The
weapons they were leaving behind were distributed with the
people in the house whom they'd shown how to use them.
Excess weapons and ammunition were being stored out in the
garage.

A pissed off looking Gordon was sitting on the couch
in the living room when they arrived. He had a small
backpack with him, his shotgun, and his pistol in a holster on
a regular black belt looped through his pants. He was
wearing dress shoes and a blazer with khakis. Randy thought
about telling him to go change into some boots and maybe
considering going a little less formal for the trip but decided to
not worry about it. All he really needed this guy to do was fly
a plane. He should be able to do that naked if he had to. As
old as Gordon was if it came down to having to run, he was
probably screwed no matter what shoes he was wearing.

A miserable and pale looking Tony came into the room about ten minutes later. He apologized for being late saying he'd gone to the wrong living room first before deciding to try this side of the house to see if it was what they were talking about.

"This is the parlor." Gordon said with a look of disdain. Randy smiled to himself and stifled the nervous laughter welling up in his chest. He'd thought about how much more disdainful that look would be if Gordon happened to take a jaunt down to the game room and smelled the destruction Tony had wrought down there. Tony looked like he might have some smart-ass comment about the 'parlor' but then decided it wasn't worth the effort. He sat down then groaned when Kelly stood up and motioned for everyone to grab their gear and follow her out of the house.

"You going to make it Tony?" Kelly asked looking at the very hung-over Tony.

"Do I have a choice?" Tony fired back.

"Nope. Time to roll." Throwing that last comment over her shoulder she made her way out the door into the backyard of the large river-side estate. Everyone filed after her down to where the truck was parked. The truck was empty now of the weapons and supplies they'd shown up with a few days ago. The supplies absorbed into the communal supply to keep the large household going. None of them had minded since they knew they couldn't take all those supplies with them in an airplane anyway.

They'd gone over this section of the plan a few times. The small private airfield was only a few miles down the road. Gordon kept a hangar there which should have all the supplies they'd need to get the plane off the ground. They'd have to get the plane prepped and make sure the runway was clear and ready to use for takeoff. None of them really had a clue what they were doing except for Gordon. He'd let them know some of the basics, so they'd been able to come up with a plan and divvy up the tasks for when they hit the airport. They'd be leaning heavily on Gordon for anything related to getting the plane ready.

Climbing in the truck Randy put Gordon in the front seat between him and Kelly. Tony got thrown in the back again. He got his revenge for being thrown in the back by opening up the sliding panels and asking a ton of annoying questions. That all ended when they rolled up to the gate to leave. They felt a chill up their collective spines as the gates slid open. They'd been safe here for a while. Behind these ornate gates and the long fence, they'd all felt a security they hadn't felt in a long time. Tony felt a sense of vertigo leaving the gates behind them. Randy and Kelly were just focused on getting to Florida and finding their children.

Gordon hadn't been outside those gates since everything had started. He was sitting in the middle of Randy and Kelly looking back and forth like he was expecting a horde of Zombies to come slamming into the truck at any time. Randy almost laughed when he saw how nervous Gordon looked. He sobered up quickly recalling how many times they'd actually experienced hordes of Zombies slamming into whatever vehicle they were in. They drove down the deserted rode in an uncomfortable silence towards the small private airport Gordon had given them the directions to. Gordon himself was doing his best not to make eye contact with them as he looked around the road checking for Zombies constantly.

They turned at a small bait and tackle shop that seemed completely out of place surrounded by the multimillion-dollar homes on the street. Once they'd turned away from the water the homes became more of the standard two to three-bedroom family homes they were used to. Randy caught Gordon staring at one bungalow style home in particular as they passed it and couldn't pass up the opportunity for a quick jab at the guy.

"Seeing how the other half lives?" He asked with a smile. He was hoping it'd break the ice and made the ride a little less awkward.

"My daughter and granddaughter were living there right before this all happened. My son-in-law was a merchant marine and out to sea. I'd invited them to come to the mansion when the news reports started to get weird, but we hadn't talked in so long that she just didn't want to come. I should've come and forced her to leave."

All of them stared over at the small house now. In the back of the truck Tony had no idea why they were all staring at the house. Due to his pounding headache he took a look over at the house and decided he didn't care enough to ask. To the rest of them it was all too obvious the inhabitants wouldn't be alive. The front door was standing wide open. A little Nissan Sentra was parked in the driveway. It didn't look like it'd been moved in over a year. A little girl's bike was barely visible over the top of the overgrown grass in the front yard. Gordon was openly crying staring at the bike in the weeds as they drove past it.

Kelly tried to comfort him, but the man was inconsolable. He was obviously in the middle of a massive self-loathing session. Thinking a little more about the situation Randy decided he didn't have much sympathy for the man. Him and Kelly were killing themselves trying to make it the length of the east coast of the United States to get back to their kids. This coward hadn't been able to go five miles down the road to check on his daughter and granddaughter. He'd left them out here to die. If it hadn't been from cowardice, then the man had let them die out of pride. Randy swallowed his righteous anger at the man and focused on the road. A couple of Zombies had appeared at the end of the street. He did the standard maneuvering to get around them. One of the Zombies was a little girl. Gordon didn't say anything, and no one asked but they were all wondering if it was his granddaughter.

They made it to the small airport without any additional issues. The airport had a chain across the access road leading to it with a big closed sign hanging off it. They parked the truck and quickly tried getting the chain off, but it'd been locked into place. Rather than screw around with it any more when they knew a few Zombies were definitely following the sounds of the truck they grabbed their bags and left the truck on the side of the road. Climbing over the chain they hiked up the long drive to the small airport.

The place looked untouched by the apocalypse. The houses and neighborhoods they'd driven past to get here had all been as decimated by the apocalypse as everywhere else. The airport was turning out to be one of the odd hold-outs they'd run into every once in a while. Places like schools that'd shut down early for the disease and locked up their fences, so no one ever went in or out of them. Places that stood out as a reminder of what the world had been once. Places that would momentarily make them doubt the nightmare around them. Places that had them looking around hopefully thinking maybe this was all a dream after all.

It never turned out to be a dream. In this case the illusion was made all the more real by the dense greenery of the forest surrounding them. Tall pine and oak trees blocked their view of the rest of the world. As they continued walking towards the small building guarding the tarmac the illusion was spoiled by the decaying corpse of an airport security guard splayed out on the front steps. Getting closer they could see a couple of large holes in the front of the security guards' uniform. The guard's gun was still in its holster. It was a scene they'd seen time and time again. Reflexively Tony moved forward and started working the holster off the corpse and checking for ammunition.

"Dude. We already have more ammunition with us than we can carry." Randy said. He was thinking the gun and the ammunition would've been laying out here baking in the sun and getting rained on for months now. He wasn't sure what good it would do them at this point to take it with them. Plus, it looked like Gordon may puke watching the corpse get yanked around like that. The rest of them were pretty much immune to the obscenity of death at this point.

"You can never have enough guns or ammunition." Tony replied casually. He started pulling the body up a little bit to pull the belt off and see if it had bullets on it. With a wet sloshing sound, a bunch of black liquid gushed out the back of the corpse and made a big puddle on the ground. A big puddle with one of the most horrible smells any of them had ever experienced and that was saying quite a bit at this point. They all backed up in disgust and started moving once again towards the terminal building. They stopped when they heard the sounds of puking and turned to watch Gordon hurling his breakfast behind the small memorial to the flying aces of WWII.

Once Gordon was done being sick, they got moving again for the terminal. Randy had idly been wondering how they'd get through the glass doors of the building without making any noise. As they got closer, they could see getting in wasn't going to be a problem. Whoever had shot the security guard had also put a few rounds through the doors to let himself in. The doors were all slightly ajar and missing most of their glass. They crunched their way across the broken glass covered floor and out the back door of the terminal. The two snack machines sitting outside by a couple of covered picnic tables had also had their glass shot out and were missing their contents.

"Looks like someone else had the same idea on how to get out of here and decided to bring some snacks." Tony said.

"Too bad for the security guard. I wonder what made them even care if someone came and took their plane to get out of here. Why would the security guard even have stayed instead of just going home?" Kelly questioned.

"Some people just have that stay your post military kind of mindset I think." Randy answered.

Gordon maintained his silence except for occasionally spitting to try to get the puke taste out of his mouth. They followed him as he made a straight path across the runway to a small hangar on the other side. Randy noticed one of the hangars on that side was standing wide open. He assumed that would've been the one the man who shot the security guard had stored his plane in. Gordon was busy pecking away at the small lock box on the front of the hangar he'd walked them over to. They all stood around and stared at him until he finally fumbled the doors open.

An hour later they'd rolled the plane out and were sitting comfortably in the plush leather seats waiting for Gordon to get it started up and fly them to the friendly skies. Gordon rolled through his preflight checklist making sure everything was good to go. He twisted nobs and stared at arcane readouts while Tony made inappropriate jokes about stewardesses and bags of peanuts. Gordon finally finished doing everything he was supposed to for the pre-flight and turned around to speak to his passengers.

"We can make it to Orlando pretty quick from here once we get in the air. The fun part is going to be finding an airport we can set down in. The main airport, MCO, is probably crawling with Zombies. Who knows? I'm leaning more towards a regional airport I used to use a lot. There's the one in Sanford and there's also a small executive airport in another part of Orlando as well. We need to leave now to get there with enough sunlight left to check out the runways and the area around them to make sure we can safely land. We'll only have enough sunlight to check out those two airports to see if they're safe. If we left tomorrow morning instead it'd be a lot safer since we'd have more time to check out potential landing spots."

"We leave now." Kelly said before anyone else had a chance to speak up. The finality of her statement left no room for argument. She wasn't about to sit around twiddling her thumbs another day.

"Ok fine. One last thing. I'm not planning on coming back here. I want to help you find your kids. I let my family down. I want to make up for that somehow. That's my deal. I'll fly you there, but I want to help you find them."

Kelly and Randy exchanged looks with Tony. Tony was shaking his head no. Randy was thinking it was a horrible idea. The old man would slow them down. He hadn't even been man enough to rescue his own granddaughter. Other than being a pilot he had no skills they needed. He was horrible with a gun and had zero understanding of how to survive in the world of today. Plus, he was old and slow and kind of a bitch. Once again Kelly took matters into her own hands.

"Absolutely. We'd love to have you. Now, let's go."
She reached forward to pat the old man on the back.
Gordon's eyes shone once more with tears at the chance to do
something to atone for his dead daughter. His shirt still had
the remains of the breakfast he'd puked all over himself on it.
Just another day in the apocalypse.

Chapter 4: The Lake House

Eric lay in bed trying to ignore the urgent requests his bladder was sending his brain. He was exhausted. All the kids were safely tucked away in the room next to this one except for Cait who was on guard duty. They'd finally made it to the lake house that morning after walking for two days through the woods and the muck. Eric insisted they stick to walking in the woods parallel to the road versus actually walking down the road. He could barely remember how they got here. He'd been in severe pain from his wrist and his back the entire time. He'd been slamming about a pill per hour from the bottle he'd been collecting pain pills in.

Codeine, OxyContin, Motrin, Aspirin or Midol were all mixed up in that one bottle. He really didn't know what he was popping in his mouth by the time they'd finally arrived at the house. He just knew if he didn't keep popping pills, he wasn't going to be able to deal with the pain from his wrist and back. Especially not while carrying Doreen. They'd slept some in the woods. Curled around each other like a pack of feral dogs. Shivering in the cold night air as the screeches of the damned split the air all around them. The smaller girls silently sobbing themselves to sleep. Eric asleep as soon as he lay down.

He lay in the bed now having to take a piss and dreading it. He'd slept long enough that the drugs had started to wear off. Without that comforting halo of numbness covering his body everything was starting to hurt again. His wrist was wrapped in gauze and some metal strips Caitlyn had found in the house. Eric vaguely remembered her working on his wrist while he was passed out in the bed. He'd been on enough drugs then that he recognized the sharp pain coming from his wrist but didn't really realize it was his own wrist that was in pain.

Now a burning sensation was hitting him from that wrist. He got up carefully trying not to put too much strain on the wrist and managed to torque his back. When he torqued his back, he fell back into the bed. When he fell back into the bed, he automatically stuck out his hand to brace himself. He then spent the next three minutes screaming into his pillow in pain. Once he felt like he'd screamed enough he carefully got back up again. This time he was able to make it to a sitting position with his legs dangling off the bed. Feeling a little too proud of himself for accomplishing that he stood up and realized he was extremely dizzy and a tad bit on the nauseous side. Like the kind of nauseous feeling you get, and you know you're eventually going to puke but you don't have to do it right that second.

Sitting back down again he noticed he was wearing a large, fluffy, extremely pink robe. That told him at least one of the smaller girls must've been awake when Caitlyn was taking care of him. She'd have taken the extra time to get the robe on him just to amuse the girls. Pink or not it did feel pretty good. Especially after having spent the previous night sleeping off a morphine high on the hard ground with the girls all trying to worm their way against him to stay warm. He took a deep breath and rocked himself up to a standing position.

He stood there for a minute waiting to see if he was going to fall back over again. When it didn't seem like he was in imminent danger of collapsing back onto the bed he looked around the room he was in to see if Caitlyn had arranged for his very own personal bucket. The room was glowing a muted green from the chem light Caitlyn had broken and left in the hallway. She had put it in the hallway on a chair in between the rooms the girls were in and the room they'd put Eric in. That way they'd all have some light at night to help them get up and use their buckets if they needed to. It would also be a major help if they were attacked in the middle of the night and needed to move quick. It was always going to be better to be able to wake up able to see than the alternative.

Eric used the bucket without falling over. He stood there thinking about puking in the bucket as well to get it over with but then decided to just try holding it down until the puking sensation went away. Wanting nothing but to get back in bed he walked out into the hallway instead. He looked down the hallway and saw Caitlyn had hung a sheet across both ends of the hall. That'd serve to keep any random glow from the chem lights from being noticeable from outside. He knew the curtains would've been closed up tight by her and Myriah as well. They'd secured enough houses by now that they all knew the drill.

Eric peeked in on the girls in the bedroom across the hall. By the light of the glowstick he could make out Myriah and the little girls all sprawled out on top of a king-sized bed. Looking around the room he saw a large easy chair sitting in a den-like area of the master suite. Caitlyn was slumped over in the chair with the M-16 sitting beside her. She'd made the rookie mistake of thinking a big comfortable easy chair was a good place to sit when you were trying to stay awake all night on guard duty. Deciding not to wake her Eric went back across the hall to his bed for the night. He'd been trying to stay awake himself since Caitlyn had fallen asleep. His bladder emptied and another random pill downed he found himself accidentally asleep again in no time.

The room was slightly brightly lit when he opened his eyes next. Caitlyn was shaking him lightly on the arm to wake him up. He came to with a start wondering how long him and Caitlyn had both been asleep. God knew they'd both needed it but that was a long amount of time to be defenseless with no one on watch right after they'd moved into a new house. Caitlyn didn't seem like she wanted to bring it up, so Eric decided to play dumb about it as well. They were still alive so no harm no foul this time. He made a promise to himself to make sure it didn't happen again though. After all, if being hurt and tired were reasons to slack off in the apocalypse then no one would ever get anything done.

He opened both his eyes wide and looked up at Cait to let her know he was awake. She stopped tapping him and took a step back.

"How's your wrist?" She finally asked.

"Hurts like hell. This little magic bottle of pills is about the only thing keeping me from crying like a baby every time I move. You could tell the bullet went in and out, right?" Eric asked.

"There was like, a lot of blood and it was dark. I looked and it seemed like there was a hole with nothing left in it, so I thought you'd be good. If it's hurting that bad though, we should take a look again while you're awake so you can look too." Caitlyn looked at him questioningly. Looking at the wound was going to require unwrapping it which was going to be extremely painful.

"We probably should be changing the dressings anyway. Sounds good. You ready to do it now?" Eric asked. He wasn't looking forward to the process but figured it was best to just go ahead and get it over with.

"Let me go tell Myriah to make sure the other kids stay in the other room and then I'll have her come in and hold a flashlight so I can see good. Be right back." Caitlyn turned and left to get Myriah while Eric leaned back against the musty pillows bunched up at the head of the bed. He thought about asking for a bottle of tequila or something like they did in the movies to numb the pain for something like this. He had no clue what kind of drugs he'd been eating like skittles though so assumed adding alcohol to the mix may be a bad idea. No matter how wonderful it sounded to be drunk through what he knew was coming next.

Caitlyn came back in with Myriah and they started working together to peel the bandages back off his wrist. Eric tried to see what was going on at first so he could help them diagnose but after a few minutes he decided his bigger job was to not scream out in pain loud enough for the whole city to hear. He lay back as the two girls tried to pry the bandages off his skin. His blood evidently had the adhesion power of super glue based on how long it was taking them to unstick the bandages. Every time they moved his wrist it was like being shot all over again.

They finally got it unwrapped and Eric came back from his virtual tour of pain land to watch them doing their best to clean up his wrist without moving it around too much. Caitlyn had a bottle of peroxide she'd found under the sink. She was dumping that all over his wrist and wiping the blood away with another sterile gauze wrap after she let it bubble on the wound for about a minute.

"Your wrist stinks." Myriah said with a crinkled nose.

That wasn't good. When someone said something smelled bad in today's world of Zombies and bucket bathrooms it meant something different than it did back in the old days. Eric would've happily exchanged the smells of most the places they slept now with any truck stop bathroom from the old world. His wound smelling bad could only really mean one thing. Eric summoned his strength up and had Caitlyn help him sit up in bed while Myriah kept the flashlight aimed at his wrist. Looking down at his wrist it was obvious the wound had gotten infected. Red lines went in multiple directions from where the bullet had punched through his skin on both sides of his arm. There was a noticeably nasty aroma coming from the hole in his wrist that the peroxide had done nothing to wash away.

"It's infected." Eric said out loud. He just wanted to get the words out in the open to see if they rang true. He knew he was probably screwed. Unlike other medicines out there that people kept in medicine cabinets and such for forever most people took all their antibiotics once it was prescribed to them. For one thing the pharmacists and doctors all emphasized you had to take it until it was gone. For another thing antibiotics had an expiration date associated with them. Even if they could find some laying around somewhere this wasn't the kind of infection that was going to be cured with the same pill's doctors handed out like candy to everyone who complained of the sniffles.

"Do we need to go find antibiotics?" Caitlyn asked.

"There's a Walgreens right up the street." Myriah said excitedly. "We used to go there before we came over here to get suntan lotion and sodas and stuff. They should have plenty of antibiotics there."

"Ok. Great. How far is right up the street?" Eric asked. He watched as the girl's brows furrowed in concentration. He understood the issue. Distance in the apocalypse wasn't the same as distance in the old world. It could take them days to move a few miles. In the old days they could've hopped in a minivan and been at Disney in forty-five minutes. They'd tried to make Disney when they'd originally met up and it'd taken them almost a week to admit defeat and turned around to limp back to where they'd started.

After some coaxing and conversation Eric calculated it was about two miles away. That wasn't an insurmountable distance. He'd just need to do it at night with a wrist that felt like it may fall off his body at any time. It also meant he'd have to leave the girls alone again. He knew they weren't going to like that idea seeing as how every time he left them alone someone seemed to show up to try and kidnap them.

"I should take you there." Myriah said. Before anyone could tell her no, she kept talking. "I know the way there and you're too sick to really be able to depend on yourself. I know you won't just let Cait and me go get it for you. We can't leave the little kids unguarded and Cait has already showed you she can handle a gun. It just makes sense. You can't go by yourself since we need you. I'm not sure you'd make it yourself as messed up as your wrist is."

Eric opened his mouth to argue and couldn't really come up with anything. It made sense to have someone go with him to watch his back. It wasn't like these were the same girls he'd first met at the church either. These girls weren't cowering in fear in a closet anymore. They were fierce. They protected the little kids with the ferocity of mama bears. They'd been through a lot since this started. They'd seen things kids should never have to see. They'd done things kids should never have to do. He belatedly realized he probably needed to start looking at them like the strong young women they were instead of as 'kids' to be protected.

"Ok. We leave once it gets dark. Let's work on setting this place up like a fortress until then. We also need to make more flyers describing this place to go drop off at your mom's house and we need to come up with some flyers to leave in this house to give your parents more clues just in case we're not here anymore either. These drugs are starting to hit me again so wake me up in about an hour and I'll help. Until then let's make sure all the windows are secure and keep the noise down."

Myriah and Caitlyn walked out. Caitlyn didn't seem phased by Eric letting Myriah go with him. Instead she'd given him a look that conveyed she thought it was about time he started treating them like adults. Eric closed his eyes thinking how messed up this was. Myriah should be getting yelled at for talking back and punished by having her phone taken away or being sent to her room. Instead she was volunteering to go on life or death missions through a wasteland filled with infected demonic cannibals. As if the infected demonic cannibals weren't enough, they kept bumping into those mad max wannabes who were trying to kill them for some reason. Or, at least they wanted to kill him. God only knew what they wanted the girls for.

Eric woke up seven hours later from his 'short nap'. He checked his watch twice to verify how long he'd been asleep. He really needed to start labeling the pills he collected in his special pain pill bottle. Groaning he sat up in bed and carefully swung his legs out over the side. His wrist burned like his bones had hot lava running through them. His mouth tasted like a Zombie had snuck in the house and took a dump in it while he was sleeping. He imagined his breath would peel wallpaper.

"What's up sleeping ugly?" Cailyn asked with a smile as she came into the room with Myriah and Zoey tagging along. Zoey was holding tight to Caitlyn's leg. Not for the first time Eric wondered how screwed up these little girls were going to turn out. They were seeing more death before their tenth birthdays than the most hardened World War II solider had walked through.

"Very funny. Why didn't you wake me up?" Eric asked.

"You needed the rest. What with the massive infection from the bullet wound and all. Besides, we wanted to make sure if we found anything good in the house, we got first dibs on it." Caitlyn answered.

"Did you?" Eric asked.

"Oreos and pepper spray. Some garden tools we can use as weapons and there's a car in the garage, but I know we shouldn't even think about taking it if we want to keep this house safe." Myriah answered.

"A decent amount of food and two of those big jugs of water like you put in the water machine dispenser things. We should be good for a week or two at least without having to scavenge too much. If you want to drag some stuff back from the drug store, I don't think anyone will complain." Caitlyn paused and looked at him a little closer. "You sure you should be going? You're covered in sweat."

"I always sweat after sleeping an entire day in a house with no AC. I'm good to go. No choice really. You ready Myriah?"

Myriah nodded and Zoey spent a few minutes begging them both not to go. Zoey was having a lot of attachment type issues lately. Eric couldn't blame her. Not much they could do about it right now though. Maybe once they got all setup on some island down in the Keys in a big house by the ocean with lobster pots and a fresh water stream they could find a book on child psychology and help her work it all out.

Once the sun went down Myriah and Eric went out the back door. Eric was carrying a shovel and had a couple of extra kitchen knives shoved in his belt next to his usual assortment of hand weapons. Myriah was carrying a hammer that she definitely didn't want to have to use. You had to get in real close to use it and no one wanted to be that close to one of the infected. Take away the fear and the fact they were trying to bite you they still just looked gnarly. Snot dripping out of their noses, drool running down their chins, all kinds of weird stains on their faces and clothes and the massive clusters of sores on their foreheads topping it all off. Add in the insane eyes and lust to rip you apart and the best weapon to take them out with in Eric's opinion was shooting at them with nukes from a base on the moon.

Eric and Myriah let themselves out the gate in the backyard and traipsed through the adjacent yard to get out to the road. Their plan was to duck into the woods once they got to the main road. For right now both sides of the small road they were on were lined with houses. Rather than try to jump fences and risk waking up any Zombies who may be nesting in the abandoned houses Eric thought it was worth the risk to just stick to the street and stay quiet. There was barely any light being given off by the sliver of a moon barely visible over the tree line.

The short walk to the main road left Eric fatigued. That worried him since he knew that meant the infection must be getting worse. He saw Myriah looking at him with worry in her eyes as he stropped to take a couple of deep breaths and try to pull himself together. Once he felt a little more like himself, he led the way across the street and into the woods. The woods along this road were mostly just a buffer between the street and yet another subdivision. They were thick and filled with weeds, but the hassle of beating their way through the underbrush was better than the risk of staying on the exposed street the whole way to the pharmacy.

They made it up the street and to the pharmacy without hitting any snags. Eric felt like he'd just run the Boston marathon while carrying an overweight, angry dwarf. He had scratches all over himself from the briars and his reserve of energy from sleeping all day had tapped out about halfway to the pharmacy. He was running on pure will power now. He needed to get antibiotics into his system soon or he may not have to worry about Zombies or heavily armed redneck militias.

The door to the pharmacy was shattered open. Myriah lay on top of the Redbox machine someone had dragged in front of the door after shattering the glass to get inside. That meant the store had previously been looted which was no surprise. It'd be pretty hard to find a pharmacy anywhere that hadn't been looted by this point. Eric wondered how many people had survived the Zombies only to die from not having their heart medicine. He was sure plenty more had died from not having access to the same antibiotics he was trying to find now. He also knew the antibiotics would've been one of those drugs everyone would've stocked up on if they were on a looting run. Antibiotics for survival and then a few bottles of Oxy for the post poc party crowd.

"I can probably wedge myself in, but I don't think we're getting you in the store unless you want to try and crawl up here?" Myriah asked in a whisper looking down at Eric. Eric wasn't sure he was going to be able to summon up the energy for the walk back to the lake house.

"Why don't you go take a look first. You're looking for any kind of antibiotics. Like a Z-Pac or amoxicillin or penicillin. Basically, anything ending in -iclliin." Eric realized that he didn't have the slightest clue what kind of medicine he needed other than it needing to be a strong antibiotic.

Myriah gave Eric a concerned look then whispered she'd be right back. She wormed her way feet first down the other side of the red box machine and walked into the store through the smashed in door. She glanced back at the door wondering if she was going to be able to get back out or not. Deciding to worry about that later she began moving through the rows of the pharmacy. She knew the first thing she needed to do was make sure there were no Zombies hanging out in here who were going to sneak up and bite her in the butt while she was trying to read medicine bottle labels.

She broke open one of the chem lights she'd brought with her and used it to provide a little bit of light as she carefully made her way through the store. The place was one huge mess. Most of the contents of the shelves had been knocked onto the floors. She saw a lot of canned food they could come back for later. There was also a whole section of drinks that were still up on the shelf. Whoever had put the Redbox machine in front of the door had done a lot to discourage looters. Myriah moved across the store as quietly as she could holding her hammer in her sweaty palm. She was so nervous about being stuck in here with a Zombie that she was sweating profusely. She got even more nervous when she realized with her palm that wet if she swung the hammer it may just fly out of her grip entirely.

She made it back to the pharmacy without any issues. The pharmacy was locked up tight. The metal roll down security screen was rolled down and locked in place. The doors leading into the pharmacy were all locked. She tried screwing around with the doors and the metal screen that was rolled down but couldn't figure out a way to get in. The only thing she could think of was to whack away at the door knob with her hammer. She wasn't sure if that would work or not, but she was pretty sure it'd make a lot of noise. It wasn't like they had much choice at this point though. She thought about going back and warning Eric, but it was a pretty long walk, so she decided to just go ahead and try out her idea.

She was poised to take her first swing when her mind flashed back to all the HGTV shows she'd watched with her mom. She'd liked the ones where they buy the 'fixer upper' and tear it apart then make a huge profit every time by putting in a fancy backsplash. What'd just occurred to her was that when they did the demo work on those shows, they normally beat the drywall to pieces first leaving the framing exposed. Myriah reared back and swung at the wall instead of the door. The head of the hammer buried itself in the drywall. Thrilled to see the drywall coming out as she plied at it with her hammer. Convinced this was the best way to get in the pharmacy she got down to some serious demo work.

It took her an hour to beat a hole through the drywall big enough for her to squeeze through. Luckily, she'd always been super skinny. She'd been a very picky eater back before the apocalypse, so she'd started off skinny. The constant running, sweating and lack of food was a great diet plan that allowed her to slip between the framing of the wall now to finally get to the pharmacy side. Once on the pharmacy side she searched the dispensers for anything that looked like an antibiotic. By the light of her glow stick she found several different '-icillins' and a dispenser labeled Keflex. She vaguely remembered that one from an infection Zoey had gotten the summer before.

She loaded the pills into the medicine bottles and looked around for a way to label the bottles. Not finding anything useful she settled for just shoving all the unlabeled bottles into her bag. She felt like she should be grabbing more stuff, but she had no idea what else they might need. She also had no way to use the label maker so that she'd be able to identify whatever random pills she dumped in each bottle. Deciding they'd need to be happy with antibiotics for now Myriah worked her way out through the hole she'd made in the drywall. Once she'd squeezed back through, she went in search of the first aid aisle she'd spotted on her earlier rounds.

She grabbed a couple boxes of sterile wraps and shoved them in her bag. Seeing a box of princess covered band aids she grabbed those as well. The kids would love them, they managed to get scraped up enough they'd probably go through a couple boxes of these in a week. Satisfied she'd gotten the supplies she'd been sent in for she grabbed some extra supplies off the feminine hygiene aisle to top off her bag and headed for the door. She made it over to the shattered front door and stage whispered towards the top of the red box machine.

"I'm back. Sorry it took so long."

"No worries. Hurry and get out so we can get the hell out of here." Myriah heard Eric's voice coming from the bottom of the red box machine. He must be lying on the ground. It made sense considering how sick he was and how long he'd been waiting. Realizing she couldn't actually get out from this side she went looking for a step stool she'd seen. When she'd gotten into the building, she'd been able to climb up the concrete ledge on the outside to get on top of the machine. Getting on the top of the Red Box machine from the inside was going to be more of a challenge.

She found a step ladder by the cashier station and used it to get on top of the machine. She made more noise than she would've liked clambering over to the other side. She hoped that noise was ok since they'd be on their way out in a few seconds anyway. By the light of her glow stick she spotted Eric lying on the ground by the machine. She dropped down beside him as he worked his way slowly to his feet.

"What took you so long?" He asked her in a quiet whisper.

"I like shopping." She said back to him with a smile.

"You look like Casper. Ok. Let's get out of here."

Myriah reached up and rubbed her face to get rid of the white drywall dust she was covered in from head to toe. That explained the Casper comment. She shoved the glow stick in her bag so it wouldn't give away their position. She went ahead and handed the sweaty, sick looking Eric one of the bottles of pills along with the bottle of water she'd snagged for him out of the drink cooler by the cash register. Eric looked at her blankly and she mimed him taking a couple of pills and washing them down with the water. As bad as he looked, she figured he should start medicating right away.

Chapter 5: Sort of Volunteering

Kyler opened his eyes with one hand on his pistol and the other reaching out to grab whoever or whatever was poking him. He'd fallen asleep late after standing watch for a couple of hours. He'd woken Sean up to relieve him when he couldn't keep his eyes open any longer. He'd actually caught himself falling asleep standing up leaning against a door frame. No one else from their patrol had shown up. It looked like him and Sean were the only two to meet the chief at the rendezvous point. Kyler's eyes focused now realizing it was the chief who was currently poking him awake. The man was standing back a few feet and warily eyeing Kyler's grip on his pistol.

"Five more minutes mom." Kyler said and faked rolling over to go back to sleep. He'd meant it as a joke but as soon as the words left his lips, he realized what poor taste they were. He had no idea if the chief or Sean had lost their moms, but it was very probable. Kyler had last seen his own mom when he was kicking her face away from his ankle trying to escape being bitten by her. He shuddered at the memory. Then he remembered the men he was with. They all put on a hard façade. Just the day before he'd been trading yo' mama jokes with a man he'd made quick friends with in the patrol. A man who was now decaying in a ditch missing the top half of his skull.

"Wake up moron. It's time to roll out. Get up and get your shit together. We're out of here in ten. Me and Sean are ready to go so actually let's make it five. Get a move on. We got places to go and things to kill."

Kyler bounced to his feet. Once up he regretted the quick movement as he realized his whole body was feeling pretty beat down from the previous day's operations. He went to the bathroom in the house to see if he might get lucky with a full bowl of water and some toilet paper but almost retched instead. He heard Sean laughing from down the hall which told him which one of his travelling companions had beat him to the bathroom. Deciding he could live with just a whiz instead he held his breath and took care of that. Then he walked back out to the living room and put on his pack. Putting on his pack was pretty much the only step in getting ready. It's not like they changed into their pajamas before going to sleep.

"I didn't hear the water running. Did you not wash your hands?" Sean asked. He was still laughing to himself over the state he'd left the bathroom in. Kyler was noticing the juvenile humor they all shared seemed to get worse the more stressful the situation got. He started to say something about Sean's mom, but Chief Presley shut him up by talking first.

"Alright. We're heading back to base. I want to get you guys checked in at central command. Once we get there, they'll want to pull you aside and quiz you on what's happened to you so far and your background and so on. They're also going to ask if you want to make your commitment more official. That means joining up more formally than you are right now. You'll find out more when we get there. Now, I'm not supposed to tell you this but in case we step outside and that sniper we were running from yesterday blows my head off you'll want to head to the mouth of the Connecticut river. There's an island about a mile up river which is where we're going to try and get today. You just tell them you were with me and looking to sign up and they should take care of you. Any questions?" The chief looked at both of them with a look that dared them to ask him a question.

"You really think that sniper is out there still?" Kyler asked.

"No clue. If it's like every other time those assholes have hit one of our settlements, he's long gone so I wouldn't be too worried. If we make it to the vehicle and start driving without our heads getting blown off, we're probably good. Anything else?"

"Why are there snipers shooting at settlements?" Sean asked. Kyler thought that was an extremely fair question. They'd all talked about the dangers posed by rogue groups out there trying to take over but talking and getting shot at were two very different things.

"Who knows. Central command may have a clue but as far as I can tell it's just some freaks out there who're too damned lazy to salvage their own food and protect their own people. So, they swoop in and try to take women and food. Maybe they have a leader trying to keep us from expanding and restoring order. No clue. I just know when we figure out where they're based out of, we'll be paying them a visit to return all the favors."

"When we get to the base should we volunteer?" Kyler asked.

"If we ever get there. You two are asking too many questions. It'll be up to you if you want to or not. I can tell you the commander is a good guy. His focus is restoring the US to as close to what it was before the virus as possible. That's what all of us want. He's also practical and he's smart enough to admit mistakes and learn from them. Now. No more questions. Once we go out this door, we go low and fast to the blue minivan by exit seventy. Let's do it by the numbers and get there alive. I don't want to have to report any more casualties from this sweep. There's a war on and we can't afford to keep losing soldiers. Not even piss poor soldiers like you two."

With those encouraging words the chief swung the back door to the house open and ran for the gate in the fence on the side of the house. Sean followed right after and Kyler counted off to five in his head then followed suit. They played this game of follow the leader by moonlight as they slowly made their way towards the interstate and exit seventy. They moved well together. People who were loud had been thinned out by the Zombies early on. Also, the people who normally lost foot races weren't around too much anymore either. If you wanted to survive out in the open in the apocalypse you needed to be able to run fast and keep it up for as long as you had to. There were no participation awards handed out after a Zombie race.

They were each covered in camouflage and weapons. Each grenade, smoke bomb, round of ammo, knife, rifle, sword, machete, hatchet, pistol, other pistol and other gear attached to them in ways to minimize the noise they'd make when they ran. Leather gloves and elbow pads gave them the option of street fighting Zombies with some protection from teeth and nails. Sean even had a pair of brass knuckles he'd taken out of some pawn shop. Kyler didn't think those were super practical. If he got that close, he had a hatchet he could just smack Zombies around with. Each to his own though. Sean was still alive which meant he must have decent survival instincts.

They were only about half a mile from exit seventy when screeching erupted all around them. They'd been jogging down the side of the road past a bunch of cars that were still sitting in a nice orderly line where they'd all run out of gas waiting for the cars in front of them to move. Kyler was still weirded out by the number of times he saw lines of cars sitting there like that. Especially when the other side of the interstate was empty. There was rarely anyone in the emergency lane or the median either. People just sat there in a traffic jam obeying the rules of the road until they were killed. He didn't get it. The inflexibility of people to be able to break rules and adapt to new situations was a key reason the virus had been able to spread so far so fast.

Kyler imagined the conversations happening in the cars sitting in the line-up.

"The Zombies are getting closer Dad!" Sally Sue said as her brother cried, and the mother sat in the front seat knitting some mittens. At least that's how Kyler saw it in his head. The cute little Sally Sue being the only one young enough not to have completely had her spirit broken by the world of yesterday. She'd need a few more years of the public-school system to accomplish that.

"I see them honey. Traffics not moving and I don't want to get a ticket though. That would mess up my perfect driving record." Kyler just couldn't imagine what'd made these idiots sit in the cars like they were. He would've been able to understand it better if there were cars all stuck in the median and on the sides of the road. At least that would've shown people taking the initiative to try and save themselves. The straight orderly lines of empty cars were one of the creepiest sights of the apocalypse to Kyler. On the other hand, it made it possible for them to use the emergency lanes now to get around the occasional traffic jams.

The chief was still in the lead with Sean right behind him. Kyler was hanging back ten to fifteen yards behind them serving as rear guard. He'd stop every few minutes and turn around to scan for anyone following them. He was walking backwards looking around behind them when the screeching broke out. They never did figure out what started it. One minute they were walking down the side of the road looking ahead for the target blue minivan and the next they were running for their lives from the horde of Zombies that crawled out from under the cars they'd been walking beside.

The screeches were coming from everywhere. There were no thoughts about trying to use their hand weapons and stay quiet. Kyler started scrambling down the side of the road towards the woods. He didn't even try to look for the others until he was almost at the tree line. He spun at the sound of shots fired and saw that Presley and Sean were only about ten feet in front of him. They had their backs to the trees as well. Flashes of fire shot out the barrels of both their rifles as they emptied their magazines in full auto mode into the mob of Zombies scrambling down from the road to get at them.

Kyler took a few shots then decided it was pretty pointless shooting at the mob coming at them. He pulled the trigger a few more times then turned and sprinted into the woods. He ignored the branches and briars ripping at his face. He ducked and crawled through one extremely dense section of briars. Behind him he heard the explosive sounds of fragmentation grenades going off. He knew that would be the chief covering their retreat by tossing as much firepower at the oncoming crowd as he could. All the noise meant this section of the woods was going to be crawling with Zombies in no time. Kyler cut left to try and move in parallel with the interstate, so he had a chance of running into the chief or Sean.

He didn't see them as he crawled into another dense group of bushes. Zombie screeches were erupting all around him. His heart was hammering in his chest as he powered through the bushes like a rabbit on crack. His back legs driving his body forward no matter the vines and sticky plants and trees ripping at his clothing and hair. He had to fight to maintain control of his rifle as it snagged on every branch he passed. He donated a good amount of his hair and some skin to the woods as his fear-fueled adrenaline pushed him to keep moving faster.

He ran around one tree in the dark and right into a tall Zombie. The Zombie had been standing still to look around and let out one of those horrific screeches once it spotted Kyler. Kyler wrapped his arms around the Zombie and drove with his feet just like if he was back in football practice. He bore the tall Zombie straight to the ground hard. His coach would have applauded how he'd got his head in the front, wrapped the Zombie up with his arms and just kept driving his legs. The Zombie was trying to snap at him and screech at the same time. It's competing instincts cooperating to keep Kyler from being bitten long enough for him to find his hatchet. Once he had that in his hand he sat back and swung it hard into the Zombies chest. The hatchet didn't seem to do much damage with the thick jacket the Zombie was wearing. The Zombie tried to sit up to get at Kyler. He smashed it in the head with the hatchet. Warm blood splattered up his arm as the hatchet cracked the skull. The Zombie kept coming until he pulled the hatchet out of its head and reared his arm back to swing again. The Zombie fell backwards and lie still. Kyler smashed it in the head with the hatchet again just to be safe.

Breathing hard Kyler got up and started his frantic pace through the woods again. A brief red glow up ahead had him reaching for his weapons until he heard a quick burst of whistling. He almost missed it with the volume of screeching in the air. He ran towards where he'd seen the red light and slid to a stop in front of the chief and Sean. They were hunched down behind a large fallen tree looking into the darkness. Kyler wanted to ask them what the hell they were looking at when he saw all the movement in the bushes up ahead and realized a good bit of the screeching was coming from that direction. The yelling from behind them would've made an avid Metallica fan reach for a pair of ear plugs.

Kyler poked Sean and the chief and ran deeper into the woods hoping they'd get the hint and follow him. There was no path forward at the moment. They were going to have to go deeper and just be happy they'd managed to end up in this peaceful eddy between the massive rip tides of death ripping into the woods all around them. Kyler held his M-16 in front of him to block the weeds and low hanging branches. There was nothing like the fear of being torn apart and eaten by Zombies to keep you from caring too much if you ripped your clothes or ran face first through the occasional spider web. All he needed was Jenny yelling 'Run Forest Run!" to complete the picture.

With the Forest Gump refence stuck in his head he ran straight into a chain link fence. He bounced off it and landed flat on his back. Standing up quickly he saw that the chief and Sean had been channeling their inner Gump as well keeping up with him on the mad dash. Without anyone saying a word they all flung their rifles onto their straps and started climbing the fence. Kyler was at the top working his leg over and trying not to fall backwards when he heard Sean start cussing. He looked back over his shoulder and saw a Zombie had come out of the darkness and grabbed Sean by the leg. The Zombie was trying to hold the leg still and get his teeth through Sean's pants while Sean was kicking the hell out of the Zombies face with his free foot.

Sean had his machete out and was trying to balance on the fence and swing the machete all while kicking at the Zombie to try and get it to let go of him. He got in one good hit on the side of the Zombies head. It looked like the ear and a bunch of skin was hanging by a flap after Sean's boot smashed down on the Zombies head. Kyler thought Sean would make it over after that hit. Then Sean lost his balance on the fence and fell hard to the ground below. Another Zombie appeared out of the woods and ran for the fallen Sean. The original Zombie who'd grabbed Sean on the fence went face first at Sean trying to get some tongue in a very unwelcome move.

Gunfire rang out and the charging Zombie fell to the ground. Screeches picked up in volume converging on their location. Kyler dropped to the ground to help Sean. The chief was already on the ground putting some rounds through the back of the Zombie trying to rip Sean's tongue out of his mouth. More Zombies emerged from the dark tree line. The chief yelled for Kyler to get Sean over the fence while he covered them. Kyler bent down and picked Sean up off the ground. Sean was blubbering and resisting him.

"Come on man we have to get over this fence or we're screwed!" Kyler yelled at Sean.

"I'm already screwed!" Sean yelled back at him cackling with maniacal laughter as blood ran out of both sides of his mouth. The laughter subsided as he gagged on the blood pouring out of this mouth. He pulled up his pants leg and showed Kyler where the Zombie had been gnawing on his ankle. Like the blood pouring out of the guys face wasn't bad enough.

"Chief!" Kyler yelled trying to be heard over the sounds of the screeching and automatic gunfire. The chief took one look back at Sean sitting on the ground staring at his wounded leg with blood pouring from his mouth like a ketchup waterfall and recognized the situation for what it was. He turned and sprinted over to them. He squatted down next to Sean and Kyler saw the two exchange some words. Then the chief grasped Sean's hand in a final hand shake and jumped to his feet.

"Get over that fence!" The chief yelled as he ran and threw himself on the chain link and climbed it with easy proficiency. The chief was already standing on the ground on the other side of the fence when Kyler was just starting to get his legs thrown over the top of it. Behind him he heard shooting as Sean covered their retreat. Presley had reloaded his weapon and was shooting through the fence waiting for Kyler to get down on the ground beside him.

Kyler landed on the ground and stumbled. The chief pulled him to his feet and told him to run for the other side of the fencing in the big open space they were in. Property of AT&T signs were revealed in the moonlight as they ran past the large concrete building at the base of the big cell tower. They got to the other side but before they could start climbing the fence Kyler grabbed the chief and asked if they should go back for Sean.

"No son." Presley said sadly while shaking his head. "We need to get over this fence and get out of here. Sean's buying us some time, but we need to move fast."

Not content with that Kyler kept his hold on the chief's jacket. "What did you tell him?" He asked.

"I told him it's been an honor and to make sure he saved a bullet for himself." The chief shrugged his shoulder hard enough to force Kyler's hand off him. Then he turned and scrambled up the fence. A second later Kyler followed him. Behind them he heard the sounds of grenades going off as Sean made his last stand. On the other side of the fence a maintenance road led the way they wanted to be going. Hoping the sounds of Sean's last battle would attract most of the Zombies in the region they began jogging down the middle of the maintenance road towards the interstate and a blue minivan that should still be sitting next to exit seventy.

Chapter 6: Coming in Hot

MCO and the Executive airport in Orlando both turned out to be a bust. Gordon didn't seem phased by that as he angled the plane to bring them in for a pass over the Sanford airport. MCO had been a mess. Airplanes and emergency vehicles sitting all over the runway. It looked like a significant number of planes had caught on fire at some point. The much smaller executive airport had looked like it may be ok to set down in. When they looked closer though there'd been a couple of military helicopters that'd landed in the middle of the runway and were surrounded by corpses. The runway had some big potholes in it thanks to the rockets that must've been getting fired out of those helicopters.

Sanford was a small regional airport. One of the places you'd go if you wanted to be able to walk to your terminal in a few minutes after parking in the garage. The kind of place you could get really cheap flights on really old airplanes as long as you were good with flying based on their route schedule. From the air it looked like Sanford must've been shut down before everything went to hell. All the planes were neatly parked in their designated spots and the runway was blissfully clear of any obstacles. There were cars parked in the long-term lots but not nearly as many as should've been there for normal operations.

"Looks like we'll be setting down here then." Gordon announced after a second flyover served to show Sanford still appeared to be the best option. Randy nodded in agreement and settled back into the comfortable leather co-pilots seat. Him and Kelly had already agreed this was probably their best option anyway. It was a straight shot from this airport back to their old house. In the old days you'd have been looking at a twenty-minute drive with no traffic.

Gordon got the small plane lined up with the runway and pushed the stick down to start their descent. They stared out the windows at the tarmac to see if they could detect any threats they'd have to deal with once they landed. The plane touched down and they rolled to a stop without any issues. They hadn't seen any large groups of Zombies or militia or anything like that from the air when they were flying to Florida. Of course, they'd settled on a course that'd kept them over the ocean for the bulk of the flight. No telling what kind of surface to air missiles the people on the ground may have gotten their hands on with all the national guard armories just sitting around. They'd wanted to fly directly over land to see the extent of the damage. They'd hoped to get a better feel for what was going on but decided an abundance of caution was the better idea.

Gordon taxied them over to the terminal and stopped the plane. They got their equipment strapped on and went out the side door of the small luxury plane. Gordon checked with them one more time to make sure they still felt good about landing here before shutting off the engine. He ran through his checklist and made sure the plane was shut down in such a way that they'd be able to hop in and start it back up again quickly if needed. Then he climbed out onto the hot tarmac to join them.

Seeing him standing there in his fancy shoes with his freshly pressed khakis Randy felt like telling him to get back in the plane and fly home. The only thing that stopped him was the selfish realization that they may need the plane to look for the kids or as an escape vehicle. Looking at Gordon standing there in his freshly pressed outfit he gave the guy a very low probability of being on this side of the sod the next time a Monday rolled around.

"Ok let's hit it. I say we go around to the main terminal and try to find a car." Kelly said. She was excited to finally have both her feet firmly planted in the state of Florida again. Now she just needed to get a car and get to looking for her kids.

"Yeah we need to find one with keys in it. Normally we look in houses and find the keys for the car sitting in the garage. I don't suppose you know how to hotwire a car Gordon?" Randy asked.

"I don't know how to hot wire a car, but I do know how to rent one when I'm at an airport. If we go look in the sections of the rental lots reserved for the frequent travelers, we may be able to find a car just sitting there waiting for us."

Randy and Tony gave Gordon a quick look of grudging respect. That was some solid reasoning the old pilot had just pulled off. Maybe he wasn't just Zombie bait after all. If he kept coming up with suggestions like that one, he may even end up pulling his own weight.

"Wouldn't they have put away all the keys and everything before they all left to go home?" Kelly asked as they walked past the main terminal building headed towards the lot with the Hertz and Enterprise signs up in the air above them.

"I think for normal situations like closing down for a hurricane or something they probably would've. For something like this I could see people skipping out on some of their normal duties to hurry home and be with their families. Or, maybe this place was full of super diligent committed rental car employees. It's possible, I just really hope not." Gordon answered.

Ten minutes later Randy and Kelly were driving out of the small airport behind the wheel of a bright red minivan. Tony and Gordon were following them in a little red sedan. They were all thankful to whomever at the budget counter hadn't bothered to remove the keys or lock the doors for the cars in their section before rushing home. A home they probably rushed to only to be eaten by the very loved ones they were rushing home to protect.

The road out of the airport was empty and the connecting road leading to the highway was pretty desolate as well. They dodged the occasional abandoned car and drove for about ten minutes before they caught sight of a Zombie. It was just standing on the side of the road staring into the trees. It turned around slowly as they drove past it. The sight of the cars slowly permeated the Zombies diseased brain and touched on a primal need to feed and hunt. The Zombie screeched and began to amble quickly after the two cars that'd left it in the dust. Nothing else moved except for the rainbow-colored tassels on a small bike lying broken in the ditch by where the Zombie had been standing.

Randy slowed down as he lost sight of the Zombie that'd been trailing them. It was just one Zombie, but the screeching could summon a lot more. He had no desire to be around when that happened. He looked over at Kelly who was leaning forward in the passenger seat staring out the front windshield as the familiar landscape rolled by. They'd driven this road hundreds of times in the past. It looked almost the same today as it had before the apocalypse. It could've been a normal drive home from work other than the overgrown median and the occasional car pulled over to the side of the road. It was another of those surreal moments he was worried may break Kelly's hold on sanity. They were now so close to where they'd left the kids that he knew it was going to start eating at her if they didn't find them right away. She wasn't the most patient of people even in the best of times.

They went through the tolls headed south towards Oviedo. The LED signs above each lane of the toll booths were dead now. Randy assumed they'd said the tolls were suspended when people were evacuating back when there was still a government to issue evacuation orders. In Florida they tended to treat any emergency the same way they treated a hurricane. He shuddered at the thought of how many people must've been urged to congregate in shelters in the beginning. Sticking people together under one roof with an airborne version of the virus circulating. He was trying to get the images out of his head of how horrific that must've turned out when Kelly tapped him on the knee.

"What the hell is all that up there?" She asked. Her brow creased as she stared down the road towards the bridge that would take them across the lake. Randy slowed down to try and figure it out as well. There were some really large things moving around on the road up ahead.

He continued to slow down as they got closer. Pretty soon they were close enough to make out what was going on. There'd always been herds of cows who lived along the edge of the lake. Those cows were now running together across the road and disappearing down the embankment on the other side. After the cows disappeared down the embankment a handful of Zombies came charging up from the other side of the road. The Zombies didn't notice the stopped cars or the people sitting in them as they were focused on catching the herd of cows. The Zombies all disappeared over the embankment. Immediately following the Zombies two low slung shapes came up over the side of the embankment and lazily crawled across the road.

"Are those alligators?" Randy asked. It was a rhetorical question as it became very obvious very quickly that's what they were.

"The cows must be running from the Zombies who must be feeding on them. I assume the alligators are feeding on the Zombies. Let's just get across the bridge before whatever eats alligators shows up." Kelly said.

"I just wish I could hear the conversation Gordon and Tony must be having right now." Randy said with a grin. He was imagining the formal and nuanced reaction of Gordon to the weird circle of life playing out in front of them contrasted to the coarse and vulgar way he was sure Tony would be reacting. Hesitating for another second to make sure nothing else emerged from the swampy lakeside to cross the road in front of them Randy let off the brake and crossed over the bridge. Looking over towards where the cows had gone as they crossed, they could see the heifers retreating around the lake edge with the Zombies following them. The alligators had gone into stealth mode, but Randy was sure they'd be able to track the alligators progress by simply watching for Zombies suddenly disappearing underneath the shallow water and never coming back up.

Still grinning Randy looked over at Kelly to see if his comment had amused her at all. One look told him she either hadn't heard him or had dismissed off-hand whatever he'd said. She looked upset and teary eyed. The weird phenomena they'd just witnessed had taken her mind off the kids for a second but then she'd snapped right back more worried than ever. With stuff like the weird alligator Zombie parade going on less than ten miles from their house it was hitting her how hard of a time the kids would've had trying to survive. They'd have had her mom with them, but this was still too much. It was too much for anyone.

Randy held her hand as they drove in silence. Neither of them could think of anything to say. Kelly was petrified anything she said now would somehow jinx them finding the kids. Randy was frozen because he couldn't think of anything to say to make Kelly feel better. There was nothing he could say right now and no tone of voice he could say it in that was going to help. He focused on the road and holding her hand and tried to fight back his own fear of what they were going to find when they finally got to the house.

They made it past the first exit after the bridge and were heading up a hill on a curvy part of the road when they saw three trucks driving the other way on the north bound side of the tollway. The trucks were packed with people in camouflage holding guns. Randy put his foot down on the pedal.

"Do you think they saw the plane landing?" Kelly asked him.

Of course, the plane would've been obvious to anyone in the area Randy thought. He was kicking himself for being so stupid. They'd cutoff a lot of risk by going around Georgia and Florida over the ocean. They should've considered how to hide the plane approaching Orlando. He didn't know how they could've done that short of flying in and attempting a night time landing with no lights on the ground. That seemed like it may have been more dangerous than three pickup trucks full of wannabe Rambos.

Randy glanced in the rear-view mirror and saw that Tony was keeping up. He was sure they'd have noticed the trucks as well. Thinking quickly Randy decided the best course of action would be to get off at the next exit. That happened to be the exit they needed to get off on anyway, so it worked out pretty well. Hopefully the guys in the trucks wouldn't be able to get turned around fast enough to see them getting off on the exit.

They got to the exit and it was completely blocked by a wreck that looked like an ambulance had slammed into a UPS truck.

"Go across the median! We can go down the other side. Or try the next exit." Kelly exclaimed from the passenger seat. She was staring at him while he sat there frozen in place trying to figure out what to do next. Deciding any action was better than just sitting there he drove slowly into the median. The median was about forty yards across at this point. It was a large, gently sloping drainage ditch in between the north and south bound sides of the tollway. The long grass and weeds that'd grown up there covered the stream that was running lazily through the thick mud at the bottom of it.

The van hit the stream and stopped. Randy pumped on the accelerator and felt the front of the van dig into the mud even deeper as they lurched forward a few feet. Behind them they heard Tony beep the horn of the little red sedan. This was exactly why they had him driving a chaser car. Randy and Kelly bailed out of the van and ran over to the red car. It took them a minute to navigate the thick mud and tall weeds to get to the car. Once there they opened the back door and piled in. Tony put the car in reverse and started driving them backwards up the hill to the side of the road they'd just tried to leave.

They hit the asphalt at the top and Tony spun the steering wheel to get them lined up correctly on the road. Then he slammed down on the gas pedal to accelerate with all the power the poor little car could muster. The tires spun out for a second on the dirt and grime covered road before gaining traction and rocketing them forward. Tony was driving while Gordon was looking behind them to try and see if he could see the trucks coming. Randy and Kelly were trying to get comfortable in the cramped back seat on top of Gordon and Tony's gear with their own gear hanging off of them at crazy angles.

"The trucks are coming!" Gordon squeaked out. If his words hadn't been so terrifying, they'd have made fun of his squeaky voice. Tony filed it away in the back of his head to use to make fun of Gordon at a later date if they happened to live through the next ten minutes.

Kelly and Randy turned around to look out the back window.

"They're back there but they don't seem like they're trying to catch us or anything." Randy said.

"Probably afraid if they get too close, we'll start shooting at them." Tony answered from the driver's seat where he was simultaneously trying to look in the rearview and keep them from crashing into anything on the road ahead.

"Do we know they want to fight us?" Gordon asked. He seemed to have gotten control of his voice for now.

"They're chasing us, and they have guns." Kelly answered sarcastically. That seemed to settle the matter for her.

They drove on. They drove for another ten minutes with the trucks behind them maintaining about a hundred yards of distance between them. They were heading up another hill when all of the tires on the little red sedan blew out simultaneously.

Tony cursed in surprise while struggling to regain control of the car. They were sliding down the road sideways at about sixty miles per hour. The car felt like it was going to flip at any second. There was no telling what they may hit. The steering wheel was completely useless in Tony's hands. The brakes weren't doing anything to slow them down either. Just for kicks Tony pulled the emergency brake. The emergency brake didn't help them slow down any at all either since they were sliding sideways on four blown tires. The metal guardrail they bounced off of a second later ate up a lot of their momentum though.

Randy was disoriented by the impact with the guardrail. He struggled to clear his head as the car finally stopped moving. The trucks were pulling up in a semi-circle around them. The men in the trucks looked like they were ready to jump out as soon as the they came to a complete stop. Randy worked the handle on his side of the car, but the door wouldn't budge. He reached across Kelly who was struggling to sit up and pulled on her door handle. Kelly's door opened easily. Randy started to crawl over Kelly to go out on that side, but she put her hand on his chest and pushed him back. She'd pulled herself together enough to know what was going on. Making sure the safety was off on her M-16 she lurched out of the car and went around to the side opposite where the trucks were working to encircle them.

Randy followed right behind her. The men from the trucks had scrambled out of their pickups and were setting up in firing positions. They were using their vehicles as cover the same as Randy and Kelly were. No shots had been fired yet. If they did need to start shooting at least they were each carrying a small arsenal.

"Now what?" Tony asked. He'd gotten out of the car and was standing on the other side of Kelly. All three of them had their rifles resting on the hood of the car.

"You cover the truck on the left, Kelly take the middle and I'll shoot up the right one. Unless you guys have any other ideas? Is Gordon ok?" Randy asked.

Gordon had smashed his face into the dashboard during the collision. He was sitting up in the front seat moaning and holding his chest where the airbag had hit him. His face was covered in blood. He looked like the poster child for severe head trauma.

"If the shooting starts, he's pretty much going to die in the crossfire if we leave him there." Kelly said. She was trying to figure out what they could do with him. The way the trucks were circling them they didn't have much in the way of cover outside where they were already standing. She was thinking they should pull him out the driver's side door and lay him down on the road by their feet when another vehicle drove up to join the party.

The black Range Rover parked beside the pickup trucks. Everyone shifted around to acknowledge the new arrival. Tony asked if they should wake up Gordon. He pointed out now they had four cars to shoot at instead of three. They waited with weapons ready until the passenger door to the luxury SUV opened up and a large man dressed in fatigues, a leather jacket and a t-shirt got out. He looked over at them and smiled.

"Hey there. I'm Amos. I'm in charge around here. I'm assuming you all flew in on the airplane earlier?"

"You always welcome visitors with spike strips and ambushes?" Randy asked in return. Amos ignored the question.

"If you folks want to put down your weapons, we'll put ours down and we can have a civilized conversation and maybe help each other out. Here, I'll start it off." Amos drew his pistol and laid it in the passenger's seat of the Range Rover. The he started walking over towards them. Randy, Kelly and Tony all had their weapons up and at the ready.

"Just stand over there. We can talk fine with you over there." Randy said. In his peripheral vision he saw the men in the trucks shifting around. If it came down to a straight up shoot out, then the guys in the pickups were going to have all the advantages. Randy knew if he pulled the trigger it was really likely they'd all die. Even if they won the fight there was no way they were getting out without getting shot up pretty bad. The guys in the pickup would have to be complete morons to let that happen. Looking over at how they'd spread out he could tell they had some discipline which probably translated into some skill with the weapons they were holding as well.

"You guys flew in to my town loaded for war. Then you drove in two stolen cars from my airport. My guess is you're here looking for somebody. Children maybe? Parents? I can tell you right now we keep tabs on everyone living around here. So, who are you looking for?" Amos looked at them expectantly.

"We're looking for our children." Kelly blurted out. "All we want to do is grab them and we'll be out of here. We can leave the guns and everything for you if you want them. We had no idea anyone considered the airport and the cars parked there to be their property. We just want to get our girls back."

A strange look crossed the man's face. He took a few steps forward to stare at Kelly then at Tony and Randy.

"How many girls do you have?" He asked.

"We have four." Kelly answered excitedly.

"Hmm. Is one named Caitlyn and one's named Maria or something like that?" Amos asked.

"Yes! Yes! That's them! Where are they? Have you seen them? Are they ok?" Kelly had pretty much forgotten she was supposed to be pointing her weapon at the guy in her excitement.

"Saw them all about a week ago. The older ones have your eyes and hair. I thought you looked familiar for some reason. We sent them to one of the houses we're protecting. I can take you over there to collect them if you'd like." Amos said with his hands spread and palms up in front of him.

"Yes. Yes. We'd like that very much!" Kelly agreed.

"Ok. We're going to need you guys to put down your weapons though. I can't allow people I don't know to go to one of our safe houses packing heat. I'm sure you understand that right."

Chapter 7: Better Living Through Pharmaceuticals

Eric swallowed the pills Myriah had handed him then sat back down again. Myriah had thought he was going to take the pills and they were going to roll out of there and back to the lake house. She squatted beside him and asked him quietly what was wrong.

"I just need another second to rest. My arm feels like it's on fire. Give me ten minutes then we'll be on our way."

Myriah nodded with a worried expression on her face. Eric wasn't the type to want to rest or to hold anyone up. He was normally the one leading them through the swamp fighting off Zombies with one hand and carrying one of the little kids with his other arm. The man had always seemed like a force of nature to Myriah. To see him weak like this was freaking her out. She sat down next to him and looked around in the darkness. She knew there was a large plaza on the other side of the street that had a Publix and a bunch of other plaza type stores. If this pharmacy had been a bust the plan had been to go across the street and see what they could find at the Publix pharmacy instead.

Myriah impatiently counted off the ten minutes in her head. Deciding it'd been long enough she nudged Eric to get his attention. Looking over at him when he didn't respond to the nudge, she saw that he was fast asleep. Judging them to still have a few hours before daybreak she decided to give him another thirty minutes to rest. Then she was going to wake him up no matter what so they could get moving. It wouldn't be good to get caught out in the open like this once the sun was up.

Myriah jerked awake. She was leaning against Eric in the doorway of the pharmacy. Eric was sleeping with his neck at an awkward angle. Myriah punched him in the arm hard. He woke up and slowly looked over at her. It looked like he was going to ask her to let him sleep another ten minutes. She watched his eyes widen as he slowly registered that they were asleep in the pharmacy alcove in full view of anyone who walked by. The sleepiness was wiped off his face in an instant as he went into survival mode.

He held his finger up to his lips to remind Myriah not to say anything. At night you could get away with making some noise here and there since the Zombies were mostly sleeping anyway. During the day the Zombies sat around hyper alert just waiting for any noises that might lead them to their human prey. If it'd been daytime when they got here looking for the medicine Myriah wouldn't have dared to hammer away on the wall like she had. It hadn't generated too much noise outside of the store, but it still would've been a lot riskier to do during the day.

Eric moved towards the edge of the alcove and began looking around. The plaza across the street was plainly visible in the daylight now. The huge group of Zombies emerging from the Publix clearly indicated that going there for antibiotics the night before would've been suicide. Motioning for Myriah to stay quiet Eric began moving out from the alcove to work his way around the cars parked in front then move around to the back of the building. Myriah had been thinking they could try ducking back into the pharmacy. The problem with that plan would have been trying to get Eric up and over the Red Box quietly. The slightest noise and they'd have been trapped in the pharmacy until the Zombies managed to beat their way in.

Myriah followed Eric. She glanced over at the Publix parking lot and felt her knees almost give out in terror. The parking lot was filled with Zombies roaming around. Several had already wandered out into the street where they were walking around in circles. The ones in the street occasionally freezing to look all around in that crazed manner they had. The stream of Zombies pouring out of the Publix didn't seem to be slowing down either. Afraid she'd freeze up if she kept looking across the street Myriah forced her eyes to follow Eric. She focused on putting one foot in front of the other as quietly as possible.

They almost made it to the corner of the store without being seen. If they'd made it another two yards, they could've ducked around and disappeared into the woods behind the store. One of the Zombies on the street noticed them though. It noticed the way they walked. Something about the way they held themselves tipped off the Zombie that they weren't one of his kind. They were prey. The Zombie screeched and sprinted towards Eric and Myriah. Behind that Zombie the same piercing screech erupted from hundreds of other throats. In a massive stampede the Zombies all turned and ran full force towards Eric and Myriah.

Eric gathered his energy together as best he could to make a run for it. The world quickly started spinning around him. His breathing sounded to him like it was coming from someone else. He wasn't going to make it. He screamed for Myriah not to look back. She stopped and pulled on his shirt to try and get him to follow her. He pushed her away and screamed at her again to run. Then he turned to face the Zombies streaming towards them. That first Zombie who'd seen them was only yards away at this point. Eric charged at the Zombie with his hammer held high. His goal now to kill as many of them as he could before they devoured him. He'd give Myriah a chance to make it.

Myriah turned and ran. Shame ate at her, but terror was driving her now. She ran like she'd never run before. She ran all out for the chain link fence separating the back strip of the plaza from the wooded area behind them. She rode the wave of the Zombies howls to the top of that fence which she scrambled over way too quickly. Her pants leg stuck on something on the top as she fell over the top of the fence. She jerked at her leg hard and the pants tore. She fell the last foot face first into that pine straw covered pavement and rolled painfully into the woods.

The Zombies hit the fence behind her. The only reason the fence didn't give right away was the bulk of the Zombies had been sidetracked trying to rip off a tasty chunk of Eric. Tears and sobs racked Myriah's body as she got to her feet and continued running like a mad woman through the underbrush. The briars and branches ripping at her long hair. How many times had they run like that with Eric leading them through the woods? Who was going to protect them now? He couldn't just be gone, could he? Heedless of the pain, she ran. Her mind picturing what the Zombies would do to her if they caught her.

She kept running until she popped out of the woods into a subdivision. It was one they'd skirted around when they originally made the trip to the pharmacy. Myriah thought about ducking into one of the houses and waiting for the Zombie herd to move past her. The last thing she wanted to do was run straight back to the lake house with the mass of Zombies on her trail. She also didn't want to get stuck in a house by herself for weeks either if the Zombies decided to randomly nest wherever she picked.

She ran. She pushed her body to the point where she was seeing black spots floating in front of her eyes. She kept going anyway. When she slowed down, she just saw Eric charging the Zombie horde with that hammer. When she slowed down, she thought about having to tell Caitlyn and the girls that Eric was gone. She'd have to tell them that now they really were on their own. They'd lost Brenda and now they'd lost their only other protector. All because she'd fallen asleep. She should've made Eric get up and leave while it was still dark. She never should've listened to him. He'd been slurping down pain pills and antibiotics like it was nobody's business. He'd been deathly sick. Myriah blamed herself for his death. The weight of that guilt was crushing her.

She ran until she just couldn't physically put one foot in front of the other anymore. She'd lost her pursuers at some point. She could hear them screeching in the background, but it was coming from a few streets over. She'd zig zagged though the subdivision trying to lose them. It must've worked. Now she realized she needed to hole up somewhere rather than risk attracting more pursuers. In her present state she didn't think she'd be able to outrun anybody else. Looking around for a place that she may be able to crash she saw the house she was standing beside had its gate to the backyard open.

Myriah walked through the overgrown front lawn to the side of the house and through the open gate. The backyard was fenced in with a high, white privacy fence. There was a pool full of green water with a moldy, mostly deflated giant donut floatie in the middle of the muck. On the side of the yard adjacent to the pool was a trampoline sitting on top of white river rocks. The grass was knee high with random weeds jutting up even higher. Nothing in the backyard signaled imminent danger to her so she shut and locked the gate behind her. She stood in the tall grass for a few minutes catching her breath.

Forcing herself to think of survival instead of about losing Eric she checked the door to the screen porch. It was locked so she took out her knife and cut out a section of the screen. Sticking her hand through the hole she'd made she unlocked the screen door and opened it. She went in and sat down on the patio furniture that was up against the wall. The part of the porch with the expensive looking outdoor furniture was under cover. Underneath the large glass table on the other side of the porch was the carcass of a large dog. It looked like it might have been a husky based on the hair stuck to what was left of it. A line of ants moving in and out connected the dogs corpse with the lawn outside.

Trying to keep her mind off anything and everything she took some time to explore the porch and see if she could get in the house. There was a little refrigerator outside. When she opened it, she found a couple of water bottles. She opened one and downed it in three big gulps. She set the other water bottles on top of the mini fridge to save for later then went to look at the large glass sliders leading into the house. She tried shifting them around on their tracks to get into the house, but they wouldn't budge. She turned around to grab another water and settle in on the patio furniture to wait out the sun.

Smash! Myriah shrieked and spilled the water all over herself. She jumped up from the couch in horror. A large, old Zombie in a stained pair of yellow boxers had just smashed into the sliding glass door. He was shrieking and smashing himself harder and harder into the glass. The glass vibrating harder every time he pounded his body into it. Myriah grabbed her bag and ran out the screen door. She looped around to the side of the house. Behind her she could hear the loud banging coming from the Zombie inside still trying to get out. She opened the gate to run out and see if she couldn't find a better place to spend the day.

Chapter 8: Any Port in a Storm

Kyler stepped out of his air-conditioned room to walk down the narrow sidewalk to the briefing he'd been summoned to. The crushed rock sidewalk was lit on both sides by bright red lights. The lights were spaced out all around the paths winding through the sprawling military complex. A year ago, the island had just been a wide spot in the river. Kyler had learned the island had been built by a group of Seabees. The Seabees had ended up here during the turbulent times when the outbreak had been airborne, and everyone had been fighting to survive.

The Seabees were a branch of the military that excelled in construction in war zones. The term Seabees originally came from the acronym 'CB' which stood for construction battalion. They'd treated the islands like they would've treated any beachhead in an active war zone. Their motto was "We Build. We Fight." That motto held true when constructing an island to hold off the hordes of infected roaming the land. They fought hard for the raw materials needed to construct what they needed. Most of it was lying around in piles in ship yards and on military bases with the infected standing over it. Some of the materials they'd scavenged from places like Home Depot and Walmart as well. The end result was pretty awesome.

Row upon row of barracks were illuminated by the red glow cast off by the LED lights. Each barracks had a working bathroom. Kyler had spent so much time in the shower someone had actually poked their head in to ask if he was ok. It'd felt so good to have the scalding hot water rinsing the accumulated layers of grossness off his skin. To be able to wrap a towel around himself afterwards and shiver in the cold air of the barracks. There was even a working TV mounted into the wall. It was hooked to a DVD player since Netflix was down for the foreseeable future. Even the emergency broadcast signal had eventually gone off the air.

All the buildings were designed to keep light and sound from escaping them as much as possible. The whole island had been built from the ground up to be exactly what it was. An island in the middle of a raging Zombie apocalypse. Walls were built all around the perimeter of the island to keep any of the Zombies who washed up on the shore from wandering into the housing areas. At night there was only the dull red glow given off above the fortress to give away the location. The HVAC units and other equipment that made noise was mounted in such a way as to make as little noise as possible. Everyone on the island was required to practice strict noise discipline when outside the barracks.

When Kyler and the chief arrived at the dock about three miles upstream from the river, he hadn't known what to expect really. The chief had been tight lipped about central command this whole time. The chief hadn't said much at all since they'd jumped the fence with Sean covering their retreat. Kyler wondered how many men had died under his command and if that was what was ripping the man apart. He'd tried to broach the subject on the drive to the dock and gotten a surprisingly introspective response from the salty chief.

"I've led men in combat all over the globe. Until a few years ago I'd never lost a single man. I thought when I did lose that single man it was going to rip me apart. It did for a while. The loss of that one man. Since this infection started everyone around me seems to be dropping like flies. I'm just treading water waiting for my number to come up. Until it does, I'm going to just keep doing what I do and hope I'm able to do some good."

He'd had gone silent after that. Kyler had never heard the man string that many sentences together all at the same time before. Unless you counted when he was yelling at him or one of the other guys. Then he'd gone into very detailed tirades about how much they all sucked and what a waste of his time they were. Kyler knew the flask the chief started sucking out of as soon as they got in the minivan had probably done its part to help loosen his lips. He'd stayed sober enough to give Kyler directions on how to get them to the dock. When they finally got there Kyler had woken him up to get the passwords needed to get them shuffled off to a short line of men waiting for the boat to take them to the island.

Kyler had expected a motorboat of some sort to show up for them to pile onto. He'd been wondering how they kept the Zombies from hearing it coming. They'd parked about a mile down the road and walked the rest of the way to the dock to keep any Zombies who may have been attracted to the sound of the engine of the minivan from following them. Instead of a motorboat cruising up to collect them a small barge silently sailed into view as if by magic. Kyler gaped at it trying to figure it out until one of the men standing on the dock told him to look down. Kyler did and saw the thick wire wrapped around the pulley system below. That explained how the barge was moving but not so much what was able to power the barge to move like that.

The power question was answered when the barge took them to the island. The rest of the men on the boat had all been there before. They were all military looking special ops type guys. They tended to take technology and the human condition in stride as they went about their day. Kyler tried to look cool but at the sight of the red glowing fortress rising out of the river in front of him his face revealed his shock. One of the guys laughed quietly at the wonder in Kyler's voice when he pointed at the submarine docked in the small marina they were headed for. Something clicked in his head and he mentioned to the chief that he bet that's where all the power was coming from.

"Good guess kid." The man in charge of guiding the ferry said. Kyler waited to see if the man was going to say anything else, but that seemed to be the end of the commentary. Some of the other guys were talking among themselves but it wasn't a very sociable group overall. Kyler personally thought they were taking the whole 'loose lips sink ships' thing a little too far.

He'd attended a mandatory orientation session his first morning on the island. It made sense to enforce the sessions as there were a lot of things that needed to happen to keep the island humming along in 'stealth mode'. There were also a lot of things on the island that could kill you if you didn't stay away from them. Defenses had been setup to ward off the infected when the island was initially set up. Over the last few months they'd started building out more defenses against human enemies as well. The human enemies were the reason for most of the increased security.

One aspect of the island that really struck Kyler was the fact that over half the population were those deemed too fragile to be sent to live in a settlement. These were the people who'd had to shoot their own children to survive. The people who'd suffered such tragic losses that they weren't able to cope out in the settlements. A lot of them were functional in that they could complete the tasks they were assigned to help with the upkeep of the island. They'd cook and clean and help out in whatever ways they were given but everyone knew to be patient with them if they suddenly just crouched down and lost themselves in their tears.

There was also a stockade. The standard punishment for pretty much everything these days was to be taken out back and shot. It's not like anyone wanted to feed and support a bunch of criminals and you couldn't exactly turn them loose either. Banishing someone just meant they'd end up working with one of the enemy factions that were starting to pop up all over the place. Or, they'd pop up as an independent looter or if they weren't very lucky as a Zombie. The simplest solution to the crimes that people actually got punished for in the apocalypse was death. The concept of what a crime was had shifted dramatically as well.

Taking advantage of others was the big one. Men who raped, murdered or otherwise took advantage of the people of the settlements were typically shot once their guilt was confirmed. The burden of guilt being a couple of eye witnesses and the mayor of that settlement being convinced the person had committed the crime. The execution was normally carried out by the mayor of the settlement. If the mayor didn't have the stomach for it then the roving patrol would hear the case when they came through and carry out the sentence. The gist of it all was that everyone should be working together to get through this. There wasn't time to coddle criminals.

The stockade was kept to house prisoners of war. It was used to house the few criminals who committed a crime considered worthy of punishment, but not worthy of death. Occasionally, it housed a Zombie or some specimen the medical team wanted to study. It was also used to house people suspected of possibly being infected until they'd gone through a week's worth of sitting there proving they weren't about to turn into a Zombie.

Otherwise, the orientation session had just been Kyler and one other guy sitting there on plastic chairs drinking bad coffee being told where the mess hall was, how to get food, and all the rules they were expected to follow if they wanted to stay out of the stockade. They'd been assigned their temporary barracks and issued a set of orders for when and where they were supposed to report in for muster. It was all run like a military base. The man he'd been in the orientation session with had been very comfortable in the environment. Kyler himself had been around military guys all his life so he hadn't been overly put off by it either.

The request to go to one of the tactical barracks so soon after being told to settle in was odd for Kyler. It seemed pretty rushed. Then again, he knew from hanging out with his dad and his dads' friends that the military was all about hurry up and wait. He couldn't even begin to count the number of times he'd heard that phrase tossed around when he'd been growing up. He was still a little freaked out opening the door to the tactical barracks to go inside.

This building looked like the barracks on the outside, but the inside had been configured to house multiple conference rooms instead of beds. This was the building the Seabees had envisioned them using to plan how they'd take back the country from the Zombies. Who'd have ever thought that they'd be holding sessions in here to discuss fighting back against other Americans. Kyler studied the map on the wall and figured out he had to walk all the way to the other side of the building for the room he was supposed to be in.

He walked down the hall noting the looks he got from the men in military uniforms who walked past him. Kyler was acutely aware he was wearing camo pants with a black hoodie opened up to a superman t-shirt. He had weapons hanging off him at different angles. Most of the men who walked by him looked neat and proper in their uniforms. Kyler kept waiting for someone to stop him and ask why he was there.

He was happy to see the chief when he walked into the conference room. They'd parted ways once they'd gotten to the island since Presley was entitled to bunk in the chief's quarters. This was the first time he'd seen him since then. He'd been starting to wonder if he'd done something to piss him off. A few other men were seated in the plastic chairs scattered around the long table in the room. A smartly dressed officer sat at the end of the table sporting a laptop he was busy taking notes on. Kyler supposed that coordinating an operation as complex as the settlements required a lot of computer time.

Presley nodded at Kyler and pulled out the chair next to him. He gestured for Kyler to come around and take a seat. Kyler did, awkwardly shifting his M-16 around to try and sit down before realizing he should just take it off and lean it against the wall behind him. Chief Presley watching him the whole time with an exasperated look on his face. Once Kyler was finally sitting down, he realized everyone in the room was staring at him. The man with the sharply creased uniform looked up from his laptop and cleared his throat to get everyone's attention.

"This the kid you were telling us about chief?" He asked.

"Yes sir."

"Your name is Kyler, right?" The officer asked after glancing down briefly at his laptop.

"That's right sir." Kyler responded. He was wondering what was going on. He'd assumed he'd been called in as part of the chief's team being sent out to the settlements to achieve some special objectives. He hadn't expected anyone to be talking to him directly. Especially not anyone who was important. The officer looked at him for a few more seconds before checking his notes again.

"This is your first time out to the island?" The officer asked looking at Kyler who nodded in the affirmative. The officer then glanced at the chief who confirmed. "Can you tell me what you've figured out so far on your visit? Also, would you mind telling us what you've observed while you've been with the patrols in relation to the island and our mission?"

"Yes sir." Kyler took a second to gather his thoughts. He was also trying to remember what he was supposed to know and what he wasn't supposed to know to keep the chief from getting into trouble. "Construction on this island was started right after the infections became widespread. The Seabees who built the place were under orders to design it to allow a long-term command center for the central east coast. They had to ensure the place had adequate storage space for food as well as barracks for people. It was built to avoid the infected from noticing it by sound or light. It serves now to secure people who can't survive on their own as well as to be the central hub for the settlements and the rebuilding of the country."

"You sound like you're reading from the brochure." The officer said with a slight smile. "What powers the island?"

"The sub, sir." Kyler answered. He'd skipped over that part not knowing if he was supposed to know that fact or not.

"How would you go about taking this island if you were an enemy?"

"I'd cutoff the barge delivering supplies and surround the land around the island with Zombies. You could pull them in with loud noises. Noises like dropping mortars on the island." Kyler replied without hesitation. He'd already put some thought into this. Mostly along the lines of making sure he had an escape plan if things went to hell. To come up with an escape plan you first had to figure out what it would mean for the place to go to hell.

The officer quizzed him for another hour. He asked him questions about the settlements and about the weaknesses Kyler had spotted there. He asked for Kyler's best guess on why someone had shot up that one settlement they'd been sent to. He asked him what he thought about the scavenging methodology and how they were hiding the supplies in different locations. Through it all no one else said a word. Everyone in the room listened closely to Kyler as he answered each of the questions as honestly and thoughtfully as he knew how. Finally, the officer stopped tapping in notes and rapid firing questions at him. He looked around the room and each person nodded.

"Here's the deal. The US is breaking up into separate zones. We've been trying to run this as a military operation in our zone. We started off trying to help as many people as we could while fighting off the infected. We made mistakes and we lost a lot of people. The zone to our south seems to have more men than we do. We're pretty sure they're the ones who've been attacking the settlements. I don't know how you define good guys and bad guys but to me they seem like the bad guys. Between the unprovoked settlement attacks and what we've heard about them doing to the people in the south I'm ok with calling them the bad guys at this point. Make sense so far?"

"Yes sir." Kyler said. He had a bad feeling about where this was all leading.

"We need to know what's going on down there. We've sent recon and we've sent spies. The recon returned with some statistics and numbers and other data we could crunch but weren't able to really get in and learn a lot about the command structure. We like the idea of sending someone who's obviously too young to have been active duty but still knows how to handle themselves. We're asking you if you'd be willing to go down south and try to get into one of their units to gather as much info as you can. Once you had enough intel, we'd make contact to get it off of you or pull you out if needed."

"You don't have to do this." The chief said loudly. "We should be fighting Zombies and saving people. Not going off on half-ass spy missions."

"Agreed chief. However, the people to the south have made it their business to attack us without provocation. If Kyler decides to go, we'll need to swear him in and give him a crash course in spy work 101, so we need an answer pretty soon. Kyler, you answered our questions in a way that shows us you have the ability to pull this off. It's dangerous though. These guys will slit you open if they find out you're a spy. You could pretty easily die just from the trip to get there. You can have a day or two to think about it if you need to. If you don't want to go, then we'll keep you in the chiefs roving patrol detail which is also extremely important."

"I'll do it." Kyler said. He ignored the hard kick to his shin from the chief.

"Ok then. We'll get the training lined up. Report back here after dinner and we'll have your orders ready for you. Good luck and thank you."

Chapter 9: No Such Thing as Too Much Ammo

"Guys. You flew all the way here to collect your kids, right? All you have to do now is put your weapons to the side and you can be hugging on them in less than ten minutes." Amos was smiling and holding his arms out as he talked. Off in the distance a Zombie screeched. With all the noise they'd made smashing the car into the guard rail Randy wouldn't be surprised if a whole herd of the monsters didn't show up pretty soon.

"I just don't understand why you didn't just ask us to pull over instead of rolling out the stop stick things. We could've been killed when the car went sideways like that." Randy said. The smile faded from Amos. He began walking backwards away from them.

"The Zombies will be here soon with all the noise we had to make to get you to stop. We claim this land and you flew in with weapons and now you're asking why we stopped you when you continued to run from my men? Drop your weapons and come out from behind the car. We'll transport you to see your children. Or, stand there and we'll shoot you down and I'll have to go tell your kids their mommy and daddy died because they were stupid."

The Zombie screeches were getting closer. Amos was all the way back to where he'd parked his Range Rover. He was reaching into the SUV to grab his pistol. Randy noticed that he didn't holster the pistol. Rather he kept it in his hand ready to go.

"How do we know you won't just shoot us as soon as we put down our weapons?" Randy yelled. He was trying to stall while racking his brain for a way out of this mess.

"You don't. I can tell you if you don't put your weapons down that we will shoot though. Either way you're going to die. You put your weapons down and at least you have a chance." Amos yelled back.

"Let's do it." Kelly said. "He's right. There's no way out of this except giving up and hoping he's telling the truth. He knew about Caitlyn and Myriah. I say we just give up and pray he really knows where our kids are."

"The handcuffs at the border." Tony said. It was the first thing he'd said during the standoff. He was referring to the other guys they'd run into from an outfit similar to this one who'd been posted on the highway to stop anyone coming through. They'd acted friendly enough as well, but they'd had a ton of handcuffs and other restrains ready to go in their guard house.

"I'm getting a real bad vibe off this guy." Randy said. "I don't trust him at all."

"I think if we put down our weapons, we'll be getting yelled at to squeal like a pig within about ten minutes. I don't know though. Your kids, your call." Tony said out of the corner of his mouth while keeping his rifle aimed at the man in the truck off to their left.

The Mexican standoff continued. Kelly wanted to throw her gun on the ground and go beg to be taken to her children, but she forced herself to trust her instincts. Even more so, she was leaning heavily on Randy to make the right decision. She knew she wouldn't be able to think clearly where her children were concerned. She knew if the wrong decisions got made now, they'd never see the girls again. They were too close to blow it all. The tense confrontation went on for a minute that felt like forever. It was interrupted by Gordon slowly standing up on the other side of the car.

He was wiping the blood and glass off his face with his sleeve and trying to see what was going on. He was rocking back and forth. He put one hand on the roof of the car to maintain his balance while he worked on his face with the other sleeve. Pretty much everyone's focus shifted to the man awkwardly standing there unaware of what was going on. Gordon reached back in the car and came out with a bottle of water that he poured over his face. That seemed to finally do the trick. He looked around at the pickup trucks with all the men pointing guns at them then spun around and saw Randy, Kelly and Tony on the other side of the car with weapons up and ready.

"Look. All I really want is the pilot who flew the plane here. Which one of you did that? We can make a trade. I'll give you your children back if you hand over the pilot. I can tell you right now the life of a pilot in our area is a pretty laid-back life with lots of perks. You've got a minute to figure it out then I'm going to finish losing my patience.

A long, loud screech interrupted everyone. A group of three Zombies were running down the road towards them at full speed. The Zombies were a good hundred yards out. Typically, most groups would've waited for the Zombies to get closer and taken them out with bows or hand weapons to keep it quiet. Otherwise, you were just asking for more Zombies. In this case Amos gave a quick command and shots rang out from the militia on one of the trucks. The three Zombies were peppered with bullets before tumbling to the asphalt.

"What's going on?" Gordon said. His voice was trembling with fear and he sounded like he might puke at any second. Probably because of the concussion.

"Those jerkoffs say they've got the kids, but we don't think we believe them. They want us to put our weapons down and go with them or trade them the pilot for the kids. Before you say anything, they don't even know who the pilot is and we're not planning on telling them. Either Zombies are going to show up in a few minutes and kill us all or they're going to open fire and wipe us out here shortly." Tony paused and looked quickly over at Randy and Kelly. "That about cover it?" He asked.

More screeches splintered the air filling the void of silence existing between the two sides of the Mexican standoff happening on the toll road. They were coming from all around now. Judging by the volume of the screams a lot of Zombies would be arriving within a few minutes. Amos had his men holding steady. They'd be able to jump in their trucks and drive off leaving Randy and crew high and dry when the Zombies showed up.

"Hand over the pilot. Last time I'm going to ask." Amos said. He'd raised his voice to mimic the guy from the game show about making a deal. All the humor left his voice as he barked his next order loud enough for everyone to hear. "Men! Fire on my command! Ready!"

"Wait!" Gordon screamed. "I'm the pilot. I'll fly whatever you want me to just return their kids and let them go."

Amos held his hand up to keep his men from shooting. It was getting hard to hear with all the screeching in the air. A couple of the militia had turned their weapons from covering them to taking shots at the Zombies who were getting danger close. Amos waved again for Gordon to join him. They watched as Gordon jogged over. Amos patted him down then had him get in the passenger seat of the Range Rover. Amos climbed in beside him.

Then the Range Rover drove off down the road. The pickups did as well. The last truck to leave left them a parting gift.

"Get down!" Tony yelled. The grenade went off a few seconds later shattering the windows of the little red car and peppering the sides with shrapnel. The noise from the grenade was echoed by the increased volume of the horde of Zombies moving towards them up the road and out of the woods.

They jumped back to their feet. Kelly was bleeding from the shoulder where a piece of shrapnel had tagged her pretty hard. Randy yelled for Tony to figure out a plan while he ripped gauze out of one of the many pockets on the utility pants he had on and tied it around Kelly's shoulder. He thought he'd done a pretty crappy job but under the circumstances it was going to have to do. Ten seconds later Randy was looking down the road at the Zombies streaming towards them. The pickup trucks were nowhere to be seen.

"Follow me!" Tony yelled. He ran around the car and towards the concrete guardrail on the far side of the road. He stopped about halfway there to empty his magazine into the oncoming Zombies before slapping in another one and yelling for Randy and Kelly to start running and shooting.

Randy got the idea and started shooting at the oncoming Zombies. They were all shooting now as they walked across the street towards the concrete barriers designed to keep cars from going off the steep hill on that side of the road. They settled into a rhythm with Randy and Tony blasting away at every Zombie they could see coming while Kelly held her fire for the ones that made it through the crucible to get close enough to be a danger to them.

Tony pulled out two grenade looking things, ripped the pins out of them and threw them over the side of the embankment. Thick green smoke started pouring up a few seconds later. They kept shooting. The gun smoke getting so thick it was almost providing the same amount of cover as the green smoke pouring up from the smoke grenades Tony had used.

"Go!" Tony yelled. Randy nudged Kelly to get over the barrier. She awkwardly moved over the barrier. Her arm in severe pain from the grenade fragment buried in it. On the other side of the barrier she put her M-16 back into her good shoulder. She tried to ignore the waves of pain so she could stay focused on covering Tony and Randy so they could join her on this side of the barrier.

Randy came over the barrier next. Tony was halfway across when a tall Zombie came out of the smoke and grabbed him around the waist. Randy stuck the barrel of his M-16 in the Zombies chest and just started pumping bullets into the gore covered Zombie until it fell over backwards. Tony jumped over the barricade and rolled to his feet. A solid wave of Zombies cresting over the barricade as Tony, Randy and Kelly all started running full speed through the green smoke down the steep hill. The green smoke screen only took a few seconds for them to run through.

On the other side of the screen they could see a subdivision that looked like it was made up mostly of long rows of townhouses. Running up the hill towards them were more Zombies. Tony took the lead running straight for the Zombies. He'd gone full auto on his rifle and was carving a hole through the Zombies coming up the hill for them to charge through. Kelly and Randy caught on to what he was doing and joined in. They had to keep moving forward at a dead run or the Zombies coming through the smoke behind them were going to catch up.

Struggling to keep his feet moving fast enough to keep him from taking a tumble down the grass and dirt covered hill Randy tried to fire as accurately as he could. He knew it wasn't very accurate but as bunched together as the Zombies were, he didn't really need a ton of accuracy to hit them. He was lining up a shot at a fat, hairy beast of a Zombie when he ran out of ammunition. There was no time to reload or switch weapons. He dodged around the outstretched arms of the Zombie and kept running.

Looking to his left he saw Kelly had pulled a little bit ahead of him. She still evidently had ammunition left. Instead of just wildly firing into the knots of Zombies coming up the hill she was waiting until she was a few feet from any Zombie in her way. When there was a Zombie right in front of her she was just pointing the gun at them and pulling the trigger. Even if the Zombies didn't go down it at least knocked them off balance enough where they weren't able to grab her as she ran by them. Up ahead Tony was using his rifle like a club as he fought his way down the hillside. The screeching all around them was reaching epic proportions.

They made it off the hill and sprinted up a short incline to reach a cul de sac in the subdivision they'd been aiming for. Kelly shot the three Zombies who were rushing down the street towards them. Tony sprinted for the first townhouse in the row and smashed into the front door. He bounced right off it and landed hard on the sidewalk he'd gone rushing down. Randy whipped out a hatchet and used it to bash through the decorative glass running around the door. He stuck his hand through the opening he'd made and tried to get the dead bolt undone so he could open the door.

Kelly had turned around and was shooting Zombies as they arrived. It was one or two still for the next few seconds, but the massive wave was surging this way. If they were here when it hit, they were dead. Tony had reloaded and scrounged in his pack for more grenades. He popped another smoke grenade and tossed it onto the sidewalk in front of them. Kelly hoped he knew what he was doing because he'd just made it a lot harder for them to shoot the Zombies before they were right on top of them. Randy got the door open and they all barreled inside.

"Up the stairs!" Yelled Tony.

"We'll be stuck if we go up there!" Randy yelled back. He was bleeding on his wrist from cutting himself on the decorative glass trying to get the deadbolt to slide open on the door.

"I've got it! Just go!" Tony yelled. They were having to yell to be heard over the screeching and gunfire. Tony opened up on full auto again as a line of Zombies started appearing out of the smoke and running towards them.

Randy and Kelly stormed up the stairs and down the hallway at the top. At the end of the hallway was the master bedroom. It was a decent sized room with a master bath connected to it with a big jacuzzi tub. Randy ran over to the windows and ripped the curtains out of the way. The view from the window was of a large weed covered field separating the house from the back of a plaza. The weed covered field was covered in Zombies sprinting this way.

"We're dead if we stay here! Now we're trapped. What the hell is Tony thinking!" Randy yelled to Kelly as Tony came bounding up the stairs. At the top of the stairs he turned and threw another smoke grenade down. The stairway started filling up with the familiar green smoke.

"Give me your hatchet!" Tony yelled at Randy. Tony was looking around the room. He'd slammed the bedroom door and locked it. "Push something against the door and throw the mattresses against the wall in front of where the bathtub is!"

Kelly and Randy hurried to comply with the odd commands. Tony ran over and started beating on the wall with the hatchet. A few seconds later he yelled at them to go get in the tub. Randy was about to ask why when he saw what Tony was doing. He shoved Kelly ahead of him into the tube and covered her with his body. A couple seconds later he felt Tony land on top of him and try to burrow down as low as he could go.

The sounds of the Zombies beating on the bedroom door were blown away when the grenade went off in the bedroom wall. Tony had hollowed out the drywall and dropped a grenade in to blow their way into the next house. Completely deaf the three of them stumbled into the shredded master bedroom and saw the hole in the wall leading into the master suite of the neighbor's house. They scrambled through that hole. Tony ran to the wall facing the plaza and stared at it for a second.

"What are you looking for?" Randy asked.

"We need one of the houses with a balcony. Neither of these cheap bastards must've paid for the damn upgrade. We'll have to go through another wall. Bathrooms on the wrong side in this one." Tony stood there for another few seconds torn with indecision. From the house they'd just left the banging and screeching was intensifying. That door wasn't going to last much longer.

Not knowing what else to do Randy pulled the mattress of the bed and used it to cover up the hole they'd made in the wall. Maybe that'd confuse the Zombies for a minute or two. It wasn't like they were being chased by an army of Einstein's after all. Tony told them to get in the tub again and he sprinted down the hallway towards the room on the far side of the house. He came sprinting back down yelling for them to put their heads down as he jumped in the tub with them. Tony had barely got in when the explosion rocked all of their ears. Pieces of shrapnel cutting through the drywall like it didn't even exist.

With their ears ringing they climbed out of the tub. They started moving towards the door to the hallway to the room Tony had hopefully just blown a hole in the wall of. As they stepped into the master bedroom from the bath the mattress Randy had put over the hole in that room fell from the wall. The mattress falling was followed by a wave of Zombies pushing to get through the hole. The Zombies were screeching their heads off as they piled through the jagged hole. Tony and Randy opened fire on the Zombies trying to get in while Kelly continued down the hall hoping they'd fall in behind her.

Running into the small room at the end of the hallway she saw the grenade trick had worked again. Another hole had been blown through another wall. Randy and Tony came crashing through the door about fifteen seconds later. Tony tossed another grenade down the hallway they'd just came from and screamed for them to get through the hole and on the ground. All three of them jumped for the hole and scrambled through then dove on the other side of the bed in the next room. Seconds later the shock wave and sound of the grenade exploding hit them again. At this point Kelly was pretty sure her hearing was toast.

Wobbling to her feet she helped Randy and Tony up. She vaguely noticed that blood was starting to seep out of her shoulder through the bandages Randy had shoved under her shirt for her. Tony ran out of the room and down the hallway with Kelly following right behind him. Randy stopped to shut the door to the small bedroom. It opened inwards so he was hoping the Zombies would get stuck against it. Worse case it'd slow them down for a minute. Even as he was shutting the door a body slammed up against it on the other side. He heard the screeching coming from inches away through the thick wooden door. Forcing his body to keep moving he followed Kelly down the hall where she was waiting to slam and lock the door behind him.

This master suite was letting in more of the fading sunlight than the last couple of rooms they'd been in. Randy saw that was because this family had decided to pay the premium to have a townhome with a balcony installed. Two big sliding glass doors led the way out of the master bedroom to the small balcony outside. Tony had both of the sliders open and was staring up at the roof. From the field below Randy heard Zombies screeching up at them. Randy and Kelly started stacking everything they could find in front of the bedroom door.

"Help me move the dresser out to the balcony!" Tony yelled. They stopped and stared at him to see if he'd finally lost his mind.

"I don't really have anything better to do." Kelly said with a shrug deciding to keep trusting Tony. He'd gotten them this far. Of course, 'this far' was trapped in a townhouse complex filling up with hundreds of the infected while they slowly depleted their supply of ammunition.

The dresser was heavy. Remembering what they'd done when they moved into their new house a couple of years earlier Randy started ripping the dresser drawers out. Kelly helped until they had the dresser light enough to drag out onto the balcony. Randy looked over the edge at the Zombies who were standing on the patio below screeching up at them. A couple of the Zombies were already banging on the sliding glass doors below to try and get in. Randy was waiting for Tony to ask for help pushing the dresser over the railing. He still wasn't clear on what Tony thought it would accomplish to squash a handful of the Zombies. He did kind of want to see it happen though.

Wondering what Tony was up to he turned around to see him working his way on top of the dresser. Standing on the top of the dresser with both his hands extended straight up he was still a little too short to reach the roof. They heard the banging start on the door in the master bedroom.

"Send Kelly up here!" Tony yelled.

Randy helped Kelly up and then watched while Tony and Kelly performed a feat worthy of a Cirque act. Randy got Kelly to use the wall to balance herself so she could stand up on his shoulders and pull herself onto the roof using her one good arm. Once Kelly was up on the roof Tony waved at Randy to climb up. Randy stood on the top of the dresser and it started rocking with both of them on it. Tony stuck out his hands and Randy almost fell off the balcony trying to climb up on Tony's shoulders.

"You try!" He yelled at Tony and made a cup with both of his hands for Tony to step into. Tony stepped in and Randy boosted him as hard as he could. Tony slammed into the roofline with his hands and started falling backwards. Kelly caught him and pulled hard to get them both stable again. If she hadn't caught him then they'd have both gone over the side. The banging inside the master suite was accompanied by the sound of cracking wood. Randy looked up at Tony and Kelly who were both hanging over the side of the roof with their arms stuck down. Like that was going to magically give him a twenty-inch vertical leap.

Rather than jumping around like an idiot until he fell off the balcony he climbed down from the dresser and ran back in the master. Looking around desperately he saw the little chair in front of the vanity. He grabbed it and ran back on the balcony as the lock to the door to the master bedroom finally gave up and Zombies poured into the room. He turned and slammed the slider closed. The Zombies slamming into it snarling and slobbering at him through the thick glass inches from his face.

Knowing he was only going to get one chance to get this right he put the chair on top of the dresser and carefully climbed up. He tried to ignore the sound of the glass door being banged into. It didn't help knowing that if any of the Zombies just pushed at an angle it would open right up. He put both his feet on the small chair and stood straight up. He couldn't quite reach the roof, but he felt Randy and Kelly's hands grip onto his wrists. He jumped for the roof.

The chair flew out from under him and tumbled to the patio below. The sliding glass doors opened, and Zombies came tumbling out. All of the Zombies in the room tried to get on the balcony causing at least two of them to fall off the balcony to the patio below. Randy was holding on for dear life to the edge of the roof trying to pull himself up while the Zombies were trying to get on the dresser to get at him. The dresser tumbled over and fell off the balcony taking another Zombie with it for the short fall.

All the weight of the supplies Randy was carrying were pulling him down. He had a pack on full of ammunition and food and gear. Unfortunately, there was no way for him to take it off with both his hands clinging to the roof for dear life. He summoned every bit of energy he had and managed to do a chin up. His face cleared the top of the roof line and Tony grabbed him by the shoulders and dragged him up onto the roof. Randy ended up lying on the roof on top of Tony. Both of them gasping for breath. Kelly stood up and looked down at her husband laying on top of Tony.

"Anything you two want to tell me?" She asked with a smirk.

"You've actually been the third wheel this whole time." Tony gasped out without missing a beat.

Randy rolled off Tony and kissed Kelly.

"Now what?" He asked looking over at Tony.

"We lay here and check out the stars for a few hours then try to figure out how the hell to get down without breaking our legs or ending up getting eaten. Hopefully the Zombies forget we're up here and start nesting for the night pretty soon." With that Tony pulled his pack off and situated it to use as a pillow. He settled in to try and rest his body for a few hours. Randy and Kelly quickly followed suit.

Chapter 10: The Deep End

Myriah looked through the open gate at the two Zombies standing out on the street. The two were sniffing and shifting their heads around looking for the source of the noise they'd just heard. Cursing herself for making such a rookie mistake she tried to slide over to the side so the fence would hide her from the Zombies. She knew she'd been spotted when she heard the Zombie start screeching. That screech was echoed all around the neighborhood by other Zombies. Myriah slammed the gate shut and ran back towards the corner of the house. She heard a crash from the back porch and assumed that was the Zombie on the back porch finally breaking through the sliding glass door.

The Zombie picked itself up from the patio of the back porch and looked around for the girl it'd seen. The Zombie was hungry. It'd eaten raw meat from the refrigerator and gnawed on the family cat but had mostly just laid on the floor of the living room in stasis for the past year. Its brain was so infected with the virus at this point that there were no memories of ever being a normal human. Its thoughts weren't even in a language anymore. It just saw things as food or sleep or kill. The screech that welled up inside it when it'd seen the girl came from some primordial part of its brain that was awakened by the virus when it burnt out the other parts.

It bashed on the glass door until it gave in. Standing up in the broken glass on the concrete patio it looked around. No sign of the food it'd seen. It knew it was on the porch for a reason though, so it walked around the perimeter of the screen. Hearing other screeches coming from all around the Zombie slammed itself into the screen a few times. The screen gave out pretty easily. The Zombie stepped into the narrow sun ledge in the pool before it could stop itself. Not seeing the food but hearing the screeches the Zombie began to walk around the yard looking to join the others it could hear screeching.

The Zombies from the street hit the gate to the backyard hard. It was the standard PVC white vinyl type fence with the different sections shoved in. As more Zombies arrived and kept beating on the fence it collapsed and the Zombies ran through it. There were ten new Zombies in the back yard within three minutes of Myriah having opened the gate in the first place. All of them walked around the back yard looking for the food they sensed should be there. None of them saw any sign of a normal human though. Not seeing anything they eventually lost interest and either lie down to rest or just stopped where they were and stood there staring vacantly in front of them.

Myriah stood in the scum coated water of the pool with her head under the floatie. She had it tilted up enough where she was able to breathe. She'd tilted the side closest to the wall of the pool to try and avoid the Zombies noticing it. She thought she was probably ok unless she made any sudden movements. It was still pretty early in the day so unless some noise distracted the Zombies and got them to leave, she knew she was going to be standing in the pool under the floatie for a long time. She felt fine now but the water wasn't warm. She was also standing on an inclined part of the ledge where the pool transitioned from the shallow to the deep end. Her legs were already getting sore from maintaining her position without starting to slip down the incline.

Realizing she wasn't going to be able to hold this pose the rest of the day she started working on a way out of the mess she was in. Ten minutes later the best she'd come up with was still standing there in the water without moving until it got dark. The problem with that being it hadn't been half an hour yet and she was already starting to get cold. Her legs were cramping up on her as well. She could hear the occasional grunt out of the Zombies hanging out around the pool. The screeches from outside the fence had died down.

Her foot slipped. She recovered quickly but the movement caused some sloshing the pool. She froze as she heard the Zombies shift around. She could imagine them staring down into the water and trying to figure out what'd made the noise they just heard. She didn't know if they'd dive in and check or just do a quick look to see if they saw anything. She waited without breathing. She froze as much as she could willing the Zombies to stop looking. She was terrified of feeling something push down on the floatie. She kept waiting to hear a splash as one of the Zombies jumped in and came over for a closer inspection.

There were no splashes. All she heard after a few minutes was the sound of her own harsh breathing under the mold coated plastic of the floatie. To her own ears her breathing seemed too loud for anyone to ignore. Based on how cold she was starting to feel just standing there in the water she was worried her teeth would start chattering soon. Thinking about making a run for it she tried to envision where the Zombies may be standing around the pool. She doubted she could jump out of the pool at this point and beat the Zombies in a foot race. She was thinking if she could slide closer to the side of the pool by the house that maybe she could pop up and run into the house.

The more she thought about it the more she thought that might be her only play. Otherwise she was going to just be standing there until she did something to give herself away or some noise randomly happened that got the Zombies to leave. She couldn't bet on the random noise happening in the next hour. She calculated she wouldn't be able to make it more than an hour without coughing or her teeth chattering or her doing something to give herself away. Once she gave herself away in the pool, she was dead. The longer she waited the harder it was going to be to force her legs to work.

Decision made she started working herself towards the shallow part of the pool underneath the floatie. She moved slowly to try and avoid being noticed. She thought about trying to swim underwater and pop up in the shallow end then run for it but was freaked out by what may be under the water. Plus, she wasn't great at opening her eyes underwater in the first place. She was also worried getting a big face full of green pool scum could cause some serious visibility issues when she could least afford them.

She slid slowly into the shallow end of the pool until she was down on her knees sliding herself across the bottom of the pool while slowly shifting the floatie above her. She hoped none of the Zombies would get curious about why a floatie was propelling itself across the pool. She bumped up against the side of the sun shelf and worked her way down to where the stairs were. She was only in a few feet of water now. She'd shrugged off her backpack and let it sink to the bottom earlier. Saddened by the loss of the medicine Eric had died for them to get. She'd hated being struck by the realization he was dead all over again.

She had her hammer in her right hand and a big hunting knife hanging off her belt. She raised her head up underneath the floatie to take one more deep breath before she slowly started working the floatie backwards out of her way. She managed to get it moved completely backwards without hearing it cause any sort of commotion. She finally got to the point where she only had to move it about another inch, and she'd be able to see around her again. She slid the raft off her face to run and looked up.

There were three Zombies standing on the end of the pool staring back at her. They must've been staring at the moving floatie the entire time. The screeching was immediate as all three Zombies plunged into the pool. Myriah dropped her hammer and dove for the deep end. She swam underwater to the other side of the pool. With her lungs burning she surfaced and looked around. The pool was frothing with all the Zombies having jumped in to get at her. None of them could swim so they were all just floundering around. The ones who'd gone to the deep end were drowning so that was good at least.

The ones still standing in the shallow end saw her head pop up and screamed their hunger at her. One of them went straight for her and became intertwined with the other Zombies slowly drowning in the deep end of the scum covered pool. The others jumped out and started running around the pool towards her. Myriah put both her hands on the ledge in the corner of the deep end and hoisted herself up and out of the pool. A tall thin gangly Zombie came running for her along the side of the pool. Myriah ran towards the Zombie to avoid the larger Zombies coming from the other side of the pool. She could also hear screeching from outside the fence again getting closer.

The tall Zombie reached for her and Myriah grabbed the Zombies wrist and spun hard with it. Using the Zombies momentum against it she dropped to the ground and tugged hard enough to send the Zombie somersaulting into the pool. Unless it was tall enough to walk on the bottom of the pool it'd drown in there with the others. It did look like two Zombies had made it out of the deep end and were working on getting out of the pool on the shallow end to come after her. Myriah sprinted past both of them and raced through the hole in the screen the original Zombie she'd seen had made to get outside.

She ran over the broken glass and through the sliding glass doorframe the Zombie had beaten out of the house to try and get at her earlier. Entering the house with her screeching pursuers right on her heels she sprinted for the front door praying her soaking wet feet wouldn't slip out from under her. Running through the living room she skidded to a stop in front of the front door and tried the knob. It didn't open, so she flung the deadbolt open. She got the door to start opening when something hit it from the outside hard. A Zombies hand shot into the crack between the door and wall. Myriah realized she'd missed the fact that the door had a chain lock on it.

She stepped back with a scream and turned to run the other way. A Zombie blocked her way back to the kitchen where the broken slider was. Behind that Zombie she saw another one coming her way as well. With her choices starting to be very limited she ran down the hallway. She saw some stairs leading up, so she took them two at a time. A door at the top was open to a girl's bedroom. This girl had gotten hooked up with her own little loft area and a bedroom off the loft area with its own bathroom. Myriah was assuming it'd been a girl's room because of all the pink and shiny things she saw.

She turned and slammed the flimsy door to the room just as the Zombie who'd been on her heels slammed into it. She was frantically looking around for a weapon when the Zombie beat its way through the door. Myriah ran into the connected bedroom but couldn't get the door shut before the Zombie shoved it's body into the room. Stumbling backwards she wound up in the bathroom. She looked around desperately for a weapon and her eyes fell on the toilet. She reached over with both hands and took the top off the toilet's basin.

She spun around right as the Zombie charged into the room. She swung the big heavy toilet lid as hard as she could at the Zombies face. She caught the Zombie with a very solid blow that rocked it backwards into the bathroom wall. Not giving the Zombie time to recover she brought the lid down hard enough to smash the dazed Zombies head in. With a caved in skull the Zombie slumped to the floor and didn't move again. Myriah took the lid out into the main bedroom where a teen age looking Zombie was coming through the door screeching. She swung at it's head in with the lid before it made it all the way in the room.

When she hit this Zombie in the head her fingers slipped, and the lid bounced off and flew into the wall. A big chunk of the lid breaking off at some point during that whole routine. The stunned Zombie had been knocked to the ground when she smashed the lid into its head. Not giving it time to recover she fumbled her knife out and stabbed it into the Zombies chest until she felt it sink deep. Blood spurted for a few seconds before it died. Myriah slammed the bedroom door shut. It was a much more solid door than the one that had been at the top of the stairs. She thought it would hold up for a little bit longer against a Zombie beating on it.

Door locked she ran over to the big window on the side of the room. It was covered in some kind of weird red velvet curtain that had little Christmas lights wrapped around it. She pulled a handful of all that to the side and looked out the window. She was on the opposite side of the house from where the gate was. She saw a handful of Zombies out on the main road, so she eliminated that as an option. She could see the house on the other side of the fence from her vantage point and it looked pretty safe. She just needed to be able to get over there.

She worked the window open as quietly as she could. She could hear Zombies out in the loft already. They could start beating on the bedroom door any second now. She looked down below. There was a bunch of tall grass and weeds in a narrow little alley between the wall of the house and the fence. A couple of air conditioner condensers took up most of the space towards the end of the alley where the pool was. No Zombies were visible down there at all.

Myriah tossed blankets and pillows out the window to try and make a softer landing for herself. She looked around for some sort of rope she could use to lower herself down. She couldn't find any rope so decided to try to use those red velvet curtains. The bottom of the floor length curtains was bunched up on the ground. Myriah figured if they went that low and if the curtain rod held, they might work to get her lowered down to the ground below. She shoved the curtain out the window and looked to see how far down it hung. Before she had a chance to look, she heard beating start on the door to the bedroom.

Trying not to think about the drop to the ground she worked her way out of the window and used the curtain to climb down the wall as far as she could get. She dangled at the bottom of the curtain gathering her courage to drop the rest of the way. In an effort to avoid being paralyzed by the fear of falling she forced herself to let go of the curtain. She landed painfully on the ground below, but all her limbs were still in working order, so she called it a successful drop.

She couldn't reach the top of the fence to pull herself over so walked down the alley to where the compressors were. She climbed up on one of those and jumped for the top of the fence. It hurt her already abused body, but she was able to scramble over the top of the fence and drop down to the neighbor's yard below. From the neighbor's yard she kept working her way through backyards until she got to the strip of woods by the last house on the street in the subdivision.

Surprised and relieved to have escaped she slipped into the woods and set a course for the lake house. She was wet, miserable, and her body hurt all over. The physical pain and discomfort were nothing compared to how she felt about losing Eric. Her stomach was upset from thinking about the fact that she was going to have to tell her sisters that Eric wasn't going to be coming back to them this time.

Chapter 11: Spies Like Us

Kyler pulled over by a green highway sign that proclaimed it was ten miles to the Georgia border. He was outfitted in the same basic clothing he'd been wearing for the last few months now. Camouflage pants, a black hoodie with a zipper running up the front and a plain black t-shirt had become his uniform of the day. The fancy TIMBUK2 labeled knapsack he had on was stuffed with spare clothes, food and weapons. He had an assortment of rifles, knives, hatchets and pistols strapped to his body in various places. The stains on his sleeves and the front of his hoodie showed he wasn't afraid to get in close for the kill.

He was riding a moped and soaked to the bone. A massive thunderstorm had come out of nowhere and soaked him as he was riding down I-95. The ride down had been uneventful. There'd been some tense moments driving past exits with signs that read 'keep going or be shot' and 'do not exit' with red marks all over them. At one of the exits he'd seen a group of men staring down at him. The men had all been armed and looked ready to shoot if he made the poor choice decide to ignore the warning signs. It'd made it hard to get gas for the moped but luckily the little machine seemed to chug along forever on just a few gallons of gas.

It'd taken two weeks at the island for them to get him some basic training in spy craft and work up some objectives for him. Chief Presley had left a week before Kyler had. The chief had headed out with a new team of young men assembled to be the next roving patrol. It was a very high turnover job. Kyler had envied them the camaraderie. He also envied them in that they were headed out to visit with people who knew their role and respected them for it. Kyler was headed out to lie like crazy to try to work his way into a group of people who'd slice his throat in a heartbeat if they learned the truth about him. He wasn't going to help people but to figure out the best way to destroy them. The chief would be helping shore up weak points in the settlement defenses. Kyler was responsible for finding weak points they could exploit in their enemies.

Shivering in the rain on the moped looking at the sign Kyler reflected he still had time to turn around. There was no rule saying he had to go do this. Presley had told him several times he thought it was a dumb idea. It was strictly voluntary. Not that anybody worried about a paycheck these days. It was all about stockpiling the kind of stuff that could help you live another day or two. Kyler figured one of the things he needed to stockpile was goodwill from the people who were going to end up ruling the world. That very much included the commanding officer of the submarine that was powering the island.

Commander Hartfield had come to the swearing in ceremony. Kyler had found out the man liked to officiate at as many of them as he could. The ceremony itself was the same swearing in ceremony members of the US military had been going through for years. In this case it'd just been made a little more generic since they weren't joining a specific branch of the military. The commander had been very specific in letting them know this wasn't an oath of fealty to him. This was an oath they were taking to serve the ideals of the USA. An oath to fight against the infection and the people taking advantage of the infection to fracture the country. He told them to take it seriously as he would hold them to it.

Once the swearing in ceremony had concluded the commander had met briefly with Kyler and thanked him for taking on the mission to the south. It'd been the commander himself who told Kyler if it seemed too dangerous or he got a bad feeling about it to feel free to turn around and come back. He'd said they could use every good man they could get here. He'd been sure to specifically tell Kyler if the spying mission began to feel more like a suicide mission he should wave off and return to base. The commanders plain spoken mannerisms and common-sense way of looking at the world had helped convince Kyler he was backing the right horse. If anyone could guide them out of this current state of devastation it was going to be Hartfield, or someone very much like him.

Teeth starting to chatter Kyler pulled back on the mopeds throttle to start riding south again. He dodged around cars. He rode past what looked like a recently killed man surrounded by the marks of a fire and what looked like a bomb blast. He drove past there quickly in case the people who'd blown up the highway happened to still be hanging around. Up ahead he saw the cars had all been cleared off the highway for the next half mile. At the end of that clean run he could see what looked like a wall of cars setup to block the highway.

He briefly considered turning back. This was his absolute last chance. He knew someone may already be staring at him through a sniper scope or a pair of binoculars, but he still had a reasonable chance of getting the hell out of there.

"Screw it." He muttered and started riding slowly towards the massive car wall up ahead. The plan was for him to drive up and argue with the guards a little bit then let them disarm him and take him to the processing center. The recon patrol who'd come through had setup and watched these guys take people in from the highway. From the ones they'd seen processed they were roughed up a little bit but eventually sent back towards the main base on a truck that came out to the checkpoint every few days.

Kyler had his cover story prepared of traveling to Florida to look for his parents. He'd never actually been to Florida before, so he'd had to sit in a room with another guy who was from Florida to learn about Florida. He'd basically borrowed that guys hometown and parents as his story. He could go deep on it if he needed to, but he hoped he wouldn't need to. He rode towards the wall of cars until he was about fifty yards away. It was raining and overcast but he assumed they had to have seen him by now. He thought about beeping his moped horn but decided he'd already lost enough man points by rolling up on the beefed-up Schwinn as it was.

Unchallenged, he rode through the cars until he could see the building the checkpoint was in. He could see people walking around the front of the building. He slowed down to a crawl as he started to get a bad feeling in the pit of his stomach. The hum from the engine of his moped finally penetrated the steady drizzle of rain. As one, the people by the guard post snapped their heads around to stare at him. Screeching split the air as the Zombies rushed towards him. Kyler gunned the mopeds engine and drove straight forward. He didn't think he'd have time to navigate the zig zag of cars to go out the way he'd just come in. He only needed to get around one more, and he'd be able to skirt by the guard post and keep on cruising south bound.

His heart was pounding. He broke out in a cold sweat as he pushed the moped to go faster. The practical vehicle had basically been a compromise between walking and driving a gas guzzling car. He hadn't wanted to try to peddle himself on a ten speed across multiple states either. He'd even pictured himself able to cruise quickly past the lumbering Zombies as they stretched out their arms for him.

In practice he felt like a toddler on a three-wheeler trying to out run a pissed off pit bull. His visions of doing a wheelie and throwing out a jaunty wave were long gone. He turned the throttle all the way back and cut hard to the left once he got past the final car. The fastest Zombie had already gotten close enough with his outstretched hand that Kyler could have fist bumped him if he'd been so inclined. He zipped right past that Zombie then his front wheel connected with a pile of what used to be a human that was strewn out across the middle of the street.

The front wheel of the moped spun helplessly for a heartbreaking second before Kyler got past the rib cage and hit the asphalt again. The back tires lost purchase a second after that. Kyler was slipping all over the place. He could feel himself losing control of the moped. He willed the tires to align as he tugged hard on the handlebars to try to get his ride back under control. A Zombie tackled him from the side, and he went toppling over. He hit the ground hard with the Zombie on top of him.

He'd been ready for the hard hit. He let his body absorb the pain and then rolled as far from the moped as he could. The Zombie who'd landed on him was crawling towards him gnashing its teeth. Kyler gave up on his rifle since it was wrapped around his back and pulled out his pistol instead. He shot the Zombie crawling towards him in the face. It crumpled to the ground with a big dark hole slowly filling with blood right in the middle of its forehead.

Sitting up Kyler took six more shots at the closest Zombies then stood up before shooting at a couple more. Screeching was coming from all around him now. The gunshots had woken up the ones who hadn't been into it quite yet. He looked around to see if he should shoot anything else once he'd changed the magazine in his pistol. Not seeing any more immediate threats, he went to pick up the moped.

There were dead bodies everywhere. Shell casings littered the ground all around him. He took in all that data as he heaved the moped back up on its tires and slung his leg over the seat to sit down. He got it started back up and carefully navigated the field of corpses to get moving south again. He began picking up speed just as the next wave of Zombies began sprinting through the field of corpses to try and get at him. Without taking the time to count he estimated there to be around fifty or sixty living Zombies back there. Who knew how many there'd been to have taken out the guard post? The pile of fresh corpses must've been part of the mob that'd stormed the guard shack.

Not wasting any more time trying to figure out what'd happened back there he settled for being alive. Now he needed to plan out his next move since getting picked up back at the guard shack was no longer an option. He supposed he could just keep going and assume a patrol would pick him up eventually. He also realized he now had a pretty good excuse to turn around and head out of Georgia. He could be back at the island in a few days. He'd have to go through the woods or something to get around the Zombie infested guard shack but that shouldn't take him too long.

The screeches of the Zombie pack at the guard shack slowly faded away as he cruised south. He was weaving in and out of cars here and there but mostly the road was clear. He kept an eye out for another outpost or more Zombies but all there was to see was mile after mile of trees. He stopped at a rest area that had a couple of cars parked in the lot in front of a large welcome center. He parked the moped and walked around to the back of the rest stop. In the parking lot behind the welcome center area he found a parked road ranger truck. He broke the back window out and helped himself to a red container full of gasoline. He also grabbed a pack of road flares because why not?

He walked back around to where he'd parked the moped right as a nice-looking black F-150 with heavily tinted windows rolled into the rest area. Kyler made sure his pistol was where he could get at it without making it too obvious. It suddenly occurred to him these men might think he'd killed the guys at the guard shack to get past them. Even if they just thought he'd snuck past them he'd still be in trouble. Just because the recon teams that'd been sent down here to gather intel had seen the people crossing the border get handcuffed and taken away didn't mean these were nice, hospitable people. They could've handcuffed them and driven them away to use as target practice. Kyler suddenly suspected that the whole recon story had been spun for him. He was here because he was expendable. He'd accepted that back at the island but now he really felt it.

Too late to worry about that now. There was no way the guys in the F-150 hadn't seen him. Kyler wondered why he hadn't bothered to ride the moped around to the back of the rest area behind the bathrooms. He'd had an idea about being able to get out of the parking lot quickly in case the rest area turned out to be full of Zombies. In retrospect, he realized that plan hadn't made a whole lot of sense. The truck drove over to within twenty feet of him. Kyler let his hand wander down to his pistol but didn't draw it.

The windows of the extended cab were tinted so dark Kyler couldn't see what was going on in the cab. He was idly thinking about that being pretty useful in the event you needed to pull over and let a bunch of Zombies run past you while you sat in the car eating a sandwich or whatever. As long as you didn't make any noise, they probably wouldn't notice you were there. The driver's window rolled down at the same time as the rear driver's side window did. Kyler also heard the doors opening on the other side of the truck. One man went to the back of the truck with a rifle and another one walked over and stood on the other side of the trucks large hood.

The men were all wearing camouflage. Two of them had on baseball hats and one had a cowboy hat he'd put on when he got out of the truck. Kyler noticed one of the men looked Hispanic and another was black. So much for the intelligence they'd gotten that parts of the south were run by white supremacist groups. Or, maybe it was a different part. At this point Kyler was hoping he'd live long enough to gather those kinds of details.

"Please move your hand away from the pistol if you don't mind. It makes us a little nervous when people do that." The driver of the truck said.

"That's understandable." Kyler said as he moved his hand away. It wasn't like he'd have time to draw and kill all four of them before one of them shot him anyway.

"That's better. Now we can have us a quick conversation. I'm Tom. What's your name?" Tom asked. He'd stuck his hand out the window of the truck as he was asking. Kyler noticed the man was wearing gloves. A smart move he'd seen lots of people adopt who were in frequent contact with the Zombies. Kyler wondered if his aversion to having sweaty hands was going to end up getting him killed. He really hoped not.

"Kyler." He said as he stuck out his ungloved hand. The driver took it and pumped it up and down a few times. Kyler half expected the man to shove a gun in his face and take him prisoner. The man didn't disappoint.

"Great to meet you. Kindly put both your hands on the side of the truck while my men here take your weapons for safe keeping. While they're doing that why don't you tell me how you got past the guard post at the state line?" Tom asked him. Once Kyler was covered by the other men and stripped of his weapons Tom lowered his pistol back out of sight.

"The outpost up the road is overrun with Zombies. Looks like there was a good fight there but the Zombies won."

"Ok. We're going to go ahead and handcuff your hands behind your back and take a little drive. Assuming what you're saying is true we need to see how bad it is before we go back to the base." Tom shifted his attention to the entrance to the rest stop getting ready to roll out once Kyler was in the back. Kyler let himself be handcuffed. The man who handcuffed him helped him climb into the bed of the truck. As Kyler and the man were getting situated in the back Tom started driving.

"What about my moped?" Kyler asked the man in the back with him.

"What about it?" The man asked. "You're not going to be needing any kind of vehicle for a while. When you do need one again the base commander will provide it. Where were you headed anyway?"

"I was going to check on my parents down in Orlando." Kyler lied. He felt like the man would be able to see right through him. Honestly though, the guy didn't care whether he was lying or not. No one really told the whole truth anymore anyway.

"Well, just so you know you're going to be taking a bit of a detour to get it sorted as to how you fit in down here. I suggest you do your best to get picked to fit in really well. People who don't seem to fit in or be good at anything tend to lead a really messed up life. People who ain't afraid to work for a living can do alright. Or, at least as alright as it's possible to do in this brave new world."

Kyler leaned back and took a deep breath. He was off to a different start than envisioned but it sounded like he was still headed in the right direction. All he had to do now was keep his eyes open and try not to die.

Chapter 12: Maximum Carnage

There was enough of a moon out to tell that they were totally screwed. The Zombies may have broken into some of the town homes and nested but there was so damned many of them wandering around below that it didn't even matter. It was like Woodstock for Zombies. Randy felt like Jimmy Hendricks looking out at the massive crowd of screaming, drugged up fans waiting for him to start playing. Except these fans were infected cannibals who were randomly screaming as they looked for humans to eat.

They were completely surrounded. It was like the whole city had turned Zombie and come to this particular subdivision to hang out. The field separating the subdivision from the Publix was literally crawling with the pus leaking human shaped bags of insanity. They did a circuit on the roof and it was Zombies for as far as the eye could see.

"So, this is working out great." Kelly stage whispered in Tony's direction.

"We're not dead at least." Randy interjected. He wanted to break up the argument before it happened. He recognized the edge to Kelly's voice. He'd been on the receiving end of that tone enough times to know it was time for Tony to duck and cover.

"We might as well be. How the hell are we going to get down off here? How are we supposed to look for our kids?" Kelly had switched her anger over to Randy now. Randy wished he'd just let Tony take the brunt of the abuse. Give him a little life lesson in marriage and understanding the mystery that is woman. Recognizing she needed him he went over and tried to hug her.

"Get off me and look for a damned way off these stupid houses you geniuses managed to get us stuck on top of. We need to be moving before daylight. I'm not sitting up here for days waiting for them to wander off. Figure something out." With that declaration Kelly shrugged off Randy trying to hug her and went to stand by herself looking down at the mass of Zombies writhing around in the field below.

Looking extremely scared of Kelly, Tony pulled Randy over to the side. "We've got backpacks full of grenades and ammunition. I know I didn't waste much space on water or food so we actually can't plan on spending too much time on the roof anyway. What if we toss a bunch of grenades off one end and then hope that opens up enough room on the other end for us to make a run for it?"

It was a pretty standard tactic they'd developed in Zombie fighting. The Zombies always surged towards the noise. Randy thought back to the Woodstock feeling he'd had earlier. Too bad they couldn't get a band to pull up and start playing some heavy metal up on the toll road. He thought of all the noise they'd made getting here already. It was due to all the grenades and gunfire that they'd attracted the crowd they had out there.

"Do you have any grenades left? You were tossing them out left and right for a little bit there." Randy asked. They started in on an inventory to see what they actually did have instead of just assuming they still had a lot of stuff. It turned out Tony's math had been completely off. He'd just taken what he crammed into his backpack and multiplied it by three. He hadn't accounted for the ammunition they'd already expended and the grenades he'd used to open up all the walls and get them safely up here on the roof. Randy had a ton of explosives in his pack, but Kelly hadn't been carrying even half as much. She was a lot smaller than either of them, so her pack wasn't as big, plus she'd actually packed things like food and water and medicine.

"We need a mariachi band being burned alive in a dumpster fire kind of distraction. Something big and loud. As many Zombies as there are, I'm not sure now if tossing a few grenades off the roof is going to get enough of them to move to give us the room we need to run."

"Propane tanks?" Randy was walking around the roof looking down into the backyards. A few of them had propane tanks in them hooked up to grills.

"Nah. I saw a Mythbusters where they shot up a propane tank and it didn't do anything. Stupid things are way too safe."

"Throwing the grenades under cars?" Randy tossed out another idea.

"I don't know. Maybe?" Tony said with a shrug. He didn't seem really keen on the idea.

One end of the townhouses butted up to a wooded area with a fence running through it. Zombies were packed in the area between the fence and the houses, but it looked empty on the other side of the fence. Staring down off the roof at all the different places they could make a run for it that one looked the best. Assuming they could make a loud enough noise on the other side to get the Zombies moving they should be able to get out and over that fence pretty quick.

"Why aren't they nesting?" Kelly asked. Randy almost fell off the roof. Him and Tony had been staring down at the Zombies and not expecting Kelly to walk up behind them and start talking.

"All the houses they're able to break into are full?" Tony guessed.

"Seems like a bunch of them are just laying down where they're at. Kind of hard to tell from up here but like out in the field they seem to be sleeping on top of one another. We probably screwed up their Zombie plans with all the noise we made. They stormed over here looking for some uninfected to eat and all they found was a field and a bunch of houses, but they don't want to leave just in case." Randy expounded on Tony's guess.

"So, what's the plan?" Kelly asked.

"Throw a bunch of grenades off the other end of the row of houses and try to get to that fence and over it before we're eaten alive." Tony answered.

"Who's going to throw the grenades and how are they going to get down to the ground before the Zombies lose interest in the grenades going off?"

They hadn't thought that far ahead yet. In his head Randy was still thinking of the plan as the 'throw grenades off one side of the roof then get eaten alive by Zombies on the other side of the houses' plan. He was hoping inspiration was going to strike him. It didn't seem like that was happening any time soon though. He thought about the garages in the townhomes and wondered if they could get a car out of one of them. The problem being the roads were all clogged with the Zombies down below. Even if they got one out, they wouldn't get very far.

"Ok. So, either me or Tony will end up being the one to sling grenades. The other two need to get down to the balcony of the house closest to the end of the row and check to see if there's a car in the garage and if they can get keys. They'll need to make sure first there aren't a bunch of Zombies nesting in that townhouse. Grenades start going off and we all meet up in the car and drive straight into the fence. We hop out and run through the woods." Randy said. He thought it was probably about the best plan they were going to get.

"Let's do it. I'll be the grenade tosser. I'm thinking about five should do it. Be ready when I catch up to you. If there's no car in the garage or that doesn't seem like it'll work for whatever reason, then let's us plan on running and gunning. Either way we'll be out of here in a few minutes and back on the way to find your kids. I'll give you two a ten-minute head start to get it all figured out." Tony said.

Tony gathered ten grenades total and split the rest of his loose gear between Kelly and Randy. He'd be coming down from the roof fast so wanted as little stuff to hold him back as possible. Once that task was complete, they found the house with the balcony on it closest to the end of street and lowered Kelly down to take a look. They were able to fashion the bandoliers from their rifles into a rope that let them lower her almost all the way down quickly and quietly. Then they waited for her to check out the house. They kept the rope dangling down in case they needed to pull her back up quickly.

She came back out on the balcony ten minutes later carrying a ladder. She folded it out so that Randy could dangle off the side of the roof and touch it with his feet. Once he had his feet planted, he carefully climbed down. They'd planned on moving a dresser out there and doing that trick again, but the ladder was a way better option. Tony gave them a thumbs up and disappeared. Kelly and Randy went down the stairs to see if they could find the keys to the Nissan Sentra sitting in the garage.

The keys were hanging on a peg right inside the door. A quick test showed the battery was still working on the car so they could be pretty sure it'd crank up once they started it. Keys ready and lever found to manually open the garage door they waited.

They didn't have to wait too long. Before they'd really settled in, they heard a series of loud explosions coming from the other end of the townhouses. The explosions were immediately drowned out by a deep and throaty roar that seemed to reverberate off the walls all around them. The army of the damned had come to life and were screaming out a challenge. It was primal. Whatever part of the human brain the virus opened up in the infected was tainted with pure evil.

It was loud enough that Randy signaled for Kelly to go ahead and start the car. Then Randy grabbed the red and white string to the manual release to the garage doors and waited for Tony to show up. He was staring at the garage door trying to will Tony to come through it when something tapped his shoulder. He spun around swinging his fist as hard as he could. Kelly ducked and he ended up throwing a haymaker into the garage door hard enough to leave a dent and hurt his wrist.

"The car died!" Kelly yelled to him over the noise of the Zombies.

"What?" Randy said with his mouth slightly opened in confusion. The damned car had been running fine like five seconds ago. Tony chose that moment to come sliding into the garage spinning his finger in a let's go motion. Seeing Kelly sitting in the driver's seat he piled into the back seat and sat there staring at Randy. He was waiting for him to open the garage door. He finally noticed Kelly shaking her head and making weird motions with her hands that in her mind indicated the car was dead.

Zombies began slamming into the garage door. Randy punching it must've been noticed by a few of them. Kelly got out of the car followed by Tony.

"We have to go now! What's wrong with Kelly's arms?" Tony said.

"I think she was trying to tell you the car wouldn't start." Despite the danger they were in, Tony took the time to give Kelly a look about the hand gestures.

"Let's go!" Kelly said. She knew they needed to get the hell out of there. Also, she was hoping they'd forget about the hand gesture thing. Fighting their way through a mob of Zombies should take care of that.

They ran to the sliding glass doors leading out to the backyard patio. There were still Zombies standing around, but it wasn't the massively packed group it'd been before the grenades. They paused as each of them took out weapons and made sure they were good to go. There were too many Zombies out there for them to have a hope of doing this quietly.

"Loud, brutal and fast. Let's get to that fence and get the hell out of here." Tony said before sliding open the glass door and stepping out on the patio with his M-16 pointed at the back of a Zombies head. The Zombie began to turn around as Kelly and Randy joined Tony on the patio. Tony pulled the trigger.

The bullet ripped a hole through the Zombie's cheek and went out the other cheek in a splatter of blood, gums and teeth. Tony had to fire again straight into its forehead to put the Zombie down. The screeching picked up in tempo at the sound of gunfire. The opening in the fence of the little patio they were in was immediately clogged up with Zombies trying to get at them. They blew away that wall of flesh with automatic fire. Watching bits and pieces of humanity get flung all over the place as the bullets cut flesh and bone to clear their way.

Charging forward Tony went through the gap in the fence. He had to jump to get over the pile of dead bodies. Kelly was right behind him with Randy pulling rear guard. He looked down before jumping when he felt splashing beneath his boots and saw that the pile of bodies had created a deep puddle of blood that was spreading across the patio. Shaking off the cold tingling shiver that puddle sent up his spine he jumped over the bodies and joined Kelly. She was standing still sending shots downrange into the Zombies coming for them. Tony had taken off for the fence to clear a path. As soon as Randy got to where Kelly was, she turned and sprinted after Tony.

Randy posted up on the spot Kelly had just vacated and shot Zombies as fast as he could pull the trigger. They were coming at them like a wave now. There'd be no way to survive if that wave crashed over him. Not bothering to look where he was aiming, he just kept pulling the trigger as he carefully walked backwards. When the firing pin clicked on an empty chamber, he dropped the rifle to hang off its bandolier and reached in his pocket for a grenade. They still had a few left and it'd been decided for Randy to throw this one into the oncoming Zombies before he turned and ran after Tony and Kelly. They'd be doing their best to clear a path to the fence. From the sound of the steady stream of shots being fired behind him they were holding up their side of the bargain.

Randy pulled the pin and tossed the grenade at the screaming wave of gnashing teeth and claw shaped hands bearing down on him. Not bothering to see where the grenade landed, he turned and ran. Tony and Kelly were all the way up by the road. Tony was blasting away in full auto while Kelly had her rifle in semi mode and was picking off the Zombies who kept heading for Randy. Tony slapped in another magazine as Randy got close to them screaming for them to run.

Kelly was already running for the fence. Tony took one look at the mass of Zombies behind Randy and he was running also. A very muffled thump behind them indicated the grenade Randy had thrown had gone off. None of them expected it to actually do much damage to the mob bearing down on them. They were running full speed now. Each of them expecting to feel a Zombie slam into them from behind at any second.

The metal fence in front of them looked to be about six feet tall. It was coming up fast and none of them had a great idea on how to get over it. Tony was the tallest of the three of them. He poured on some extra speed and slid on his knees to the fence. He put both hands on the ground and let Kelly use him like a springboard to scramble over the fence. Without missing a step Randy put one foot on top of Tony's back to help himself spring over the fence behind Kelly.

Kelly bounced to her feet instantly once she landed on the other side of the fence. She had her rifle barrel shoved through the gaps in the fence firing as fast as she could into the oncoming Zombies. Randy joined her a moment later trying to slow the Zombies as much as possible to give Tony time to get over the fence. Tony put both hands on the top of the fence and jumped like an Olympian. He cleared the fence by a good foot with his whole body before crashing down on the other side. It was a nice jump, but he lost a ton of style points on the landing.

The Zombie wave crashed into the metal fence. Directly in front of them the Zombies had lost some momentum due to being shot in the face a lot. They'd also had to hop, skip and jump over the dead bodies of their comrades to get to the fence. That didn't hold true for the Zombie wave crashing on either side of them into the fence. With loud snapping and grinding noises that temporarily cut through the screeching of the Zombies the fence began to give in.

Not wanting to be there when the fence completely collapsed Randy and Kelly helped Tony to his feet. They quickly continued sprinting through the weeds and the bushes and briars towards the subdivision adjacent to this one. In less than a minute they were running down a sidewalk with a pack of the faster Zombies trailing them by about fifty feet. They needed to get back into stealth mode and lose these pursuers as quickly as possible. Instead of turning and shooting them they began weaving in and out of yards. They'd run into a gated backyard and jump the fence to get to the next yard then run through a house.

The ones that caught up to them they killed. They used knives and hatchets and attacked any Zombies that got too close. All of them would pounce on the pursuer and drag it to the ground to stab to death. They repeated that gruesome task ten times until they finally were clear of their pursuers. They could hear screeching all around and knew the subdivision would be filling up soon, so they kept moving rather than risk getting stuck again. They jogged across another parking lot to the main road. They jogged up the road past a Publix and across the street to the pharmacy on the corner.

There was a DVD vending machine blocking the front door, so Tony and Randy pulled that out. Kelly slipped through the gap they'd made and with her pushing and them pulling they got it open enough for the two men to slide in beside her. They pushed their way through the store grabbing snacks and water. Kelly was hoping the pharmacy would be open and not looted yet. She'd love to get them all some antibiotics and pain killers and settle in for the day to heal up from that last push to escape. Her arm was totally useless to her at this point and the pain kept hitting her in waves when she wasn't expecting it. She wanted to be healed and healthy by the time the sun went down so they could start the search for the kids.

When they got to the back, she saw that the iron curtain had been pulled down and locked for the pharmacy. Looking to the side she saw where someone had beaten their way through the drywall to get at the drugs inside. Whoever it was they must've been super skinny to fit through that hole. Not wanting to make a ton of noise beating on the wall any more right now Kelly sat down with her back against the end of the aisle. Randy sat down next to her and reached over to hold her hand. Tony wandered up with a six-pack of warm Corona and sat down to drink himself to sleep. Randy glanced at Kelly's face expecting to see a big scowl directed at Tony for deciding to get drunk again.

"What are you smiling about?" Randy asked surprised by the look on her face. Kelly was staring across at the broken drywall with a dreamy look in her eyes and a small but goofy grin on her face.

"The drywall just reminded me of watching HGTV with the girls. I have a feeling we'll be seeing them again soon."

"Me too babe." Randy echoed. He let go of her hand so he could wrap his arm around her and pull her in close.

Chapter 13: Death is Harder on those Left Behind

Myriah kept to the woods and skirted around the backs of houses until she arrived back at the lake house. She was wet and miserable. Her body hurt all over from the fall out the window and then slamming into the fence. She focused on the physical misery. It was a million times easier to endure than those moments when her mind would replay Eric charging the line of Zombies. She'd remember him playing Candyland or cards with them then she'd slip and remember the sounds from behind her when he fell. She didn't remember a scream or anything. She wondered if Eric had held in the pain on purpose to keep her from stopping and looking back. One last unselfish act to protect the girls whose lives he'd been entrusted with. That seemed like him.

She didn't think she could cry much more. Then she'd think of something else that'd set the waterworks off again. There was no rule saying Eric had to stick with a bunch of girls and try protecting them. There was no rule saying he had to pick them up in the first place. If he'd just stuck with his original group of men, there's a good chance he'd still be alive today. He could've dropped them off somewhere and just kept his niece with him. It was amazing he'd survived as long as he had considering how often he'd put himself between the girls and danger. Now he was gone. Gone because she hadn't made him wake up. For some stupid, lazy reason she'd let him sleep. She'd slept. Eric's death was on her.

She found herself in the yard behind the lake house. She didn't know how to get Cait's attention without scaring everyone in the house. She knew she didn't want to startle the scared teen girl with the automatic rifle. Cait was probably expecting Zombies to attack at any second. She tried the door. It was locked. That made sense considering Cait had been a bit paranoid even before the apocalypse. She'd always locked all the doors and turned on every light in the house when their parents had gone out for date night.

Myriah took her knife out and started lightly tapping on the door. She kept it up until Cait appeared out of the depths of the house. She watched Caitlyn's face register that it was Myriah standing out there and not a Zombie. She was enormously relieved when the barrel of the M-16 shifted away from being pointed at her. She hadn't realized how large that barrel looked until she was staring down it. Caitlyn unlocked the door and slid it open so Myriah could come in.

"Where's Eric?" Cait asked. She was looking into the yard expecting Eric to show up out of the darkness at any second. It was a logical response as he'd trailed behind them plenty of times to provide a rear guard. Myriah shook her head from side to side and started bawling. Caitlyn slid the door shut and pulled Myriah into a hug. They stood like that for a long while.

"What do we do now?" Myriah said when she was finally able to talk. She was ashamed to say how Eric had died.

"What happened?" Cait asked.

"We fell asleep. He wanted to rest before we came back. We got the medicine and everything he needed then he wanted to rest. Then he had to charge the Zombies to save me. He died for me." Myriah started bawling again. Tears and snot dripping down her face. She wiped at her nose with her sleeve and avoided Cait's eyes.

"What do you mean you fell asleep? Why would you fall asleep?" Cait asked. She was trying to grasp what'd happened. How could they have lost their protector over something as trivial as him falling asleep. There was no chance she was getting an answer anytime soon. Her questions were sending Myriah even deeper into her depression. She was inconsolable now.

Cait told her it was ok and that she loved her. She kept repeating those words while she took Myriah to the spare bedroom and got her tucked in. She was careful not to say anything about sleeping but hopeful Myriah would get the hint and rest. She tugged Myriah's boots and clothes off. She wondered how come she was soaked but decided to ask about that some other time. For now, she just went with getting Myriah tucked in. Zoey and Ali came in with Doreen in the middle of them. All they seemed to grasp was that Myriah was sad. They all crawled into the bed and snuggled together around Cait and Myriah.

Caitlyn hadn't slept since Eric and Myriah had left the day before. Lying in the bed surrounded by all the kids and torn apart with depression she closed her eyes. Within about thirty minutes all of them were asleep on the bed except for Zoey. Zoey got up to go down to the bathroom to pee. They'd been using milk jugs filled with water to wash down the pee and flush the toilets. One of the big advantages of the lake house being that it was on a lake.

A loud noise scared Zoey. She pulled her clothes back on quickly and decided not to waste time trying to flush her pee down the toilet. They'd been mostly trying to let the toilet fill up a little bit before flushing it since none of them were positive how long the trick with the water jug would keep working. There was the sound of glass shattering and something beating on the front door. Zoey cracked open the bathroom door and saw men in the hallway with guns. She saw one of them dragging Caitlyn out of the bedroom while Cait screamed and swore. Myriah and the other kids were marched out of the bedroom at gun point a minute later.

Zoey did what she'd been told to do if something like that happened. She jumped in the bathtub and closed the curtain. A second after she got in the tub a man kicked open the door and stepped into the bathroom. Zoey stayed as quiet as she could. She was pressed up as close to the side of the tub by the curtain as she could get. The man stuck his gun into the shower curtain and moved it to the side. He took a quick peek but didn't look far enough over to see Zoey. As quickly as he'd blown in to the bathroom he left. Zoey was shaking with fear. Tears were streaming down her face. She wanted to run out into the hallway and find Caitlyn.

She stuck to what she'd been told to do. Eric had drilled into their heads to hide if bad men broke into the house. They'd even had designated hiding spots in case something like this happened. Zoey wasn't in her spot right now, but she was in one she knew Eric would've approved of. Knowing it was what she supposed to do kept her pinned there almost as much as the fear in her stomach did. She'd never really thought this might happen. She didn't know what to do now. What if the bad guys took everyone away with them and left her in the house all by herself? Who was going to take care of her?

Caitlyn had gone for the M-16 when she'd heard the glass break. By the time the men entered the room she'd been standing bleary eyed at the foot of the bed with the rifle in her hands. The men had come in fast. Yelling at her to drop the weapon or they'd shoot her little sisters. There were a lot of them, and they all had rifles too. Not knowing what else to do Caitlyn pointed the M-16 at the floor. One of the men had walked confidently into the room and backhanded her after grabbing the M-16 out of her hands.

Myriah and the other girls on the bed were all crying and yelling at the men coming in the room. When one of them hit Caitlyn and yelled for them to all shut up if they didn't want to get beaten, they all shut up. The man shoved Caitlyn out in to the hall. Another guy with a big bushy beard got the other girls to get up and get out. Myriah was busy getting dressed as she was shoved out of the room. In the hallway Myriah happened to glance over her shoulder and saw Zoey peeking out the bathroom door. Hoping Zoey would take advantage of the distraction to hide Myriah started cussing and yelling at the men who'd just thrown her into the hallway. It didn't take a lot of motivation to yell at them since they'd shoved her out before she even got her boots laced up.

"Is this all of you?" A tall man in camouflage asked. He'd come in from the main living area in the house.

Caitlyn hesitated. She knew Zoey must be hiding somewhere. She didn't know if they should try and find her so she could go with them or if Zoey would be better off left alone in the house. She didn't know if they'd have a chance to come back and get her later if they left now. She did know these appeared to be bad guys. She just didn't know how bad they were.

"This is all of us." She answered. The man looked at her closely. He'd noticed the hesitation.

"You sure this is everybody?" He asked again. Getting close to Caitlyn's face. He'd pulled a knife out at some point as well and started flipping it in the air and catching it by the handle. Caitlyn gulped hard.

"We're all that's left. Everybody else is dead." She stuttered out.

Gunshots rang out from the front of the house. One of the men poked his head in the hallway from the front of the house and yelled that they needed to get moving. Without asking any more questions the men herded the girls out the front door of the house. Multiple Zombies were coming through the woods on the opposite side of the street and approaching the house. The noise from shattering the sliding glass doors must've carried.

Caitlyn and Ali were shoved in the back of a Ford Expedition. Doreen and Myriah were put in the back of an extended cab Nissan Titan with windows tinted well beyond any reasonable expectation of legality. Caitlyn had no idea why they were separating them unless it was just to keep them from all trying to escape together. She watched out the windows as Zombies started getting close to the men. The men had swords and spears out now as they dealt with the single Zombies attacking them. A couple of men were standing in the backs of the pickup trucks with bows in hand taking shots as well.

In less than a minute the first wave of Zombies had been put down and everyone was in a vehicle. More Zombies were streaming towards them though. The trucks all rolled out down the road. Some Zombies followed them, but way more than Caitlyn expected kept running towards the house.

"Why are the Zombies still headed for the house?" Caitlyn asked the sweat covered man sitting in the seat in front of them. The man had somehow managed to stay fat this far into the apocalypse. He smelled like fried chicken, body odor and booze.

"We left a boom box going inside. It's screeching out all kinds of sounds like people talking and screaming and gun shots. Stuff like that. Works really good to distract the Zombies. Most of them will probably hang out at that house until the batteries die." The man responded.

Caitlyn took in his words. She thought about it for about a second before urgently asking the man to turn around. She told him her little sister was still in the building. All Caitlyn could think of now was that she'd left Zoey to die. How could she have been so stupid. Of course, Zoey was better off with them than she was alone in a house by herself. Especially a house that'd been set up as a honeypot for the Zombies. Caitlyn should've dragged her out of her hiding spot and made sure she came along with them.

Consumed with worry she listened as the man talked on the radio.

"Detainee number one is saying there's still a juvenile female back in the building. She didn't confirm prior as she was worried about our intentions. She wants to turn around for the juvenile. Over."

"Negative. We need to get out of this sector. The herd is danger close. We don't have time to search for the juvenile. Over."

On hearing that last transmission Caitlyn leapt for the door handle. She tried her best to get out of the moving truck before they could stop her. The man guarding her tried pulling her back and yelling at her to sit down. He finally pushed her to the ground with the help of another man in the truck. Caitlyn struggled and hit one of them in the face with her elbow. He leaned back leaking blood out of his broken nose. The man with the bloody nose kicked her hard in the back of her head. Her forehead bounced off the floor boards. The world swam in her vision before everything faded to black. Her wrists were zip tied together and she was tossed into the back seat on top of a tearful Ali.

The men followed the truck in front of them that had Myriah and Doreen in it. Doreen was in Myriah's lap with both her arms wrapped tightly around her neck. Her face was buried in Myriah's shoulder soaking her shirt with snot and tears. Myriah was freaked out about leaving Zoey behind. She couldn't just jump out of the truck though. She had Doreen to think about. In the seat in front of her Myriah saw a man playing what she thought was a video game. As she watched the monitor, she saw the man was seeing an aerial view of the area they were in. One side of the screen was undulating with motion.

"What's all that stuff moving around on the side?" Myriah asked curiously.

"Not really supposed to talk about this with outsiders. Since you're staring at me and fixing to be sent off to bride school though I'll let you in on it. This is how we found you and your sisters. We were actually looking for another group of people right near here when I saw you pulling all those shenanigans in the pool. That's how we tracked you down. All that motion on the side of the screen that looks like some kind of glitch. That's the herd coming this way. Which is why we're going the other way." The man answered. He turned back around in his seat with finality indicating the conversation was over.

By the time they'd turned the corner Myriah was desperately trying to think of a way to escape and go save Zoey. Based on what she could make out on the screen the herd was seeping through the woods and around the local streets to converge on the house her little sister was currently sitting in. She wouldn't stand a chance.

Indecision about leaving Doreen behind got Myriah caught reaching for the door handle. The other man sitting in the seat in front of them had been watching as Myriah's eyes drifted over to look for an escape route. He moved back to sit next to them. He took out a couple of zip ties and calmly tied Myriah's wrists to the metal part of the headrest on the seat in front of her. Forced to lean forward Myriah watched on the video as the herd moved out of the woods and converged on the house they'd just left. They were already well on their way out of the neighborhood.

Knowing it was pointless to protest. Thinking to herself that her sleeping had just gotten someone else she loved killed Myriah did her best to comfort Doreen. They cried together. Myriah picturing Zoey's sweet face and little girl attitude. Doreen was missing everyone and scared and had no idea what was going on. Myriah was so concerned about Zoey that she never even thought to ask what the man had meant when he said they were going to be going to bride school.

Back at the house Zoey lay huddled on the cold, hard porcelain bottom of the bathtub. She'd shut the door when everyone left but she couldn't get it to lock now. The lock must've been broken when the attacker had kicked the door in earlier. She'd pulled the jug of lake water and all the towels into the bathtub with her. She shut the shower curtain and pulled the towels over her body as she heard the boombox start shrieking out it's welcoming song to the Zombies. Minutes later she heard Zombies ripping through the house. She burrowed deeper into the towel mound she'd built for herself and tried to keep from crying too loud.

Chapter 14: Deep Cover

Kyler bounced around in the back of the oversized pickup truck. He'd expected one of the men to stay in the bed to keep an eye on him, but the guy had just said that riding in the back sucked then left Kyler there. Kyler agreed. Tom would never win any awards for smooth driving. It was like he went out of his way to find bumps. It didn't help that he seemed to like going through the median to get around the few cars blocking the roads versus just weaving through them. He was driving via the median to keep from having to slow down. What it ended up doing was bouncing everyone around like potatoes on a trampoline.

They weren't able to drive all the way to the guard post that trip. They were a little over three miles away from it when they ran into a mass of Zombies coming down I-95 from the north. There was an exponentially larger number of Zombies than Kyler had seen earlier that day. He supposed they may have been in the woods nearby or maybe they'd been following Kyler down I-95 the whole time. Either way, when Tom turned the truck around to get moving south again Kyler couldn't see an end to the mob of Zombies marching down the interstate.

What he could see was a handful of the fast ones bounding along the road towards them. Tom had taken his sweet time turning around. He'd probably been recording the mob on his phone or making notes or having a snack or whatever. Which was fine for him to be doing in the cab of the big truck with all kinds of weapons strapped to him. It wasn't so fine for Kyler since he was in the open air of the truck bed with no weapons and his hands tied behind his back. He was soaked and starting to shiver from the miserable drizzle of rain coming down.

He forgot all about his discomforts from the rain when the first Zombie caught up to them and leapt into the air. The monster landed on the roof of the cab of the truck and started trying to claw its way in. Kyler stayed as quiet as he could hoping it wouldn't notice him. Tom accelerated and the Zombie slipped off the roof of the cab right into the bed of the truck. It sat up about two feet in front of Kyler and stared right at him. Kyler was considering jumping over the side of the truck when the sliders on the window into the cab of the truck opened. Someone held a large pistol out of the window aimed at the Zombie.

The Zombie went for Kyler just as the gun was fired. Bullets impacted and shattered the skull of the leaping demon. Kyler was splattered with all kinds of Zombie gore as the remainder of the head fell into his lap with the body flapping around behind it. Happy to be alive Kyler decided he didn't even care that he probably had muzzle flash burns on his neck and his hearing was pretty much gone on that side now. He turned around to thank the guy with the pistol when it started firing again. The big barrel was only a few inches from his face.

Kyler moved backwards away from the gun and huddled in the corner of the pickup truck bed. Yet another Zombie jumped into the bed with him and was shot until it stopped moving. The bed of the truck was sloshing around with a Kool-Aid like mixture of blood and water. The truck finally picked up enough speed where even the adrenalized Zombies weren't able to catch up. Kyler was bouncing around in the back now with a couple of dead bodies and a whole lot of fluids. He wanted a case of hand sanitizer and some of those green scrub pads to use on his skin. With the wind whipping everything around he was hopeful he may actually dry off before he died of hypothermia.

The truck pulled over briefly for a bathroom break. Kyler was given a bottle of water with a straw to sip out of. Tom finally took pity on him and cut the zip ties so Kyler could hold the bottle himself. Tom and the other guys used some poles to push the Zombie carcasses out of the back of the truck. They left the bodies to rot in the ditch and drove a few more miles before exiting the interstate.

Once they pulled off the exit the truck pulled over to the side of the road again. Tom walked back around to the back of the truck. He motioned for Kyler to climb down and turn around so he could tie his wrists back together.

"We're going to head through town here and then take a couple back roads to the camp. This is where we take the people who cross into our territory for interrogation and on-boarding. I know you were headed down south to see if you could find your parents but at this point, I'd advise you to suddenly become very interested in joining up with us. If you get accepted, then you'll probably be assigned to a unit like ours. You'll get weapons and food and a safe place to stay. If you don't join or don't get accepted for whatever reason, then the places you go and the things you end up having to do aren't really pleasant. I think you'd fit in good here for what it's worth."

Kyler nodded. This was all fitting into the plan pretty nicely except he liked Tom and the team. They seemed like the same kind of men who made up the roving patrols back in the settlements. He was having a hard time reconciling that they'd be the ones attacking and killing for no reason. They'd hit on this in his training with the instructor bringing up the fact that if you happened to know German you could probably have sat down and had a beer with the same men who operated the gas chambers during the holocaust. The worst monsters in human history all looked like normal men. Most of them had incredible charisma as well. Of course, there was also the possibility that these people had nothing to do with the attacks on the settlements. That's what he was there to find out.

"Thanks Tom. I appreciate the heads up. Also appreciate you letting me ride this far without the tie wraps on. These things suck."

Tom laughed. "Agreed. I've had them on me too. Alright, we probably should've put these ties on after you were in the truck. Oh well. Let's see if you can get up there without killing yourself. We'll call it your first test."

With the tail gate down Kyler was able to awkwardly climb into the back of the truck with only a little help needed from Tom. They drove quickly through the tiny town by the interstate exit consisting of a couple of gas stations and two dive bar looking restaurants. Kyler didn't spot any Zombies hanging out so assumed the camp had come through here and cleaned out the area to make it safe to exit the interstate. That level of safety was going to change quickly once the giant herd following them reached the exit.

The camp they were going to turned out to be an actual campground. There were a bunch of cabins tucked into open spaces along a single road. There was a small store for campers to buy liquor and band aids in under a large KOA sign. There was an administrative building tucked in among the other buildings. The administration building was the first one visible after they turned in. There were a few armed men walking in between the cabin to the administrative building. He looked for anything useful to report as part of his spy role, he didn't see anything that he thought anyone was going to really care too much about. The recon patrol had already located this camp anyway.

A man walked out of the administrative building to meet them. Tom saluted then shook the man's hand as they talked. Kyler couldn't make out all the words, but it was obvious Tom was telling the camp commander about the guard outpost on the state line being overrun. Even more concerning to the commander would be the news about the herd heading down the interstate in this direction. Tom finished up his report and walked back to the truck with the commander.

"Tom tells me you're interested in joining up." The commander said to Kyler.

"Yes sir." Kyler said back respectfully.

"Ok then. Climb on out of the truck and I'll take you to the intake clerk. He'll ask you some questions and have you fill out some forms. Once we check you over for bites, we'll get those ties off of you. If you can go ahead and climb down, we'll head in now." The commander and Tom shared a few more words quietly as Kyler worked out how to get out of the truck with his hands tied behind him. Once on the ground the commander motioned for Kyler to follow him and they headed into the administrative building. The commander dropped Kyler off in the care of another uniformed man.

The man took Kyler into an examining room. There was a sheet of plexiglass with a door in it that had been added to cover half the room. There was a hole in the door big enough for someone to stick their hands through to get a zip tie cut off once they got in the room. The man opened the door and cutoff the zip tie. Then he had Kyler go inside and strip down. Once completely undressed the man had Kyler spin slowly in a circle so he could inspect him for any bites or suspicious scratches.

"I don't see any bite marks or scratches on you. Any health issues we need to worry about? We have some doctors if you do have anything. As long as you don't have a condition that requires medicine with an expiration date, we can hook you up." The man looked at Kyler who shook his head no and started getting dressed. Once dressed Kyler went through a very similar on-boarding process to what he'd done in the settlements. It kept striking him how similar all of this was to what he was used to up north. Once the questions had all been asked and answered the clerk locked Kyler in the room and left to go make his report to the commander.

An hour later there was a few hard raps on the office door and the camp commander walked back in. He sat down at the desk and leaned forward to look at Kyler.

"In the old world you wouldn't have been able to legally buy cigarettes or vote yet. You'd be wondering if you were going to get lucky at the prom. Now you're probably wondering if we're going to take you out back and shoot you. Well, we're not so you can get that out of your head. What I am going to do is very simply ask you if you want to join up with us. Tom gives you a good reference and the clerk says you check out. You've got the skills and experience to get put into one of our teams despite how old you are. Does that sound good to you?"

Kyler paused to look like he was thinking about it. "Sir, I was hoping to go check in on my parents down in Florida. If I do this will I be able to get down there?"

"Sure. You'll get sent where you're most needed, but you can absolutely put in to get down to Florida. It may take some time but eventually you'll get there. We're working hard to make Georgia and Florida into a safe place to live again. You can be a part of that. Sound good?"

"Yes sir. I'm in." Kyler said. They both knew he didn't have much of a choice anyway. The commander welcomed him aboard then sent him away to one of the cabins. He let him know to report back to the administrative building the next morning to get his orders.

A few minutes later he found himself walking down the road looking for cabin number twenty. They hadn't put a guard on him. He wondered if it was a test and they had someone watching the cabin to see if he'd try and sneak off in the middle of the night. He found the cabin and went inside. There was a pile of MREs sitting on the small table in the dining room area. The fireplace looked like it was a real one if he wanted to try and get a fire going. Not knowing what else to do he used a knife he found in the kitchen to cut open an MRE and make himself dinner. He lay down on the couch thinking he'd get up and go to the bed when he got too tired.

He woke up on the couch the next morning with the light streaming in through the kitchen window in the cabin. Time to go report in and see what new kind of weirdness this day would bring him. With a full stomach from breakfasting on another MRE and a sore neck from falling asleep at an awkward angle on the couch Kyler opened the door to head to the administrative building and get the weirdness started.

Chapter 15: Home Sweet Home

Randy woke up pissed off at himself. They hadn't set a watch. They hadn't even really tried to hide or secure the doors. Tony had worked his way through the six pack of Corona and a bottle of red wine before passing out. Kelly had said she was too excited about looking for the kids to fall asleep then promptly fallen asleep. Randy had been left in an uncomfortable position supporting Kelly while trying to balance on the edge of the shelf he was leaning up against. He hadn't been too concerned about himself falling asleep considering the discomfort of the position he was in. He'd sat there with his arm around Kelly while the sun filled the store with shadows.

Randy's arm was completely numb from the awkward position he'd slept with it in around Kelly. The sound of broken glass crunching drifted to him from the front of the store. The snuffling noises the Zombies made when they were on the hunt but hadn't seen anything yet came next. They always reminded Randy of the noises the Black Riders had made in the Lord of the Rings movies. The noises a rabid dog would make sniffing at the carcass of its owner after it ripped out his throat.

Randy sat up straight and put his hand over Kelly's mouth before rocking her sharply to try and wake her up. It took a few tries as he didn't want to wake her so quickly, she was scared and woke up swinging or screaming. Her eyes grew big when she came to and realized someone had their hand over her mouth. She had a knife in her hand reaching to saw at the arm of the person holding her when she finally figured out it was Randy. He watched in relief as she lowered the knife and became aware of the sounds from the front of the store.

With Kelly awake Randy looked over at Tony. The man's head was back against the cooler section at a painful looking angle. Drool was trickling through his scroungy looking beard down to this neck. The Corona bottles had been set down carefully beside him in a circle with the wine bottle sitting in the middle of it. So now Tony had become OCD on top of working on becoming an alcoholic. Randy knew the stress of what they went through on a daily basis was enough to break pretty much anyone. He just didn't care. The end result was they needed to find and protect their kids. On top of their kids Randy needed to protect Kelly. If Tony was going to become a hindrance to that then they'd have to have a conversation at some point.

A few loud noises from upfront had Randy trying to carefully move to take a look over his shoulder. Kelly had moved so she could try to look down the aisle on her side. Randy saw a flicker of movement to his right and whipped his head around to spy Tony moving into position on the aisle adjacent to them. Hungover or not Tony was moving smoothly and had weapons out and ready to go. It looked like they could postpone having any conversations about the alcoholism any time soon. It was the end of the world so as long as you were a functional alcoholic who really cared. It was highly unlikely Tony would live long enough for liver damage to become a concern anyway.

The snuffling sounds continued coming from the front of the store. Then the sound of feet slapping rapidly across the floor as the Zombie ran down the aisle a few aisles over from them. When it got to the end of the aisle it'd easily be able to see them. Without even thinking about it they all slid around to the insides of their aisles to avoid being seen. The sound of the feet slapping on the floor stopped and the snuffling noises started up again. The loud sound of items from the shelf being swept to the floor filled the room. A startled Kelly slapped her hand over her mouth after emitting a quick squeal at the sudden unexpected noise.

A loud snapping sound was followed by more items hitting the floor and more loud noises. The snuffling was suddenly right on top of them. Randy looked straight up and saw the Zombie was standing on the top of the shelf right above them gazing around. It jumped to the next shelf and kept looking around trying to see if it'd actually heard anything. Randy popped Kelly in the shoulder with his elbow and got to his feet as quickly and quietly as he could. Once he was upright, he pulled his knife and stabbed it overhand as hard as he could into the back of the Zombie's thigh. Before the Zombie even had time to acknowledge the pain Randy pulled hard on its good leg.

The Zombie smashed down into the items on the top of the shelf. It's legs and lower torso dangling over the edge of the shelf. Kelly was whacking at the monster with her machete scoring lots of hits. Blood flinging back from the machete blade every time she pulled back to strike again. The Zombie was scrambling to turn over so it could get at them when Tony started hitting the top of its head with a claw hammer from the next aisle over. He struck until the skull caved in. Bits of brain and blood stuck to the top of the hammer falling to the ground like ketchup covered clumps of biscuit mix.

Kelly stopped swinging the machete once the body stopped thrashing around. She was covered in blood. The dingy white tile floor had a big puddle of blood on it. Tony came around the corner covered in blood as well. Randy worked his knife out of the things leg and stuck it back in its leather sheath after wiping the excess blood off on his pants leg. They froze when they heard another series of crunching sounds coming from the front of the store. Realizing that if they didn't go seal up the front of the store, they'd be dealing with this until nightfall. The three of them began quietly moving up the aisle towards the source of the noise. They left three sets of blood-soaked footprints on the dust covered white tile behind them.

They paused about ten feet from the end of the aisle and listened to the sounds coming from the front of the store. It sounded like it was just another single Zombie who'd come through the hole to see the inside of the store. They needed to kill it and seal up the hole without attracting any more visitors. Tony motioned to keep moving to the end of the aisle. As he turned to wave to them a waif of a Zombie appeared at the end of the aisle. Long stringy blond hair hung down from an emaciated face. Exaggerated cheekbones stuck out of the sore and scab covered face. The eyes were coated with some sort of thick yellow pus that seemed to have congealed in place.

They all froze in place as if the Zombie wasn't going to see them squatting ten feet in front of it. Randy looked intently at the things face. The eyes really were completely covered in the yellow pus. The creature was snuffling and starting to take some tentative steps towards them. Its mouth hung wide open as it took small stumbling steps in their direction. The Zombie was so covered in sores and dressed so plainly it was impossible to discern the sex of the creature. It could've been a heroin model twenty something woman or a gangly teenage boy.

They all stayed squatting. Weapons in hand waiting to see what would happen. With no warning the Zombie screeched at them in a high-pitched voice and charged them. Tony stood and swung his hammer in a sideways arc that pegged the creature hard on the side of its head. It leapt and carried Tony to the ground wrapped in its embrace. Randy jumped on its back and grabbed the dingy blond hair pulling backwards as hard as he could. He looked like he was trying to pull the reins back on a bronco at a wild west show. The creature bucked and tucked it's head up to try and roll over and get at Randy.

Kelly hacked at its throat. She hit it in the face with the blade first causing the pus to explode out of one of the eyes. It squirted outwards along with the warm blood that poured from the cut. Her second strike landed on the Zombies throat and shut it up permanently. The voice box was ripped apart by the deep penetration of the machete. Kelly swung again and hacked deeper in to the neck finally killing the Zombie. Randy dragged it by its hair off of Tony and shoved the cooling body against the cash register.

Tony stood up drenched in blood and goo with a disgusted look on his face. They all looked and smelled like they'd been rolling around in a slaughterhouse. The scraping sound of the vending machine outside the front door being moved around caught their attention. They rushed over to the front of the store to see if they could figure out a way to block the broken door and stop the steady stream of unwanted guests.

Randy stopped and looked through the broken glass door. He saw what appeared to be a bloated Zombie trying to squeeze through the narrow gap afforded by the vending machine in the entryway. Tony raised his hammer and slid through the frame of the front door to position himself behind the vending machine. He raised the hammer in preparation for smashing in the things head if it made it through the crack. Kelly evidently had another idea as she raced through the hole in the door sliding past Tony to position herself right in the path of the mass of moving flesh trying to get into the store. She put the machete horizontally against the ribs of the giant Zombie and pushed as hard as she could.

The machete pierced the skin sinking deep into the Zombie. The Zombie let out a loud bellow of pain and started thrashing around. Its massive hand swatted Kelly to the ground. She left the machete in the monster's side and crawled back through the front door. She stood up picking pieces of glass out of her palms with little facial tics revealing the pain she was in. Randy moved over beside her to see if he could help her at all. Tony stayed at his post behind the machine as the thrashing Zombie slowly bled out. He'd been ready to bash in the things head if it managed to make it through.

After making sure Kelly was ok Randy went and peeled back the posters from the window by the door to look outside. He looked out towards the street for a minute then waved Kelly and Tony over to take a look for themselves. Outside the drug store they were in was a gas station on the corner. On the other side of the street there was a large Publix shopping store in a big plaza. In the parking lot of the Publix and in the parking lot of the gas station there were Zombies randomly wandering around in packs of twos and threes. There were also a fair number of single Zombies moving around.

Those were scary enough but once you looked past them towards the road and saw the group these wandering Zombies were a part of that was the bone chilling part. The road looked like a river. A river of Zombies flowing down it. They couldn't tell where it ended and where it began. They immediately recognized this must be the herd that'd had them trapped on the roof the day before. They watched as the herd continued to pass for another ten minutes. As the herd started thinning out the other Zombies in the parking lot and around the area left to join back into it. Randy and the others walked back to the back of the store to talk.

"Good thinking on killing that fat one in the gap. Blocked it up so none of the others can get in." Randy whispered as soon as they were far enough from the doors that he didn't think their voices would carry. The last thing they wanted was the herd heading back their way.

"The fun part will be getting out. I want to roll out of here as soon as the suns been down for an hour. We can be at our house in thirty minutes to get started looking for the kids." Kelly whispered back. Randy nodded in return. That wasn't giving the Zombies a lot of time to settle down for the night, but it was a decent chunk of time given how excited Kelly was about getting to their house. He wasn't about to try and tell her they should wait longer. If it looked like the coast was clear an hour after sundown then they'd head out.

"In the meantime, I suggest we find the baby section and use as many moist towelettes as it takes to wipe this gunk off." Randy said.

"There's not enough moist towelettes in the world for me to ever feel clean again." Tony said. Randy looked at him in the dim light and nodded. They were all covered in nastiness. There were some socks and underwear and touristy t-shirts for sale up by the counter they could use to freshen up a little bit. They had minimal clothing in their packs since they'd tried to shove as much firepower in them as possible. Tony had joked about not needing fresh underwear until after the firefight. If you wasted space on underwear before the firefight you may be too dead to care about feeling fresh after the fight. Lifting his pack now Randy noted it was depressingly light. They'd managed to run through most of their munitions already.

They spent some time freshening up then took turns peeking out the front windows. The Zombies had mostly cleared out by the time nightfall rolled in and covered the parking lot. Kelly took one last, long look and announced it was time to dig through the big, fat dead guy at the front of the store. She was the one to announce it and the one who was in the biggest hurry to leave but she definitely wasn't the one she thought should be doing the digging. She stood aside as Tony and Randy squeezed through the front door to take a look at the bloated, bloody mess stuck between the red box and the wall.

"I don't know if it's the texture or the smell that's worse." Tony whispered. His complete disgust at what they were about to do outweighing his ability to maintain noise discipline. Randy just nodded as he reached out to poke at a dirty, pale, white roll of flesh covered in half-dried blood. They pushed and pulled on the over-sized cadaver without getting anywhere until Kelly showed back up with two bottles of Wesson oil. Fighting down his urge to vomit Kyler detached his mind from what was happening. He couldn't believe his life had reached the point where lubing up an obese cadaver to try and escape from a building in the middle of the night without being seen or heard by Zombies was an actual thing.

It worked. The body slid right out in a big flabby mess once they'd gotten the oil rubbed in all over it. Tony added a little bit of puke to the pile when the body made some disturbing noises while being pushed. The corpse cork popped they turned and went back into the store to give any curious Zombies who may have heard the noises a few minutes to show up. Randy and Tony both changed into new t-shirts and went through another couple bottles of hand sanitizer along with an enormous quantity of moist towelettes. Randy was sure he was never going to feel clean again. Every inch of him felt covered in the Wesson oil mixed with the other random bodily fluids that'd been leaking everywhere.

Kelly finally stopped the two of them from scrubbing themselves with moist towelettes. She continued to maintain noise discipline but even in the darkness they could both feel her attitude radiating over them. She needed them both to man up and quit trying to remove cadaver flesh from underneath their fingernails long enough to start working their way over to the house. Neither of them was happy about it. Tony rebelliously squirted some more sanitizer on his hands, but they began to make their way to the front of the store.

There was no sign of any activity in the parking lot. The moon was barely visible through the clouds. Kelly led them across the street past another plaza towards the road that would take them to the subdivision they were looking for. They moved quickly and quietly. There was no room for playing around when you were out in the open like this. Each of them had a blade or a hammer in their hand. Guns were all neatly holstered up. As close as the herd was if they had to draw their guns, they were screwed.

In the end it was very anticlimactic. They jogged down a side road to the gated entrance to their subdivision. The gate had been wrecked by a car crashing into it, but the pedestrian gate was working fine. They passed through the gate and headed for their house. Tony followed along behind them trying to be extra vigilant. It was obvious Randy and Kelly were just focused on getting to their house and seeing what was there. The moon came out from behind the clouds as they jogged revealing a nightmarish scene in their front yard.

The black Elantra was sitting in the middle of the driveway with a desiccated corpse handcuffed to it. Their other cars were missing. The road around the house and the driveway were littered with dead bodies. Kelly barely noticed all the dead bodies as she rushed into the home though the front door. Randy following closely behind her noticing out of the corner of his eye that the front door was barely hanging on by a single hinge and there were bullet holes stitched across it. Tony hurried to catch up. Randy freaked out for a second when he lost track of Kelly. Looking around he spotted her sitting down on the ground reading something. She looked up at him with her face covered in tears and a huge smile. She held out a sparkle glue covered letter to him.

"Our little girls are alive!"

Chapter 16: Bride School

Caitlyn woke up in the back seat with her head in Ali's lap. Ali was running her fingers through Caitlyn's hair and making soothing noises. Caitlyn sat up and looked around. Her head pounded from being slammed into the floor of the vehicle they were in. She could taste blood on the inside of her mouth. The man in the seat in front of them gave Caitlyn an exasperated look. One of the man's eyes was blackening up pretty good. Caitlyn vaguely remembered tagging him with her elbow before she'd been stomped right out of the fight.

"We're sorry about your little sister. It was too late to go back. Why didn't you tell us she was in there?" The man asked.

Caitlyn ignored his question and continued to look around the inside of the van. She didn't see anything that was going to help her. She wasn't sure what she'd been looking for anyway. A loaded M-16 someone had accidently left on the floor would've been nice. With no loaded weapons lying around in easy reach she focused on the man asking the questions.

"Where are you taking us?" She asked him back. She ignored his earlier question.

"We're taking you to the refugee camp. Once you're there you and your sisters will be processed and assigned a destination. You'll also spend some time learning your new roles."

"What are you talking about?" She asked him. Her head hurt and this guy was talking crazy. Zombies covered the countryside. This guy and his friends had nothing better to do than hunt down survivors.

"You'll find out in the training. It's hard to explain it all without giving you some background first. It's a dangerous world now but we're fighting to make it a better place. I can tell you're a fighter." The man smiled and patted his black eye.

"I'm just not a big fan of being kidnapped. You people and your organization killed my little sister. You want me to just forget that?" Caitlyn was mad now. She hadn't realized how far she'd leaned in to yell at the guy. He moved back from her to avoid the spit flying out of her mouth. He was also probably worried about her head butting him or doing something else they hadn't constrained her from being able to do.

"Why don't you just focus on keeping the other ones alive?" The man snapped back. He'd dropped the act of trying to be her friend. It obviously wasn't getting him anywhere with her anyway. "Lean back in your seat now or I'll knock you back in it." He finished. He moved forward and bared his teeth at her. He had his fist cocked back to slam into her face if she didn't comply.

"Woah!" A smiling man moved into the seat next to the overly aggressive guard. The smiling man moved the angry man gently over to the side and told him he'd handle the girls from there. Then he stuck his hand out to Caitlyn to see if she'd shake it. Caitlyn stared at the hand like he was handing her a dog turd on toast. The man withdrew his hand but kept the big fake smile plastered on his face. He handed Caitlyn and Ali each a water bottle.

"Thank you." Ali said.

Ali talking brought Caitlyn back to reality. She knew Zoey was out of her control now. All she could do was pray the Zombies missed her and she somehow made her way out of that house. Ali needed her though. Myriah and Doreen needed her too. She had to be strong for them. She could harbor all the ill will she wanted towards their kidnappers, but she needed to change how she was approaching them. She needed to do like Ali and show some appreciation. Attempt to be sociable with them. Pretend she was thankful to be kidnapped while her little sister had been left to die.

If she could get them to trust her then their guard may go down at some point. At that point she'd figure out a way to kill them all. Once these clowns were all dead, they could try and rescue Zoey. She just had to keep the steps in mind. One of the first steps was knowledge. She was completely lacking in any of that. Looking out the window wasn't cluing her in to where they were at. She'd been unconscious for over half the time they'd been driving now.

"Yeah. Thanks for the water. Where's the refugee camp?" Caitlyn asked trying to take on a nicer tone. The guard probably wasn't fooled by the tone change at all but took it in stride. The guy would've made a great timeshare sales person.

"We're almost there. Once we park, we'll have to hike about a mile to get to the actual camp. We don't have cars pull right up to it in case someone happens to be trailing a ton of Zombies behind them."

"Aren't you watching everything with those drones?" Caitlyn asked. She was wondering how she was going to be able to escape if they had those things flying around all the time. She guessed they could make a run at night if the drones didn't do infrared or sense heat or anything fancy like that. She was hoping they just had the standard personal drones.

"We watch the main areas, but we don't have the man power or the drones to watch everything all the time. We have other ways we watch. We're learning how to live again. I think you're going to like the camp. It's at least got some security compared to how you've been living." The man seemed to recognize that the security discussion was probably pretty awkward since the thing the girls had been trying to guard against had been them. He rushed to change the subject. "We're almost there. If you'll promise not to try to escape or beat anybody else up, I'll go ahead and cut off those tie wraps so you can move your arms around again. Sound good?"

They pulled to a stop next to a line of other vehicles that'd been parked along the side of the road. There was a steep drop into a culvert on both sides of the road, so the vehicles were all only about halfway off the road. This meant one of the lanes was blocked for all practical purposes. Caitlyn sat in the back with her hands freed watching as four men in camouflage walked up the road towards them. The men had emerged out of the woods almost as soon as they'd parked. The group was led by a large black man with a shaved head who was flipping a hatchet in one hand as he walked. The rest of the men were pointing large caliber rifles at them.

The man in the driver's seat of the van they were in got out and talked briefly to the man flipping the hatchet around. A few minutes later Caitlyn and Ali were reunited with Myriah and Doreen to begin the trek to the camp they were being taken to. Two of the men they'd been riding with came with them. The rest had gotten back into the vans and disappeared on some other mission. Caitlyn wondered if they were just driving around with the drones trying to find more survivors they could kidnap. Or, refugees they could save as they probably thought of their actions to themselves.

"How far is it?" Myriah asked one of the men escorting them. He muttered something about it not being very far and motioned for them to hurry up. He seemed nervous to be walking around out in the open.

"Is it safe out here?" Caitlyn asked. She'd picked up on the man's nervousness. She was worried for Doreen if they got swarmed by a group of Zombies. The two men with them were both well-armed but there was no telling if they'd protect them or just take off running at the first sign of trouble.

"As safe as anywhere is these days." The other camouflaged man answered. He looked like he might be on some sort of drugs. The way he was acting was just a little bit off. Not a lot but enough to make Caitlyn think he must be on something. She'd never actually seen anyone on drugs anywhere except on the Chicago Med TV show but the way the man was acting kind of reminded her of that.

They trudged onwards through the muggy hot day. They were surrounded on both sides by thick green Florida vegetation. Mosquitos were enjoying every inch of exposed skin they could find on the marching girls. Another side effect of the fall of humanity was the increase in the mosquito population. Without the mosquito control people driving around spraying poison on the still bodies of water the bugs were getting out of control. It'd gotten so bad that the girls barely even noticed the thick clouds of mosquitos anymore. It had become just another part of the misery of being outside in this post-apocalyptic paradise.

At the end of the long road there was an intersection with another road that was slightly larger. They turned on that road and walked past the entrance to a park. A man stood by the park entrance sign with an M-16. He waved to the men escorting them and then stepped back into the vegetation to continue guarding the entrance to the park. The park itself was visible through openings in the trees. Several of those large green canvas army tents had been setup across the overgrown baseball diamonds. They could see people moving around between the tents but for all the people they saw there was barely any noise reaching them out on the road. It was more people in a single place than the girls had seen in a long time. Caitlyn thought there may be a couple hundred people camped out in the fields.

Another hundred yards past the park was the entrance to the county fire department. Their escorts took them up to the booth by the large rolling gate and turned them over to another guard. He had them wait while he used the radio in the booth to call someone to come get them. Ten minutes later a man came out of a side door in the large building and walked over to the gate. The guard pressed a button and the gate rolled open. It'd been so long since the girls had seen something as simple as a gate opening at the press of a button that it seemed like witchcraft.

The gate closing behind them felt like the cell door closing on a man thrown in jail. Caitlyn felt trapped. Hope drained from her body. How was she going to escape the tall fences around her? How could she sneak a bunch of kids past all these guards with drones watching from the sky? She started to tear up thinking about Zoey in that house with the Zombies rushing in. Zoey trying to hide and wait for her sisters to come save her. She'd feel abandoned and alone. That's how her little sister was going to die.

Myriah must've been thinking along the same line as she jumped when the gate clanked shut behind them. She didn't look scared though. She looked pissed off. She looked ready to fight. Unfortunately, they didn't have much of a chance with no weapons against grown, armed fighting men. The man who'd come out to greet them was trying to say hello to them.

"Is this bride school?" Myriah snapped at the man. She made it obvious the way she said it that she was sickened by everything the phrase implied.

"Where'd you hear that from?" The man asked her with a smile.

"The guards." Myriah said. Before the man got a chance to answer Caitlyn jumped in.

"Our sister got left behind in a building that's being surrounded by Zombies. How do we get someone to go rescue her?"

"I'm going to assume you let your guards know about your sister, right?" The man asked. When Myriah and Caitlyn nodded their heads in affirmation he continued. "Then I'm sure we're already doing everything we can to save your sister. The best thing you guys can do is start getting adjusted to your new lives. I think you're going to like it here."

The man opened the door to the building and led them inside the dimly lit interior. The walls were concrete and seemed to go on forever. The long hallway was lined with doors on both sides. An armed guard was seated at a desk by the door. He nodded at them as they came in and directed them to a room with 'intake' written in black sharpie on the door.

Inside that room they were made to take off their clothes to be examined by a hatchet-faced woman with little to no bedside manner. Feeling violated and embarrassed they were covered in some sort of delousing powder and then handed wet sponges to wash themselves off with. Caitlyn held Doreen and took care of her as gently as she could. At least they were still together. There was still hope they could break out and go rescue Zoey somehow. When the nurse was done with them, she sent them back out in the hallway in new clothes where they stood against the wall under the watchful eye of the guard.

A little while later a man and woman dressed in camouflage came down the hall. The woman stopped and talked to the nurse briefly then addressed the girls.

"Say your goodbyes for now. We split everyone up by age groups for training. You'll be reunited once you've finished the training. We'll give you a minute to do that while we grab the gear you'll need."

Caitlyn's world crumbled around her. Ali and Doreen were both freaking out at the thought of being separated from them. Myriah was crying softly trying to comfort the two little ones. Caitlyn found herself trying to reason with the woman when she came back.

"Doreen and Ali really need to be with us. They've been with us since the beginning. you can't just take them away like that."

"Say your goodbyes now. You'll be put in different groups for training."

Doreen started screaming she wouldn't leave. A man came out into the hallway and tried pulling Doreen away from Caitlyn. Myriah jumped at him raking her nails across his face. He backhanded her across the room. Caitlyn jumped in swinging a fist wildly at the man. More men appeared from another door and Caitlyn found herself pinned to the ground. The taste of blood in her mouth again. Sobs wracked her body as she watched her family torn apart. Doreen and Ali disappeared down the hall tossed across the broad shoulders of the camouflaged soldiers. Myriah was zip tied and marched into another room. Caitlyn could feel hope draining from her body. She lie still on the ground as zip ties were secured around her wrists before she was yanked painfully to her feet.

Chapter 17: Herd Reversal

Kyler walked out his cabin door and down the path to the administration building. Entering the building he saw there was a whole lot of activity going on. Not sure who to ask for his orders Kyler meandered over to a small table someone had set out some snacks on. He was trying to figure out how old the slices of cheese were when someone poked him in the back. Turning around he saw that it was Tom standing there with his hand stuck out. Kyler shook the older man's hand wondering what the deal was.

"Welcome aboard. You're supposed to be getting orders for reporting to one of the training depots but you're going to be doing some OJT first. Got all your weapons and gear in a duffle bag out in the truck. Come on out with me. You're going to be with me and my crew today."

Kyler walked outside with Tom over to the pickup truck where the guys were busy loading boxes of grenades and ammunition.

"We declare war on a small country while I was sleeping?" Kyler asked.

"Nope." Tom said. "The Zombies in that herd we saw yesterday are rolling past our exit right now. Once they get past it a little bit more, we're going to hit them from behind and try to get them to follow us. Once they're following us, we'll hide and hopefully they'll keep heading north."

"We're supposed to get that many Zombies to just turn around and follow us?"

"Oh yeah." One of the guys loading boxes in the truck answered. "We'll just come up behind them and start laying into the rear of the pack with grenades. The ones in the back will start screaming and chasing us and the rest of them should spin around and do the same thing. We might not get all of them to follow us, but it should be most of them."

"Added bonus." The guy Kyler recognized as the one who'd tied him up and left him in the back of the truck the day before looked over to chip in. "The ones in the back of the herd are the slowest ones. Hopefully we won't have any more of that hopping in the truck with us garbage."

Tom handed Kyler his bag with his gear in it. Kyler happily started strapping his weapons back on. He'd felt naked the day before walking around without the familiar weight of holstered weapons pulling at his belt and shoulders. It'd been even weirder to wake up in the morning and not be able to reach out and put his hand on some sort of weapon. He'd gotten used to sleeping with a knife or a pistol near his hand. The kitchen utensil he'd shoved under his pillow like a lost tooth hadn't been a great substitute.

Sliding a hatchet into the back of his belt he hopped up on the tailgate and swung his legs around to climb into the bed of the truck. This time one of the other guys was going to be stuck back there with him. There was also another truck that'd be driving along beside them in case anything happened. That truck just had a single driver in it. If they got a flat tire or the engine blew up on them, they'd be able to hop out and switch trucks before the Zombies could catch up.

It made sense from a mission point of view as well since the Zombies stopping to kill and eat them if they got a flat tire would slow down their northerly momentum. The whole idea was to get them moving as fast as possible in a direction that was out of Georgia. Kyler hadn't heard anyone express any concern as to what would happen to the citizens of South Carolina because of this plan. He couldn't think of a way to casually bring that up in conversation either without it raising a bunch of other questions he'd rather avoid. He decided for now he'd just perform his role and not worry about it. It'd be a good chance to gather operational data about how these guys worked. Plus, if they pulled it off this'd be a neat maneuver to be able to duplicate up north.

Kyler sat in the back thinking about how this kind of maneuvering could end up looking like a ping pong match between the two states while he waited for them to get moving. If South Carolina pulled off the same maneuver and flung the herd back to the south to be dealt with. Zombie herds being used as WMDs between the two factions. He didn't think that was the idea here though. The idea here seemed to be more of just getting rid of the Zombies before they did too much damage to the south. The damn things had come from the north to begin with so why not send them back that way? For all they knew the people to the north were responsible for the herd moving this way.

The sound of the engine turning over brought him back to reality. They'd been waiting on confirmation that the herd had moved past the exit before heading in that direction. They must have received that confirmation as Tom started driving them down the road towards the interstate.

"I'm Pete." The big guy sitting next to him announced. It was the first words the guy had said to him since telling him to move the day before when he'd started shooting the Zombies jumping in the back of the truck.

"Kyler." Kyler stuck his hand out and Pete gave it a quick firm handshake.

"Ok. Well between Tom's driving and me being stuck with a kid who hasn't graduated high school, I feel like today may end up sucking. We've got a box of grenades and a shitload of loaded magazines to run through. You know how to shoot at least?" Pete asked.

"Yep. I can also tie my own shoes and pull the pin out of a grenade and toss it behind us. How many times have you guys done this?" Kyler asked. He was trying to figure out how proficient they were at it. Any useful tips he could pick up to stay alive today would be appreciated as well as possibly turning out to be valuable intel.

"You mean how many times have we attacked the rear column of a massive mob of tens of thousands of insane infected to try and get them to turn around and go the other way?" Pete smiled at him. "Counting today that would be exactly one time. This is not a normal daily thing for us. Killing a few Zombies here and there no problem. Getting a few hundred to move from one side of some deserted town to the other no problem. Tens of thousands marching down the interstate towards our major centers. Problem."

Kyler absorbed that bit of unwelcome information as they drove. Over the steady hum of the engine and the howling of the wind around him in the open truck bed he picked up a roar that sounded like a waterfall. He sat up and looked over the edges of the truck, but they weren't going over a bridge and he didn't see any bodies of water running beside them. The noise grew louder as they drove until it dawned on Kyler it was probably the roar of a few thousand Zombies going down the interstate less than a mile from them.

They stopped again. This time Tom made a point of indicating they shouldn't speak. The roar from the Zombies passing was so loud Kyler doubted they'd be heard anyway but he agreed with Tom on not risking it. He knew he wasn't super excited about what they were preparing to do. Getting the attention of that many Zombies on purpose was akin to suicide. Then after they got the attention of the Zombies instead of driving like madmen to get away from them, they were going to stay close enough to tease the mob along.

It occurred to Kyler at this point that there would also be a lot of stragglers for them to dodge. Not all of the Zombies would've been able to keep up with the main mob. Just like there'd be some of the supercharged freaks who ran ahead of the pack there was also going to be a whole section of laggards they'd have to dodge. This would consist of mostly the wounded and slow Zombies so that was a plus in being able to avoid them but if there were enough of them spread out across the road it could seriously interfere with their plan. It was one thing to dodge one Zombie with a missing leg. An entire road full of them crawling along would be a different story.

The roaring subsided so gradually that Kyler couldn't have pinpointed the time it went from deafening to distant. From the constant roar of Niagara Falls to the muted rumble of a distant thunderstorm passing. Tom made a little circle gesture with his finger and drove the rest of the way up the road into the area Kyler recognized as having the dilapidated gas station and the other small businesses. The place had probably looked bad before the apocalypse but now it had completely fallen apart. With the support vehicle following closely behind them they turned and headed towards the I-95 on-ramp.

Tom rolled to a stop at the top of the ramp. Looking down they could see a steady stream of Zombies trudging their way southwards. Looking northwards the line of stragglers continued until the road curved and Kyler couldn't see any farther. This plan was already FUBAR. No one had anticipated the line of Zombies to be this long. It had to be at least a few miles long between the leading elements rushing forward and the slower Zombies trudging and limping along in their wake. For this to be successful they needed to lead the Zombies on a chase in a northerly direction and right now that didn't look like a possibility. If they went down there now, they'd just be overwhelmed by the stragglers after they made some noise trying to get the bulk of the Zombies to move the other direction. A new plan occurred to Kyler. It wasn't a great plan, but it was way better than the drive onto the interstate and toss some grenades around until overwhelmed and eaten alive plan.

Ignoring the no talking rule Tom had laid down Kyler stuck his head in the cab of the truck through the slider. "Hey. Instead of leading the Zombies out of here via the interstate which isn't going to work why don't we lead them down this road instead? Does it go somewhere it's safe for us to get the Zombies going to?"

"Good thinking Kyler. Yeah. I'm not sure where the hell this road goes. I don't think we have any people this way though. Then again, this'll pretty much end this exit as a camp for us. At least for right now. Let me see what the commander wants us to do." Kyler bit back a remark about how everyone seemed to like using the word commander. That would've been a dead giveaway that his cover story had some major holes in it. Kyler slid back into the truck bed listening to Tom talk on the radio.

"Good thinking." Pete said. He was staring in awe at the long line of Zombie shambling around. He was trying to be calm, but Kyler saw that his fingers were shaking as he loaded more bullets into a stack of magazines. Kyler didn't blame him. That long line of death snaking up the highway could easily snap on them.

"Let's do it." The command came from Tom in the cab. "Load up and get ready to cause some havoc. We're going to curve out of here then take some backroads northerly. None of these routes have been checked out so fingers crossed."

"So, a slightly higher chance of dying today than we had about twenty minutes ago. Sounds about right. You want to take the million on the left or the million on the right?" Pete asked sarcastically. He already had the pin pulled out of a grenade he was gripping tightly in his hand.

"I'll shoot. You throw." Kyler said. The idea being Pete would make the big booms that would attract the whole column of Zombies while Kyler would keep the faster Zombies from jumping in the back of the truck and killing them. They both really hoped the plan worked. Especially the not getting killed by the leaping Zombies part.

Tom turned the truck around to point it back eastwards and drove in reverse down the on ramp. Everyone in the truck fixated on the undulating river of diseased flesh flowing down the road in front of them. The Zombies at this end weren't screeching and roaring as much as the leaders were but they still gave off a loud moaning sound. They were still completely terrifying. A parade of soulless people covered in filth and gore moving mindlessly in pursuit of their prey. They followed the group in front of them in the hopes that the group in front of them had caught site of a normal. Grey haired grandmothers walked alongside gore covered toddlers. All of them missing chunks of skin. Their faces covered in huge black boils. Pete tossed a grenade.

They watched as the grenade sailed through the air. Kyler made a mental note to ask Pete if he'd ever played ball professionally or maybe just in college. The grenade went over the bulk of the Zombies on this side of the interstate and disappeared into the median. Kyler was wondering if it was dud when it finally blew up.

Instant insanity. The Zombies on the road below erupted into piercing shrieks. The whole area in front of them erupted into an insane swirl of bodies. It was a massively morbid mosh pit set to the music of their own screams. The Zombies still hadn't noticed them sitting fifty feet up the on-ramp staring at the chaos they'd created. Pete started tossing grenades like he was playing some kind of carnival game. The Zombies who weren't ripped to pieces by the shrapnel finally noticed them and surged forward with a collective screech.

That screech echoed up and down the interstate as far as they could hear. That was the signal Tom had been waiting for to be sure they had the Zombies attention. He began driving back up the on-ramp. Pete kept tossing grenades at the clumps of Zombies following them. Kyler was shooting every second now at the Zombies who seemed to be edging too close to them. On top of the ones coming up the road for them others started running through the underbrush right up the side of the hills towards them. The men sitting on the passenger side of the cab both had barrels stuck out their windows and were shooting away at the Zombies who'd gone off-road to get at them.

Accuracy sucked in the back of a bouncing truck with a zillion Zombies screeching towards them. Accuracy wasn't the point though. They just needed to make noise and keep any of the Zombies following them from getting in the truck. As closely packed together as the Zombies were in the confined space between the trees it was almost impossible to take a shot and not hit one of them. They made it to the road at the top of the on-ramp without being swamped by their pursuers. The truck bed was full of hot brass and Pete was running out of grenades to throw. They were burning through bullets at a pretty alarming rate. Kyler breathed deeply and stopped pulling the trigger every time he had a target. He knew he had to conserve some ammunition to keep the adrenalized Zombies off of them once they started coming.

Tom slowed them down as they followed the lead truck onto the road leading west away from the interstate. The Zombies surged forward in a mass through the wide-open area of stores and gas stations off the exit. Kyler and Pete shot at any Zombies who seemed to be getting too close. They tried to get a shot off at least once every thirty seconds to keep the Zombies at the back of the pack interested. They were almost all the way through town to the point where the road narrowed to a blacktop two lane when a group of the adrenalized Zombies came bounding towards them through the parking lot of the last gas station on the road.

Pete and Kyler spotted the Zombies at the same time and opened fire. There looked to be about seven of the adrenaline Zombies headed their way. Two of them had jumped off the roof of the gas station towards them. The other five were running through the mass of Zombies already moving their way. Occasionally the five running through the other Zombies would jump over the heads of the Zombies in front of them and keep sprinting for the pickup trucks. Tom had seen the issue as well and sped up. The lead truck had accelerated quickly to give Tom plenty of room to maneuver.

With deadly intensity Pete and Kyler lined up their shots on the fast-moving predators headed their way. They both sighed a little bit in relief when they realized they were surrounded on both side by tall trees and not out in the middle of the plaza any more. The Zombies were still barreling towards them with the fast ones in the lead but now they were confined to a straight approach. The Zombies confined on the road between the trees were much easier for them to shoot down. Kyler ejected a magazine and slammed in a new one. He lined up a sight picture on a large skinny male Zombie who was only about thirty feet behind them and coming up fast.

Kyler pulled the trigger at the same time as the truck hit something that made it bounce hard. Kyler and Pete's shots both went wild as they were tossed around. Kyler slammed his head painfully into the side of the truck bed after unleashing a few rounds in the general direction of the tailgate. He realized his ass was wet and everything smelled funny. Pete was yelling something at him over the roar of the pursuing Zombies, but he couldn't quite make it out. He came out of the fugue state cracking his head on the side of the truck had put him in and placed the smell as that of gasoline. He realized belatedly that he was sitting in a truck bed full of hot brass and gas.

He raised his rifle and shot at a Zombie that'd just jumped into the truck bed right beside Pete. The Zombies head snapped backwards, and it flipped out of the truck. Pete gave Kyler an appreciative nod before sighting in on another Zombie that was danger close. The truck skidded sideways with a loud bang. Pete's shot went wild and the danger close Zombie jumped for them. It landed on Kyler who began kicking the Zombie and trying to keep it from getting close enough to bite him. The stained teeth flashed at him from the black sore covered face.

Then the truck bed caught on fire. They'd had the big red jug of spare gasoline back there with them. All Kyler could think of while he struggled to keep the Zombie off him long enough for the fire to burn him to death was that either him or Pete must've put a bullet through the gas container in all the crazy shooting. He had no idea why Tom would've stopped the truck when he did or what'd actually set off the puddle of gasoline.

"Let's go!" Someone was yelling loudly now. It sounded like a great idea to Kyler if this Zombie he was holding would just go away. All of a sudden, the Zombies head exploded. Pete had placed the barrel of his rifle on the things forehead and pulled the trigger. Now he was reaching down to grab Kyler's hand and help him out of the burning truck bed. Kyler grabbed the offered hand and jumped to his feet. Pete and him both jumped over the side of the truck away from the crowd of Zombies that were moving quickly up the road towards them.

"Get to the other truck!" Tom was shooting and yelling. The other guys in the truck were shooting at the incoming Zombies while trying to work their way out of the cab. Two of the fast Zombies landed on the roof of the burning truck. Kyler raised his rifle to take a shot at them before realizing he was in quite a good bit of pain. Pete tossed him down on the ground.

"Roll around! You're on fire!" Pete yelled at him. He was busy shooting at the adrenalized Zombies coming at them from every direction.

Kyler rolled around on the ground a few times. Weary of wasting too much time rolling around on the ground he popped to his feet hoping he was no longer on fire. The two guys in the cab were out of luck. The cab was filled with squirming Zombies trying to push their way in to get at the man flesh being ripped off the bones by the other Zombies. There were piles of dead and wounded Zombies all around them. The lead truck pulled into view and Pete, Tom and Kyler ran for it. Everyone else from the main truck was dead now. It was a miracle they weren't all dead already. The driver of the lead truck was screaming for them to hurry up. He had his window down.

Kyler watched in horror as the man was jerked out of the truck through the driver side window and down to the ground out of sight. Tom jumped in through the passenger side and stuck his head out the driver's window looking to help the unfortunate driver. Whatever he saw on the ground below evidently told him it was too late for the former truck's driver. Tom slid into the driver's seat himself while pressing down desperately hard on the button to roll up the window. Kyler and Pete wedged themselves into the passenger seat and slammed that door shut. Kyler worked his way over the console into the back-bench seat in the extended cab truck. Tom already accelerating quickly down the road away from the Zombies who were busy ripping apart the bodies of their teammates.

The Zombies who couldn't easily get at the flesh were running flat out in pursuit of their truck. Kyler started sifting through the piles of supplies he was sitting on to try and find more grenades and ammunition. The first wave of the Zombies pursuit looked vicious behind them. Tom accelerated gaining them fifty feet of room then a hundred feet of room. They roared around a tight turn and almost collided with a school bus that was pulled over to the side of the road. A bunch of kids and a few adults were running out of a dilapidated looking dollar store towards the bus.

Tom slammed on the brakes and turned the steering wheel to bring them to a smoking stop in front of the bus. He looked over and caught the attention of an older man with a head full of grey hair who was carrying two kids and pushing a couple of others along.

"Get them in the bus and get the hell out of here. We'll hold them off!"

Chapter 18: Hide and Seek

"The herd was headed towards Donna's house. I think we need to check all the local places before we storm off towards Disney or the beach or any of those other places. Maybe we save Donnas for last and hope the herd has moved on by then." Randy said. They'd been reading the letters and the writing on the walls and trying to figure out what to do with the breadcrumbs their kids and Kelly's mom had left behind.

"Disney was only mentioned in the earlier letters as the main place they were headed. It's just an option in the later ones. I'm pretty sure my mom would've stayed around here as long as it was safe to wait for us to show up." Kelly said. She still had a big grin plastered to her face. Now that they had proof the kids had survived and her mom was with them Kelly felt like they were so close to finding them. She knew they just had to work the clues they'd been given. She was wracking her brain trying to figure out the best places to search first.

Her mom's house was only a few miles away. That was the most obvious one for them to be at if they were still local and hoping Kelly and Randy would eventually show up. There were a few friends around the area and of course the kids had spent a good deal of time at Kelly's friend Donnas house. Caitlyn had spent plenty of time over there dog sitting and housesitting as well. Comparing the letters to the intent of the letters and thinking of all the places the kids could be started to overwhelm Kelly. All this time she'd really just thought it would all resolve itself once they made it here to the house. Now they were standing here in the house and they still had a lot of work left to do to find them. Kelly vacillated between feeling like they were only seconds away from finding the kids and being overwhelmed at having to figure out where to go next.

Tony had kept quiet during the whole exchange. He'd mostly been walking the perimeter of the house and performing sentry type duty. The next time he walked by close enough to hear them Randy asked if he had any opinions.

"I don't know. You guys know your kids and your mom the best. Where do you think they'd have gone? I don't really have any idea where we'd go after here. I'm still in shock that we found all these envelopes and everything."

"If you didn't think they were going to be here then why'd you come with us all this way?" Kelly asked him. The wording was aggressive, but the tone of the question was more curious than agitated.

"I may not have the same level of faith and belief you two have in your kids and your mom, but I do have faith in both of you. Once I got on that train it wasn't like it would've been easy to get off. Besides, what the hell else was I going to do? Join up with one of these moronic militias cruising around?"

Kelly got up off the couch and walked over to give an embarrassed looking Tony a hug. She told him thanks and then Randy came over and echoed the sentiment.

"The herd!" Kelly said out of nowhere. Right in the middle of their kumbaya moment. Randy and Tony stared at her.

"The herd was going up the road past the pharmacy." Kelly continued after neither Randy nor Tony said anything in response to her outburst. She looked at them both with exasperation. "The herd was moving towards my mom's and Donnas houses. If the kids are hiding in one of their houses, then the herd may be onto them. We need to move now and check both houses."

Kelly had that look in her eyes that Randy knew meant she wasn't about to stay here another second. He hoisted himself up to his feet and made sure he had all his gear strapped on. He heard Tony doing the same and was silently impressed that Tony didn't even bother complaining. He evidently understood Kelly a little better at this point as well.

"Well. We've got a few hours of darkness left so if we're going to go poke around a huge number of killer Zombies in the dark let's get moving." Randy said. He was being droll about it, but he felt a bit of the energy Kelly was putting off. His need to find and protect his daughters was driving him as well. Being in their house and seeing their writing on the walls and in the letters had reinvigorated him. Now he was twenty times more fearful for them than he'd been before. Being this close to where they'd been and seeing the evidence that they were still alive was almost unbearable.

They went back out the front door a few minutes later. None of them looked back at the house they'd been trying so hard for so long to get to. Without the kids there it was just another pile of wood and concrete slowly molding away in the blazing humidity of Florida. The only reason they hadn't left immediately was Kelly had insisted on spending a few minutes searching the house to make sure they had all the letters and had read all of them to see if there were any other clues. They hadn't found any clues, but Tony had been struck by how sure the kids seemed in their letters that Randy and Kelly would come for them. How sure the mom had been that her daughter would endure. He wasn't able to even think of a way to begin to describe how powerfully moved he was by reading the letters.

They hiked out to the gate and continued to retrace their steps all the way back to the intersection by the drug store. At the intersection they turned right instead of heading across the parking lot to the drug store. After the discoveries back at the house they all had questions and things they wanted to say. They just weren't able to actually talk about anything as they had to maintain strict noise discipline. In the dark walking along the side of the road their visibility was extremely limited. To make it a little more miserable clouds had moved in and they were slowly getting drenched by a light rain that started falling. The clouds that brought the rain also blotted out the moon. This had the effect of making it even darker which made it a lot more treacherous to hike the sides of the overgrown road they were on.

Kelly slipped in the mud on the side of the road and bit her tongue to keep from cursing in frustration. They were sticking to the sides of the roads and with the rain and overgrown vegetation the sides were slick and treacherously steep. Picking herself up and wiping mud and water off the legs of her pants she kept on moving forward. She was tired. She was so tired, but she was driven by a need to find her kids and make sure they were safe. A primal urge to find and comfort them. This instinct and drive were so strong sometimes it amazed even her.

They moved forward in the night. The moon occasionally making an appearance to give them the brief hope they'd be able to actually see where they were going to step before disappearing once again behind the dense cloud cover. Miserable and soaked they moved forward. The spark of hope burned bright in Kelly's heart. They were so close and the letters she'd just seen spurred her on. Randy was on a different level. His thoughts tended to the more pessimistic side. He was spurred on by the ideas that they were too late. That all they'd find was the pathetic decaying corpses of his children. He thought if maybe he moved faster, they could prevent that. He had to fight over every step he took to try and tell himself it wasn't a mistake. To tell himself they had to go to one place then the next. He couldn't be everywhere at once.

His frustration came to the forefront as they began to encounter Zombies. Leading the three of them Randy was the first to have his foot connect with one of the sleeping beasts. Peering down he saw the mud-covered face of an elderly woman curled up into a fetal position covered in dirt and leaves. Her eyes were closed, and she didn't seem to even register the jab to her leg from his foot. Pulling his foot back carefully he raised his machete over his head. Making sure he had room to swing the blade without hitting either Kelly or Tony he chopped down as hard as he could while maintaining his focus on the woman's head. He dropped to one knee to complete the downward chopping motion and was rewarded by the sound and feel of the machete popping through a skull and sinking into the soft gooey center.

He put his foot down on the cracked open skull and worked his machete out. He briefly wondered how long it'd taken for Kelly to consider it normal to have to pause to wait for her husband to work his blade out of the head of a dead old woman before continuing forward. There was nothing normal about any of this. A few steps later he encountered another sleeper. This one was a young boy. Swallowing his natural pity for the small frame he smashed the boy's skull in half with a strong downward strike of the machete. Feeling as though he'd left part of his soul behind him with the tiny corpse Randy kept moving forward.

Tony brought up the rear of the small party. His thoughts were miles way from where they were at right now. He was a single guy with no kids of his own, but he had plenty of nieces and nephews. He loved them all. He felt like that gave him some sense of what Randy and Kelly must be going through. His head was on a swivel as Randy led them deeper into the sleeping herd. He knew one misstep could spell the end for all of them. He knew they shouldn't be rushing into this with zero planning the way they were. He understood why they were doing it though. He understood that drive Randy and Kelly must be feeling. He envied them for having that strong of a purpose. He felt like he was just along for the ride.

Their progress kept slowing as they encountered more and more sleeping Zombies. Normally the Zombies would've found a house to nest in but since they'd moved this way so fast, they assumed the Zombies must've just lay down where they were standing when they got tired. That meant the herd probably had stopped in this general area somewhere. Randy was in the lead and knew that if the herd had stopped here that meant there was a good chance that they were bunched up around Donna's house. The problem was he only had a vague idea of where Donna's house was. He stopped and waited for Kelly to catch up. Then he stared at her until she got the idea and took the lead.

Randy fell back into the middle of the pack. He followed behind Kelly as she led them deeper into the miserably humid night. She gradually moved them from walking along the side of the road to walking in the middle of the streets as the ditches filled up with sleeping Zombies. Feeling super exposed but making way better time they marched briskly down the middle of the road towards Donna's house. Kelly sped them up as she mentally did the math to figure out if they'd have time to check both Donna's house and her mom's house that night. She wasn't letting herself think they'd actually find the kids quite yet. She was scared to let herself hope for that much. Scared of how low she'd go if it didn't end up working out.

Soaked to the bone they followed Kelly until she came to a stop in the middle of the asphalt looking over at a medium sized house. It looked just like all of the other houses they'd been passing to Tony and Randy. Randy had only ever been there one time when he'd dropped off Cait or Kelly to take Donna's dog out or something like that. The rest of his family had been over a lot more than that which was good since Kelly was able to recognize the house. Randy looked closer and saw that the windows and front door had all been ripped out. A few lumps littered the lawn which he assumed were decomposing bodies.

Given the density of the bodies they'd passed lying in the ditches and on the cold hard ground he knew the house they were looking at was probably packed to the rafters with nesting Zombies. The same as all of the other houses on the street. That meant they were going to have to poke around in a house filled with Zombies in the middle of the night to see if there were any other clues. Randy was thinking they really needed to slide between the houses and find a space somewhere to meet and quietly discuss next steps when Kelly took off down the sidewalk straight towards the house. Seeing that she obviously wasn't in a planning session mood Randy cracked his neck and tested the weight of the hatchet and machete he held in his hands.

Kelly walked quickly towards the front door of the house. She felt a stronger sense of urgency as she got closer and saw the front door had been ripped off its hinges. The foyer to the home was dimly lit by the moon peeking through the rain clouds above. They were going to need to search every room in the house. That meant they were going to need to kill a lot of Zombies. She didn't care how many Zombies they had to kill she was going to search the house from top to bottom.

In the foyer of the home the trio of would be rescuers stood motionless listening to the sound of the nesting horde all around them. It was a larger house on the inside than it had seemed from the street. There were plenty of windows to let in the dim outside light. By this sliver of illumination Randy was able to make out how screwed they were. Zombies were literally covering the floor and furniture. Several were stacked on top of one another grunting and writhing around to find the best place to sleep. The smell in the house was awful. The deep moist scent of fecal waste and the acidic smell of urine mixed with a whole new level of body odor coming off the sleeping piles of sore covered bodies in waves.

There was no way they were hacking their way through this house. Not if they had any desire to live through the next few minutes anyway. They were going to need to tiptoe around the bodies and try to find clues. Not that there was much hope of finding anything useful in this Zombie carpeted pile of garbage. It was going to be like a group of drunk teenagers trying to find a lost set of car keys in the dark at the city dump while pit bulls were on patrol. Randy wanted to pull Kelly and Tony out and go try Brenda's house. He didn't bother trying though since he knew she wasn't going to leave until they'd at least made an effort to cross this house off the list.

Kelly sobbed silently as she slowly led them deeper into the darkness of the house. The smells were assaulting her, and she felt like she might vomit. She couldn't see anything. She had no idea what it was she was trying to find in this mad house. She knew she may be leading her husband and their friend to a horrible death. One misstep and this whole house could become a giant tomb for them. They'd die in a storm of undulating teeth and clawing Zombies. Kelly almost turned back. Her foot hit something though. She bent over to figure out what it was and found a bunch of electronic components that came out of some sort of boom box that'd been smashed to pieces. She'd hoped for something that would've persuaded her to go deeper into the house.

She reached up and grabbed Randy's hand and motioned for them to leave the house. He put his finger to her lips signaling her to stay quiet and wait for him there. He wanted to finish searching the house just to make sure. More to keep Kelly from trying to get them to come back in here the next day than because he thought he might find anything else. Moving his feet in a semicircle in front of him with every step he worked his way down the hall. Occasionally he'd be forced step over piles of bodies on the floor. The occasional contact wasn't really a huge deal in the dark since the Zombie's just assumed it was one of their own poking into them to try and get comfortable.

He made it down the hall and looked into the bedrooms which were covered in piles of sleeping Zombies. Not seeing anything in there of interest he turned and went down the hallway towards the last door he figured he'd check before leaving. He could barely make out the broken door at the end of the hallway in the dim light. On the borderline of checking out the last room or not he went with his instinct to check out the anomaly of the broken interior door. He carefully made his way over to the door and moved it around on the broken hinge to slide into the room he now recognized as a bathroom.

Standing in the small space of the tiled bathroom he sensed an urgency to get out of the house. Kelly and Tony were standing out in the middle of it all with no chance to survive if something happened to wake up the Zombies. He turned to leave, and the bathroom door squeaked on its hinge and fell off completely. Randy caught the door as best he could and turned around to awkwardly try and lean it against the wall. Trying to avoid making too much noise he still managed to get the end of it caught in the shower curtain. Going with the flow he started to lay the door down on its side in the tub with the top still tangled in the shower curtain. He was doing everything with exaggerated caution now to try and avoid making any more noise.

The door hit an empty jug on the side of the bathtub that fell into the tub and landed on a pile of towels and other rags. Randy couldn't see anything in the dark moldy room. He felt around on that end of the tub to try and see what had just fallen. He finally got the door settled to a point where he didn't think it was going to fly around anymore. Not really finding anything in the pile of rags he got up to walk out of the bathroom. He heard a little whimper come from the tub. He froze.

Not sure of exactly what he'd just heard he turned and walked back towards the tub. He knew a Zombie could be curled up in the tub and making noises. He knew he should just walk out and tell Kelly he hadn't heard anything. He knew he couldn't do that. If there was the slightest chance it might be one of their kids in that tub, he had to check it out. He just wasn't a fan of sticking his hand down where a Zombie could decide to snack on one of his fingers. He knew that was exactly what he needed to do though.

He walked over to the tub, knelt down on the floor and reached into the tub like someone sticking their hand in a garbage disposal. He gingerly pulled the pile of rags to the side. A small body sprang out of the tub and jumped on him. Randy fell over backwards with the little banshee he'd let out of the tub. The silent banshee proceeded to scratch and punch him all over his body. Randy had his machete up and ready to strike when it dawned on him that a Zombie would've bitten him by now. A Zombie would also have been screaming it's head off. His attacker jumped up and tried to run around him. He reached out an arm and wrapped it around the small person dragging her back to him kicking and flailing. He pulled the kid over to where he could whisper in their ear.

"Not a Zombie. Let me help you get out of here." Then he picked up the random survivor he'd managed to find.

"Daddy?" Randy almost dropped his little girl he was so shaken hearing her voice there in the darkness. A new fear threatened to paralyze him. He realized he had to get her out of there alive. He pulled her back in close and went to a corner of the bathroom.

"We can't talk here baby girl. Are your sisters here? Just nod." He whispered as quietly as he could directly into her ear.

Zoey shook her head for no. Randy kissed his brave little girl on the forehead and took a deep breath to calm his nerves. Once he felt slightly more secure, he went through the open doorway and out into the hall. By the extremely dim light filtering through the windows he was able to see Tony and Kelly's eyes get bigger when they saw he was carrying someone. As they moved into the living room and she realized who it was he was carrying Randy saw a host of emotions flicker across Kelly's face. Her first instinct had been to see if the other kids were still in the house. She stared at Zoey then gave Randy a questioning look. He shook his head no.

As soon as they got out the door Kelly took Zoey from Randy. Tony moved in close with a big grin on his face and patted Randy hard on the back then gave him a big thumbs up. Zoey had been kicking her feet and trying to get to her mom as soon as she saw her. Kelly held Zoey tightly in her arms as they started walking down the middle of the road away from the lake house. The lake water Zoey had been drinking from the jug in the tub got the best of her and she spewed a stream of clear vomit all over her mom. Kelly just held her little girl closer until the sickness passed and then kept on walking down the road. It was surreal how elated she could be covered in puke walking down a road bordered on both sides by sleeping ghouls.

Elated to find Zoey and chilled to the bone that the other girls were not with her. Tears of joy, fear, and sadness intermingled running down the fierce mom's cheeks as she carried her baby down the street.

Chapter 19: Solitary

She had no tears left to cry. They'd thrown her into an empty supply closet and locked the door. The cramped space smelled like pine sol and vomit. Caitlyn tried to think what she could've done differently. How she could've made sure they didn't end up like this. Nothing popped out at her. After all the Zombies they'd dodged the biggest threat to them had turned out to be other survivors. If everyone else on the planet had just turned into blood thirsty Zombies, they'd have been fine.

Bloodthirsty Zombies they could deal with. Those scenarios made sense. Groups of survivors hunting down other groups of survivors with drones and throwing them into closets for reeducation didn't make any sense at all. Splitting families apart was just hurtful and mean and small minded. She'd cried for hours. She'd let the self-pity and sadness and hopelessness consume her as she sat on the hard floor in that dark confined space. When that tired her to the point of exhaustion, she'd passed out with her head braced against the wall.

At some point they'd opened the door and slid in a bottled water and some kind of granola bar. She'd been in the middle of a nightmare when they opened the door. A nightmare that turned out to be true when she realized she really was locked in a closet. She'd really lost Myriah, Zoey, Doreen and Ali. In her dream her mom and dad finally found her. They'd been carrying the bodies of her dead little sisters. They'd stared at Caitlyn with revulsion.

She felt around in the darkness looking for any sort of weapon she could use. She told herself she'd be ready the next time they opened the door. She wasn't really sure what it was she'd be ready for, but she knew she'd feel a lot better if she had some way to go on the offensive. She didn't take to just sitting in a closet waiting for someone to open the door and decide if she lived or died. They hadn't killed her yet so she felt she could be reasonably sure she might survive the next time they opened the door.

She ate the granola bar and drank the water. She'd hesitated to drink the water at first fearing it might be poisoned. Then she'd realized all they had to do was open the door and shoot her in the head if they wanted her dead. Plus, the bottled water cap made a little click and a hissing noise when she got it opened. That settled it for her as she couldn't really see a group of men working late into the night to perfect putting the lids back on poisoned water bottles to take out unsuspecting young girls they'd locked in closets.

She only drank half the bottle to try and avoid the inevitable outcome. Trying to avoid that outcome meant it became the one thing she could think about. Less than an hour after drinking half the bottle of water she had to pee. She had to pee pretty bad. She didn't have a problem just doing it in the closet. She did have a problem doing it in the closet and then someone opening the door either as she was going or right as she finished. Not knowing what else to do she knocked on the door a few times and called out softly to anyone who may be listening that she needed to use the restroom.

No one answered so she sat there a little longer before swigging down the rest of the bottle. When she'd finished all the water, she then had a place to pee. She carefully took care of that need as sanitarily as possible given the circumstances and settled back in to wait. She fiddled with the door hoping to find a way out of the closet. It was locked which wouldn't be that big of a deal, but she could also tell they had a deadbolt across the front of it. That posed a more complicated obstacle.

She climbed to the top of the closet but there was nothing up there besides a vent too small for her to fit through. She'd been hoping to find the entry point to an attic or air duct system. As she'd pulled her way up to check the ceiling, she'd envisioned herself crawling the duct system looking for her sisters. That scene playing in her head was the same one in virtually every spy movie ever made. She figured there had to be some basis to it. There may very well be, but it wasn't something that was going to hold true in the closet she was currently stuck in.

Eventually the door opened. A tall, stern woman in comfortable looking camouflage pants and blouse looked down her nose at Caitlyn. Caitlyn was aware she hadn't bathed in a while and that she'd let her hair go a little wild, but she didn't feel she warranted the look of mild disgust etched on the woman's face. She briefly considered emptying the water bottle full of pee on the lady's head to see if that helped with her expression. She bottled up that urge having decided she needed to start cooperating as fully as she could if she was going to get a chance to escape.

"Are you ready to act like a civilized young lady?" The woman asked. She had a southern drawl wrapped around a hard, cultured voice that spoke of higher education and tea times and charity balls. Those things were a thing of the past now which explained the hint of desperation and craziness that tinged the aura of culture and sophistication she presented.

"Yes ma'am. Can you tell me how my sisters are doing?" Caitlyn asked as respectfully as she could. She'd slid the bottle of pee into the corner out of the woman's sight as she stood up to walk out of the closet.

"I'm sure they're fine. Please grab your bottle of urine and come with me." The woman answered.

Blushing despite herself, Caitlyn squatted back down and grabbed the slightly warm bottle of pee from the corner she'd shoved it into.

"Do you have some place I could throw this away?" She asked.

"There's a trash receptacle over in the corner. You can leave it in there for now. I'm happy to see you used the bottle. Half of the girls we bring here just drink the water then go all over the closet floor. I open the door and they're squatting in their own urine like animals. One was even napping in it. Some of the girls we've brought in have gone quite feral during their time out in the open. I suppose living on their own like animals in constant fear of being eaten by the infected will do that to a young person. Especially if they started life without a strong moral compass to begin with."

Caitlyn agreed with that assessment. If her and her sisters hadn't had their grandma and Eric to take care of them then there was no telling if they'd be alive now or not. There'd be no telling what their state of mind would be. She shuddered at the thought of trying to survive all of this on her own. She hadn't heard any sympathy in the woman's voice for those girls who'd gone feral though. She'd heard more derision and disgust than anything else. Caitlyn had gotten the sense this woman was important. She felt sorry for the girls the woman decided were too feral to be raised around the rest of them.

"My sisters and I've been pretty lucky. We've been on the move most of the time, but we've had one another to keep us sane." Caitlyn answered. They'd reached the end of the corridor they'd been walking down. Her escort opened the door to a large room with multiple cots and footlockers set out in it. There were some shelves along the walls holding books and other gear. The whole room was illuminated by a narrow window along the top of one of the walls.

"This is where you'll be staying for your testing and at least the first phase of the training. Your class leader is Sandra. She should be returning any time now. There are guards stationed all around the exits. Do us both a favor and don't do anything stupid. Have a seat on one of the empty cots and wait for Sandra and the rest of your class to get back." Without waiting for any sort of response the lady turned and exited out the door.

Caitlyn sat in the dim room staring at the door leading out of the room into the corridor. She was tempted to just open the door and take her chances with the guards. She needed to find Myriah, Ali and Doreen so they could escape this place and try to rescue Zoey. She remembered Myriah had attacked one of the guards earlier. She wondered if Myriah had been locked in one of the closets in the same room she'd just been taken out of or if she'd been punished harsher. Caitlyn sat and waited. A dark and heavy cloud of depression crushing her into the cot she sat on.

Chapter 20: Custards Last Stand

Kyler stared at the group of kids climbing into the bus with the adults hurrying them along. Where'd they come from? He respected Tom for telling them to get in the bus and they'd cover them, but he also knew they didn't have any kind of chance of slowing down that river of insanity that was rumbling towards them. They were going to be inundated with a wall of death dealing Zombies before all those kids managed to even get on the bus. Tom, Pete and Kyler standing by the run-down storefront blazing away with the rest of their ammunition wasn't going to accomplish a damn thing.

Tom did a quick turn in the middle of the road. He was hoping to block the road a bit better with the truck. Tom and Pete both stuck their guns out their windows and waited. Kyler sighed and jumped out of the false safety of the trucks cabin down to the road. He climbed into the back of the truck and got into position right as the first Zombies came bounding around the corner towards them. The adrenalized Zombies were leaping at least five feet into the air. They would've all gone in the first round of the NBA draft if they'd been able to channel their bouncing abilities that well before they got infected and their rational minds melted away.

Kyler aimed, fired and repeated. In the cab right beside him the harsh bark of Pete and Toms guns threatened Kyler's already endangered hearing. He wondered if normal people thought about using ear protection when they were in the middle of a fire fight trying to halt a mob of blood thirsty freaks from eating them alive. He fired until the loud, dry click told him he needed to swap out magazines. He did that quickly and continued firing. There were too many Zombies now to really bother trying to pick specific ones to kill. The leading wave of the Zombies was going to crash over their truck in less than twenty seconds if they didn't do anything. Kyler did the only thing that occurred to him in the moment. He switched his rifle to full-automatic and got set to take as many out with him as he could. His mind getting stuck on a really bad pun associated with the ice cream store in the plaza.

Tom chose that moment to whip the truck into motion. Kyler looked up from adding another fresh magazine to his rifle and saw the bus was starting to accelerate as well. Tom must've decided he'd been courteous and brave enough for one day as he left the bus in their dust. Kyler looked up and saw wide eyed kids staring down at them as they bounced along the side of the road passing the bus. The bus accelerated much slower than the hemi-powered truck they were driving.

Tom pulled off the side of the road in front of the much slower bus. Kyler had a clear view of the Zombie wave crashing into the bright yellow bus. Zombies were hanging onto the back of it and attempting to climb it. One or two of them had actually managed to get on the roof of the bus. More disturbing than the ones on the roof of the bus were the ones who were getting sucked under the tires. Kyler watched, afraid to shoot since he may hit a kid, as the bus slowly began to pull ahead of the mass of Zombies. Both of the Zombies who'd been on the roof were thrown off as the bus lurched forward suddenly.

Something happened that flipped the bus over on its side in a flurry of sparks and dust. Kyler thought it may have been the Zombies who were getting sucked into the giant wheel wells and crushed by the tires. He screamed and banged on the window for Tom to stop the truck. Tom slowed to a stop a good fifty yards from the bus then began slowly reversing towards it. The bus was barely visible underneath the Zombies piling on top of it trying to get to the kids trapped inside. Kyler started shooting when they got close enough for him to pick out targets. All that accomplished was causing some of the Zombie's on the outskirts to leave the bus alone and start charging for them.

Kyler saw when the Zombies broke through the windows and started pouring into the bus. He imagined he could hear the screams of the kids over the inhuman screeching of the Zombies. He pulled the trigger on his rifle with it pointed vaguely in the direction of the Zombies charging for them. He couldn't even see them through the tears spilling from his eyes. All he could think of was the kids looking down at him from the bus as they'd driven past. The goofy looking smiles and curious expressions. Now those kids were trapped in an overturned bus being eaten alive. All because Kyler had the idea to get the team to lead the Zombies down this road instead of just staying on the interstate.

Tom accelerated quickly back down the road. Kyler stayed in the back of the truck. He kept his rifle loaded and methodically shot down the Zombies streaming towards them. His mind was a million miles away from their mission at this point. All he wanted to do was put as many of the Zombies permanently on the ground as possible. He'd forgotten he was supposed to be a spy. It all seemed so stupid to him now anyway. Based on everything he'd seen so far this place was basically working just like the settlements he'd been part of up north. It was just people banding together and trying to survive. Trying to stay alive and sane in a world that had gone completely to hell.

He'd imagined it more like a giant band of skinhead Nazis had taken over the southernmost part of the USA and were running around being evil. He wasn't sure exactly what he'd expected but it wasn't this. He felt as close to Pete and Tom as he had to his comrades in arms up north. Someone was attacking the settlements. He understood that needed to be figured out. He was thinking now the better course of action for figuring that out would be to capture one of the raiding parties and torture the info out of them. Sending him down here to pal around with a bunch of the soldiers wasn't going to get them a ton of valuable intel unless he happened to overhear their top-secret evil plans at the proverbial water cooler.

Tom had the truck going at a speed where they were staying just in sight of the lead Zombies. In theory this would keep them screeching and following along. Hopefully the interstate was being cleared of the Zombies and they could get them turned away from Georgia. It sucked to be in South Carolina or wherever the conga line of death ended up at, but Kyler didn't see a real way to deal with that issue at the moment. The Zombies had to go somewhere. They had boxes of ammunition and grenades back here in the truck but even if they sat here and shot with hundred percent accuracy all day long, they weren't going to be able to make that big a dent in the massive number of Zombies trailing them.

He'd been shooting in a trance. His mind elsewhere while his body went through the robotic motions of lining up shots and pulling the trigger. He was acquiring the next target when his trance state was disrupted. It was a little boy running towards the truck. The boy was dark skinned, his face was one big rash of sores. The mouth was curled in the typical grimace of hatred as he roared out the screeching noise the Zombie's made on seeing live prey. Kyler hesitated on pulling the trigger then let the barrel dip down as exhaustion and grief overwhelmed him. Grief for a dead world. A dead way of life. Grief for Mike and his mom and all the kids in his boy scout troop.

He'd built a wall around all those memories and emotions. For some reason the sight of this Zombie kid broke the dam and the raw pain flowed out. It hit him hard. Head bowed and tears flowing once more he sobbed openly in the back of the truck. He tried to pull himself together then remembered the faces of the kids in the school bus they'd passed. The faces of the kids he knew their mission had killed. Those kids had become collateral damage because of him. He angled himself so that Tom and Pete hopefully couldn't see his face. He knew they'd probably be able to tell something was wrong since he'd stopped firing and his back was shaking from the massive sobs wracking his body.

He finally pulled himself back together. Wiping his face, he cleared off the snot and tears then pulled the rifle back snugly into this shoulder. He looked down the barrel through the sights at the trees zipping past them then focused in on the road trying to find the Zombie kid who'd set him off. He didn't see the kid but did see a female Zombie streaking down the side of the road at a speed that should've been impossible. The woman was wearing a dress covered in dirt and weeds and the stains from her victims. Only patches of the original dark blue color were visible on the frayed dress. She had long dark hair blowing out behind her as she ran.

As close as she'd gotten to catching them it still took three shots before she lost her footing and went sliding to the ground. In this kind of chase Kyler didn't have to make sure the Zombies stayed down as long as they went down. No need for fancy head shots or any of that. Before the lady in blue dress had even stopped tumbling to the ground Kyler was busy acquiring another target. He took out a bounder with a couple of shots then put some rounds down the road in the general direction of the main mob chasing after them. Then they came to a T-intersection and Tom turned right to get them moving northwards again.

"Hey when they come around the corner let's makes sure the leaders see which way we went and then toss some grenades out to keep the other ones heading this way." Pete had opened the back slider to talk to Kyler as Tom slowed down.

"Sounds good." Kyler said back over his shoulder. He hoped Pete assumed he was focused on the rapidly approaching Zombies. In reality he didn't want anyone to see how red his eyes were from all the tears he'd shed.

Something was nagging him about this plan, but he couldn't put his finger on it. He was fixing to ask Pete if he knew where they were headed when the first few Zombies popped out onto the road they were now on. Kyler shot at them. They didn't want the fastest Zombies after them. They wanted the bulk of the Zombies after them. Tom stayed parked in the spot he'd stopped them in on the trash and dirt covered asphalt of the back-country blacktop road. Kyler felt the truck shift around as Pete hopped into the back with him.

They didn't have time to talk as more Zombies popped out on the road behind them. Pete started digging though boxes until he found the ones with the grenades. He thumped on the window separating them from the cab and Tom started driving slowly down the road. Pete pulled the pin out of a grenade and tossed it in the direction of the Zombies coming for them. He counted off two seconds then tossed another grenade in the same direction and ducked down in the back of the truck pulling Kyler with him. Muffled explosions sounded over the screeching of the Zombies moments later. The explosions were accompanied by a couple of metallic pings as shrapnel from the fragmentation grenades hit the tail gate their heads were against. One of the flying metal fragments took out a section of the trucks back window.

Kyler and Pete both popped back up. Kyler with rifle in hand and Pete with another couple of grenades to throw. The road behind them was littered with broken bits and pieces of Zombies. They were only able to see that nightmare landscape for a few seconds before the broken bodies were hidden by the next wave of Zombies. Pete tossed out three more grenades as Tom kept them moving steadily up the narrow road. Kyler shot at a couple of the Zombies who'd gotten too close before ducking down next to Pete and waiting for the grenades to do their job.

Once he'd counted off three explosions, he popped back up next to Pete again in the back. Tom was yelling at them through the broken window from the cab, so they spun around to see what he was trying to show them. Kyler was expecting to see a car blocking their path or maybe a few Zombies coming down the road towards them from the other direction. They'd been making enough noise it was inevitable there'd be some Zombies coming from the other direction at some point. He thought they were pretty much in the middle of nowhere, but you never knew where a bunch of Zombies may have ended up.

"Oh crap." He heard Pete say beside him. It was a major understatement. Kyler felt like Pete could've really expanded his vocabulary on that one. There was a freaking plethora of Zombies coming from the other direction. You couldn't see the road up ahead there were so many Zombies coming down it. Tom had stopped the truck and was getting out.

"Let's go!" Tom yelled as he grabbed his backpack and a box of ammunition out of the back of the truck.

Pete jumped over the side of the truck with his pack on then reached back in to grab the box of grenades. Kyler stood up and shot at the leading Zombies coming at them from both directions. He jumped over the side of the truck then had an idea when his boots hit the ground. He reached back into the truck and grabbed the box of grenades. Sorting through them he grabbed the last fragmentation grenades and a couple of the smoke grenades. He pulled the pins out of all of them one by one starting with the smoke grenades and tossed them in the back of the truck. Then he turned and followed Pete and Tom at a full-on sprint as they smashed their way into the woods.

Behind them came the loud explosions as the truck bed was ripped apart by the exploding grenades. Kyler hoped the grenades would start a chain reaction, but it didn't sound like that'd happened. It'd been pretty loud though. He knew the smoke bombs would be pouring out smoke by now. He hoped the smoke would confuse the Zombies even more and help throw them off their trail. He caught up with Tom and Pete who were leaning against trees trying to catch their breath.

"Nice job on the grenades." Pete said with a thumbs up in between his panting.

"Yeah. Now we just need to work our way north around this group and get the whole mob of them moving again. What a cluster." Tom said. "You did good Kyler. That was fast thinking."

A Zombie came bashing through the weeds behind them. It managed to come out of a bush right beside Pete who was waiting for it with a raised machete. He brought it down hard directly in the center of the Zombies skull. The Zombie dropped down to the ground with a thud. It was dead before it hit the ground. Pete tried to work the machete out then gave up when they heard other rustling in the bushes around them.

They stopped talking. They snapped and strapped their loud weapons back into place and pulled out their preferred melee style weapons. Kyler had a hatchet in one hand and a short knife in the other. They all took one last breath before Tom led them north in parallel with the road. All they had to do now was get around this new group of Zombies and set the whole dangerously flawed plan back in motion again. Assuming they could find a truck and some more noise makers along the way.

Chapter 21: The Best Laid Plans

Randy stared down at his wife and daughter sleeping in the bed. Zoey was turned sideways beside her. They'd found a house a few miles from the herd and managed to get into it without being discovered before the sun came up. Tony had set himself up in the living room and told Randy and Kelly to go spend some time with their little girl. Zoey had fallen asleep in Kelly's arms on the way to the house. Randy and Kelly both wanted to quiz Zoey on where her sisters were but hesitated to do so.

For one thing, Zoey needed sleep. Who knew how long she'd been stuck in that nightmare scenario surviving in a bathtub under a pile of rags surrounded by monsters? They were also both a little scared of the answers Zoey may give. Something had to have happened for Caitlyn or Brenda not to be with Zoey. They also couldn't get past just staring at her sleeping. Randy couldn't take his eyes off her. Kelly snuggled with Zoey and ended up falling asleep staring at her. The rough and tough sleeping habits of their little pre-tween would typically lead to them tossing her down to the foot of the bed. Neither of them could care less now.

Randy took a tiny foot to the nose and decided that was his cue to go get some water and see how Tony was doing. Carefully extricating himself from the bed to avoid waking anyone he padded on bare feet out to the living room. The light from the sun coming up filtered through the tightly drawn curtains. Tony had already gone around and made sure that all the windows were covered as well as he could.

"Anything going on outside?" Randy asked Tony quietly. Tony was sitting in a comfortable looking recliner he'd dragged over beside one of the windows.

"A Zombie went wandering by down the road earlier but otherwise I haven't seen anything. How's Zoey?" Tony asked.

"I really don't know. She seems healthy overall. She's exhausted and dehydrated from being in that tub and drinking that nasty water but that should go away with some rest and fluids. She's been asleep since we got here so we haven't had a chance to talk to her yet. Once she wakes up, we're hoping she may know where Brenda and her sisters went off to."

It was left unspoken by both of them that the most likely answer to that was the sisters and Brenda hadn't gone anywhere. They were either wandering around the house they'd discovered Zoey in as Zombies, or their bodies were lying around somewhere in that same house. Neither Randy nor Tony was able to come up with a likely scenario that didn't revolve around everyone being dead except for Zoey. Randy could even picture Caitlyn or Myriah being the ones who hid her in the bathtub before they were overwhelmed and killed.

Randy grabbed a couple of warm bottled waters Tony had found somewhere and headed back to the bedroom. Kelly was sitting up in bed running her fingers through Zoey's hair. Zoey was still fast asleep. She didn't look like she was planning on waking up anytime soon either.

"We found her." Kelly said looking up at Randy. Her voice cracked a little as she said it. Randy rushed to sit in the bed and hold her as tears started streaming out of her eyes. He intuited what she was thinking, and he started running his fingers through her hair in a mimicry of what Kelly was doing to Zoey.

"We'll have the others soon enough. Caitlyn and Myriah and Doreen wouldn't be far from Zoey. Once she wakes up, we'll find out where they're at and go get them."

Kelly nodded in an absent way that told Randy she really wasn't listening to him. That was fine he was just trying to fill the air with comforting words at this point. After a few more mumbled platitudes between the two of them they sat there in a comfortable silence watching Zoey sleep. Neither of them quite believing they'd managed to get their little girl back. In a world so full of death it was miraculous they'd found her. Now they just needed the miracle to be a repeated a few more times until their family was complete.

Randy looked over at the window to the bedroom and saw that it was curtained up tightly already. Tony must have slipped in during the night to verify they were secure. He glanced down at Zoey. Both her eyes were wide open staring up at him. He smiled expecting a big smile or a hug or a kiss. Instead her hand flew up and grabbed his nose hard. Then she yanked on it. Randy reached up and gently grabbed her wrist away before she could grab any other parts of his face.

"You're real! Mommy too!" Zoey blurted out as she spun over on her side to stare at her mom. Kelly smiled and pulled Zoey in close for a long needed snuggle. Randy piled on top of both of them to get in on the snuggle action. They must've gotten a little too loud because Tony came into the room and cleared his throat to get them to quiet down. When Randy looked up at him, he was grinning from ear to ear.

"Hey honey. This is Tony. He helped mommy and daddy make it all the way back to Florida to find you." Kelly politically left out the part about how Tony's journey had begun as a hostage kidnapped at gunpoint by them. Zoey broke out of her mom and dad's grip to jump down on the floor and run across the floor to give Tony a huge hug.

"Thank you for helping my mommy and daddy! I missed them so much. I dreamed about them all the time. I thought last night was just another dream when I woke up. Thank you so much!"

Tony looked like he may have gotten something in his eyes. He blinked a few times while awkwardly patting Zoey on the back. Zoey said thank you to him again before rushing back over into Kelly's arms. Kelly didn't look like she planned on letting go of Zoey anytime soon. An awkward silence filled the room while each of them tried to think of the best way to ask Zoey about her sisters and her grandma. Zoey saved them all the hassle by launching into her story on her own.

"Are we going to go rescue Caitlyn and Myriah and Doreen and Ali now? The bad men who killed grandma have them. We need to get to them soon before they hurt them." She blurted out. Kelly and Randy shared a quick glance.

"What bad men honey?" Kelly asked her. She was trying to process the other news Zoey had just casually dropped in their laps. Brenda was dead. The air seemed to have been sucked out of the room with that announcement. She wanted to ask Zoey more about how her mom had died but she knew that would lead to tears and they'd get off track. Brenda may have died but she'd kept the kids alive long enough for Randy and Kelly to have a chance to reunite with them. Kelly knew her mom would've been proud of having the girl's survival as her legacy.

"The ones who kept chasing us everywhere. They came in the house we were staying in. I hid in the tub and they took everybody." Zoey's lip started to quiver as she told them about losing her sisters. Kelly wrapped her in a tight embrace and let her cry for a few minutes. When she seemed to be under control again Kelly very gently asked if she knew what'd happened to her sisters. After some back and forth with a tearful Zoey it became obvious, she had no idea where the men may have taken her sisters.

"It's probably the same guys we ran into on the road." Tony chimed in quietly. He'd been hanging back after the hug Zoey had given him. He knew this was a powerful moment for Kelly and Randy. He wanted to give them some family time but at the same time he sensed the trail was growing cold to find Zoey's sisters. He'd never really thought they were going to find any of them, so he was surprised at himself for how determined he now was to rescue the rest of them. A plan started to form in his head as to how they might be able to find the others.

"Yeah that'd make sense. They seem to be controlling this area for now. We need to figure out where they're keeping the girls at and go get them." Randy said.

"What if we don't go to them?" Tony said. The plan forming in his head had a ton of holes in it, but he wasn't coming up with anything else. He knew it wasn't a great plan, but a bad plan well executed would work better than a good plan they came up with too late. It wasn't like they'd planned most of what'd happened that allowed them to find Zoey in the first place. He was working through his idea in his head when he noticed he had Randy and Kelly's complete attention.

"You going to let us in on the plan? I can see the hamster wheel in your head spinning." Kelly asked. She said it with a smile, but she was feeling the urgency to do something. Having found Zoey and knowing the rest of her children were within her grasp was driving her crazy. She needed to get to them and make sure they were safe, and she needed to do it right now.

"I don't know if I'd call it a plan so much as the beginning of a pretty suicidal set of ideas."

"That's more than we've got." Randy answered for him and Kelly. They were both staring at Tony now mentally willing him to have a better plan than he was letting on.

"We don't go to them. We get them to come to us." Tony said to blank stares from Kelly and Randy. "They've found the girls a few times based on what Zoey said. They were able to coordinate and ambush us on the road. That means they must be watching the area. I'm not sure if they've got regular roving patrols, or they've accessed the CCTV system or they're flying drones around or whatever but they're obviously monitoring the territory somehow. That means we just need to drive around outside, and they'll eventually come to us. Then we get them to take us to wherever the girls are."

"So, your plan to free the girls is to get us captured and locked up too?" Kelly asked. The expression on her face revealing her opinion of his plan.

"Remember I said I didn't necessarily have a plan. Just the beginning of one, I think. I can't think of a way to find them without one of us getting caught. We have to get them to come to us somehow since we have no clue where they're based out of." Tony wandered off staring at the others. Now that he was saying it out loud, he was realizing what a horrible idea it was. There was a huge list of things that could go wrong with it forming in his mind. He saw the same list forming in Randy and Kelly's minds. Zoey was staring at them all waiting for the adults to make everything alright.

They talked about it. They argued about it. Voices were raised and Zoey cried again. Finally, it was decided that Randy and Tony would be the ones to wander out the door to try and attract the attention of the men who'd taken the other kids. They didn't want to risk Zoey being caught up in this and Zoey needed someone to take care of her. If Tony and Randy died, then Kelly would be the one to figure out if her and Zoey should cut ties and leave or if they would try to reunite with the other kids another way.

Neither Kelly nor Zoey were happy with the arrangement. Kelly didn't like Randy putting himself into the kind of position he was talking about getting into. Zoey didn't want to lose her daddy so fast after finding him. They all thought this was crazy. In what kind of world do you have to risk being killed or taken prisoner to try and rescue your kids. In what part of crazy town do you purposefully wander aimlessly around in streets crawling with Zombies trying to be seen by some unknown party who may or may not be looking for you.

They threw some other ideas around but the only plan that seemed like it had a chance of working was the one where they wandered around until caught and taken prisoner. After a tearful goodbye Randy found himself jogging down streets and through the alleys between homes with Tony. He was wondering if they may need to show themselves a little bit better when he saw something glinting up in the sky. He pointed it out to Tony, and they kept moving down the same road they'd been on before. They went another mile dodging around groups of Zombies before breaking through to the other side of the herd where the streets were mostly deserted. They began walking down the street checking car doors to see if they could find something easy to get going in.

Fifteen minutes after spotting the drone up above they heard cars coming their direction. Tony looked back at Randy who pointed at a house they were currently walking past. They ran up the sidewalk leading towards the house and tried the front door. It was locked so they took turns kicking it until it finally opened up. They heard the sounds of cars pulling up into the driveway as they sprinted into the house and threw themselves behind the moldy couch in the living room. Breathing hard they squatted there waiting for the men outside to come in looking for them.

"Do we fight them when they come in?" Tony asked. He had a pistol in his hand and a wild look in his eyes.

"If we shoot at them then they'll shoot back, and we'll have Zombies all over us. We need to get them to take us but not take our weapons. Go with the 'we want to join up plan'?" Randy answered uncertainly. It was occurring to him how supremely stupid this all was. There were way too many things that could go wrong. They put their backs to the couch and waited. It was going to be a play it by ear and try to keep their cool kind of engagement. The couch shifted slightly with both of them leaning against it.

Suddenly Tony sprung into the air squealing in fear. Randy spun around pointing the shot gun he was carrying in the general direction of Tony's feet. A fat black snake that had to have been at least six feet long casually slithered out from under the couch. They watched it slither across the fake wood tile in the living room and disappear into the garbage on the kitchen floor. Tony wasn't a fan of snakes. Randy was motioning for him to squat back down behind the couch again.

The front door flew open and a group of men rushed in yelling and waving assault rifles. The men were all dressed in camouflage with balaclavas covering their faces and rugged looking leather gloves with the fingers cut out. Randy found himself being pushed to the ground and his hands being zip tied behind him. Someone yanked him back to his feet and shoved a sack over his head. He was marched out and pushed into the back seat of a running car. Within seconds he was sitting in the car with the sack over his head feeling the breeze as the car started moving quickly down the road.

Randy took a deep breath to calm himself. He was in the back seat of an enemy vehicle with a sack over his head and his hands tied together behind him. He had no idea where he was being taken. He hoped it was the same place they'd taken his kids and the other girl Zoey had told them about. Ali, the niece of the man who'd protected his daughters until he'd died guarding Myriah from a group of Zombies. They obviously owed Eric so if they could find his niece, they'd take her with them as well.

Riding down the road with the sack over his head and his hands painfully secured behind him Randy felt something he wouldn't have anticipated feeling. Despite the circumstances he was filled with confidence they'd be able to find his daughters and rescue them. Every bit of common sense hinted at them being executed gangland style on the side of some random dirt road, but he felt like they were going to be able to pull this off. He didn't know how but he knew he'd get it done. He really didn't have a choice since his daughter's lives depended on it. He'd make it happen somehow.

Chapter 22: Spare the Rod

Myriah was in a sturdier closet than the one they'd locked Caitlyn up in. This one was in a main hallway, but it still smelled like piss and pine sol. The floor was hard concrete, and the walls painted concrete block. The small space had just enough room for her to stretch out in. She'd been tossed into the closet by two guards. She'd been sitting there wondering what to do next when the door had opened, and the guards had tossed in a blanket and a bottled water. She'd gone through the same process with the water as Caitlyn. She turned the cool water into a bottle of warm pee she slid into the corner of her closet.

She cried until her throat hurt and the tears stopped coming. She beat on the door and walls until her knuckles bled. She slept and when she woke up, she was still trapped. She was still seeing the house out the back window of the car as they drove away. The house that was due to be overrun by Zombies. The house that had her little sister hiding in a bathtub. Zoey was being protected from certain death by a cheap shower curtain. Every second she was in this closet was another second closer to death for her little sister.

Why? What did these idiots want with them? Why was she locked in a closet when she should be out there trying to save her little sister? Where were Doreen and Ali and Caitlyn? For all she knew they may all be in a situation where they could die any second. She was going mad with worry. She yelled at the door for a little while. She screamed for them to let her out so she could save her sister. She screamed to know where her sisters were being kept. She made threats. She was ignored. She eventually slept again.

When she woke up there were two more water bottles and a little bag full of trail mix. She devoured the stale trail mix washing it down with the water. About fifteen minutes after eating the trail mix and drinking the water she was beyond groggy. She couldn't even manage to put any coherent thoughts together. She collapsed into the corner of the closet and watched as the closet door opened. She willed herself to jump for the man who'd opened it. She needed to rip out his throat and make a run for the exit. From there she'd go to find her sister. The drugs in the water she'd drank kept her from remembering her sisters name.

She managed some completely ineffectual punches on the back of the man who scooped her up and threw her over his shoulder. He carried her out into the hallway. The other man stayed behind to clean out the closet. He made a note of the fact that Myriah had used the bottle instead of relieving herself on the floor. It was a crude test, but it did seem to separate the ones who were going to make it from the rest. The ones who'd maintained more of a sense of normalcy did much better in this environment than the one's who'd regressed. The ones who'd gone feral as the principal liked to call it. They typically shipped the feral ones off to the camps without bothering to waste any time attempting to groom them.

Myriah slowly came back to life sitting in a swivel chair. A man and woman sat across from her talking about supply runs and shipping issues. Myriah didn't really understand everything they were saying but she chalked that up to the massive headache she had. She tried to get out of the chair but discovered her hands had been tied to the arm rests. Her legs were loose but that didn't help her since she would still be attached to the chair. She shifted around trying to figure out how to free her arms.

Burning pain across the top of her thighs. Myriah cried out and pushed herself backwards. Looking up she saw the man had gotten up out of his chair and was standing over her with a wooden rod in his hand. Her legs burnt badly from the sting of that rod being whipped across her thighs. She doubled her efforts to free her arms and got another hard strike across her thighs. Tears leapt unbidden into her eyes. She screamed out loud in pain and frustration. She fixed her gaze on the man who'd been hitting her. He reached back and started to bring the rod down again when the woman cleared her throat.

"You do know you can't win this right? You're tied to a chair in a locked room facing a man with a weapon who's under my protection. I'm trying to decide if I admire your spirit or if you're just supremely stupid. I'm leaning towards stupid but please prove me wrong. Or, we'll simply get rid of you. We can always use more scavengers and Zombie bait. If you happen to survive until you come of age, we could give you to a common soldier as a reward."

"Or you could shut your dumbass mouth before I get my hands loose and shut it for you." Myriah stuttered out. She tried to have it come out like a zinger from an action hero in a summer blockbuster. She felt like her voice cracked hallway through it and the fear was perceptible in her voice though. She hated herself for the weakness. She hated whoever these people were.

"Ok. Well we're going to try one more thing to see if we can get you to cooperate. If not, then there's plenty of other girls out there we can pull into the program." The lady turned her head slightly towards the open door to the hall and called out to someone out there to bring someone else into the room.

Myriah glanced over towards the open door wondering what this new ploy was. Her heart sank when she saw who they were marching into the room. A tearful Ali was leading Doreen into the room by the hand. Doreen and Ali both smiled when they saw Myriah. Doreen started running towards Myriah with her arms spread and a big grin on her face. Both Ali and Doreen looked like they'd had baths and haircuts recently. They were both wearing pretty little flowery dresses and crocs.

Before Doreen had gotten hallway to Myriah the lady nodded. The man stepped forward with the cane pole and whipped it across the back of Doreen's thighs. Doreen fell to the ground screaming in pain. Ali jumped forward to help Doreen and was rewarded with two strikes to her back. Both girls were on the ground in pain. Myriah was screaming and cursing and alternately begging and threatening the lady and the man. Ali crawled across the floor to wrap herself around Doreen to shield her from any more blows. The man stood over both of the with cane pole held ready to strike and looked over at the lady.

"I'm sorry! That's enough! I'll do whatever you guys say! Stop hitting them!" Myriah shouted. The lady looked over at Myriah then back at the man.

"I don't think I believe you quite yet." She nodded at the man who whipped Ali in the back and arms until she rolled off Doreen. Then the man gave Doreen a few more whacks. Blood was seeping out of cuts in Alis and Doreen's brand-new dresses. Neither of them looked freshly bathed anymore. Myriah was sobbing and saying over and over she'd do anything. She kept saying how sorry she was. Seeing the blood on her sister's pretty new dress she meant it. Watching Ali try so bravely to protect Doreen she meant it. A tiny voice in the back of her head told her to apologize and beg for now but a day of reckoning would come.

"Do you believe her now ma'am?" The man asked. He looked like he was losing his stomach for beating the little girls at his feet with the cane pole.

"I believe I do." The woman turned her face from where she'd been watching the children be beaten to look again at Myriah. "What was your name again?" The lady casually asked her.

"It's Myriah ma'am. Doreen and Ali there are my little sisters. I'm so sorry for how I've acted. I can follow orders. I can –" The lady cut her off with a swipe of her hand through the air.

"You may address me as 'principal'. Only the guards and other adults are allowed to call me ma'am. You will, of course, follow orders moving forward. If you don't follow orders, we won't bother hurting you. We'll whip your little sisters instead. The only real reason we have to waste our resources on a girl her age is to help keep you and your other sister in line. Starting now you will do what you're told or there will be consequences. Understood?" The principal waited for Myriah to confirm she understood.

Myriah nodded her head in affirmation. The principal pointed at her and the man she'd brought as her enforcer stepped forward and whipped Myriah hard across the thighs. Myriah looked up in shock.

"Let's try that again. When I ask you a question you will answer the question out loud. You will never nod your head or mumble anything to myself, the guards, or the other adults in this building. Or you will be punished. Understood?" The principal stood in front of Myriah with an evil grin resting on her lips.

"Yes. Understood principal." Myriah said as loudly and clearly as she could manage over the searing pain emanating from the tops of her thighs.

"That's better. Now tell your little sisters goodbye. You won't get a chance to speak to them again for a while. Then you'll follow Mr. Abrams to your room assignment. I don't expect to hear of any more trouble from you." The principal got up and left the room. Leaving Mr. Abrams and another guard in the room with them. Myriah assumed the other guard must be the one who'd be taking Doreen and Ali to their areas.

Mr. Abrams came over and untied her wrists so she could get up out of the chair. He watched her impassively as she painfully knelt down to hug Doreen and Ali. Myriah had to be careful as it seemed like every spot her hands touched on either of their bodies made them wince in pain. Doreen and Ali were both crying as they all tried to hug each other and wish this nightmare away. Myriah was thinking Zoey might actually be the lucky one to not have ended up here.

In what seemed like no time at all the other guard signaled it was time for them to go. Mr. Abrams told Myriah to follow him and walked out the door briskly. Not knowing what else to do and hating herself for her weakness Myriah peeled Doreen's hands off of her and left the room quickly. She didn't look back. She knew she had to play their game for now, and she was determined to do it. Until the time was right not to play their game anymore.

Chapter 23: So Now What?

"This sucks." Pete said looking down at the writhing mass of Zombies undulating on the forest floor. They were high enough in the tree where you had to peek between the limbs and foliage to see them. The height didn't seem to diminish the sheer volume of that many Zombies. They howled like a team of demented hunting dogs with a bear cub treed. They were high enough in the stout old pine tree that the limbs were dangerously thin. Every time one of them shifted their body around to get more comfortable they were in serious danger of plummeting to their deaths.

"It could be worse." Tom said from his perch slightly below Kyler and Pete. He was heavier than either one of them so had stopped trusting the limbs to hold him slightly before Kyler and Pete came to that same decision. Since he was the lowest, he was on guard duty. Guard duty in this case mostly consisting of waiting until one of the adrenalized Zombies showed up and made a play to get up in the tree with them. Tom was doing his best to shoot them out of the tree with minimal use of ammunition.

"How exactly?" Kyler asked. He was ok with taking the bait. Anything to get his mind off the fact they were probably going to die stuck in this tree. He didn't know why but it really bothered him that he didn't really have a clue where he was right now. It probably didn't say much for the quality of his supposed spy craft that he wasn't even sure he was still in Georgia. He imagined showing back up and providing the report to the commander. Be careful of that tree in the southeast part of the USA because there's a lot of Zombies underneath it. Really useful intel he was going to be able to provide. Lucky for him he'd be dead long before he was going to have to make any sort of report at this rate.

"We could be one of those things down below howling up at the tree instead of one of us losers sitting up here in it. The way I figure it we already did better than ninety percent of the population just to still be alive at this point." Tom stopped talking to draw a bead on a skinny little Zombie who looked like he was dressed in a kimono. It was getting difficult to tell the race and sex of the Zombies now that their faces were covered in boils and pus. They were starting to look more and more like the orcs out of the Lord of the Ring movies than anything else. Except their faces oozed blood and pus and they had a yellow jaundice tinge to them and always looked greasy. It wasn't a good look.

"Nice shot." Pete complimented Tom on the head shot he'd just scored. They'd all seen the Zombie do a backflip when the round took off most of its skull. It'd come running up the ladder leading to the deer stand attached to the tree. The same deer stand they'd used to get up in the tree when the smoke grenades hadn't worked out as well as Kyler had hoped. If the deer stand hadn't turned up when it did to provide them this flimsy escape, they'd probably be dead by now. If they'd been able to just climb the tree and sit there most of the Zombies would've just wandered by underneath and everything would've been fine and dandy.

They couldn't just sit there though when the random adrenalized Zombie kept jumping for them. Kyler was hoping that with the setting sun the Zombies may settle down and forget they were up in the tree. Then with any luck at all the Zombies would wander away in a day or two and they could climb down. It was going to suck living in a tree for that long, but it was definitely better than the alternative. Kyler shifted around to try to get a little more comfortable on the two branches he was straddled across. With his back against the tree it actually wasn't too horrible.

"We should go into quiet mode as soon as it starts getting dark. The sooner we do that the sooner these Zombies will wander off." Tom said from below Kyler. Following his own advice, he shut up after that and stopped shooting the Zombies who crowded around the deer stand with hands extended up towards him. As long as none of them exhibited any Michael Jordan jumping skills, he saw no need to take shots at them. They were actually serving to keep the more coordinated Zombies from getting up the ladder to get close to them.

Kyler was starting to think they might actually be able to pull this off when he saw the Zombies start going ballistic beneath them. He shifted around trying to see what was going on down below. He figured it out about the same time he smelled the smoke. Deer and other animals were tearing through the forest all around them and running into the mass of Zombies radiating out from the tree they were stuck in. The Zombies were jumping around like crazy trying to grab the food so conveniently running past them. Kyler assumed the animals were fleeing from a fire.

Kyler further assumed the fire was probably emanating from the area where he'd set off all the explosives to try and cover their retreat. In retrospect blowing up a truck bed full of gasoline and explosives next to a forest full of kindling might not have been the smartest move. There was no ranger patrol to call in airplanes full of fire retardant. No volunteer fire fighters to be driven up to clear brush and dig ditches to stop the spread of the flames. This fire was going to spread and wouldn't stop until it ran into a river or a thunder storm.

"You've got to be kidding me. How can anyone's luck be this damned bad." Pete whispered loudly. "Like being in a tree surrounded by Zombies isn't bad enough there's seriously got to be a forest fire heading towards us. Did we blow up a church or something on the way here? Why does God hate us?"

"We may need to make a run for it soon if the fire keeps heading this way." Tom said ignoring Pete's questions. There were a lot of days he wasn't sure if having survived made him lucky or not. He lived every day knowing his family had all died already.

"How exactly are we going to make a run for it through all those Zombies down there? They're not going to care if a fire's coming. They'll stand there and burn waiting for us to come down. Especially if the fire keeps us visible to them. Plus, all the screaming we're going to start doing when the tree catches on fire around us." Kyler knew Tom was just trying to think of a way out of an impossible solution but that didn't mean he had to go along with it. Also, if you couldn't be a little grumpy in the situation they were currently in then when the hell could you be irritable?

"The wind could always blow the fire the other way. Let's wait and see." Tom said.

"We all know which way the damned wind's going to blow. We must've blown up a church and when it fell over it caught an orphanage on fire. Like an orphanage for kids and kittens. Or one of you guys is a prick of epic proportions to have this much bad karma coming at us." Pete continued to blabber on. Talking was a coping mechanism for him. Between the screaming Zombies and the steadily increasing roar of the fire no one could really hear him anyway.

A huge red glow reflected off a giant wall of smoke moving towards them. Below them on the ground the Zombies didn't seem to care that it was getting much hotter. Kyler was wondering if the smoke inhalation would kill them faster or slower up in a tree than it would if they were on the ground. For about the millionth time since this had all started, he yearned for the ability to whip out a smart phone and google the answers he needed. He knew there was probably hundreds of websites that could assist him with his urgent forest fire related questions.

Hot ash started raining down on them even as more waves of heat drifted up. Kyler was having a hard time breathing and his eyes were tearing up like crazy. There was no way they were lasting much longer sitting in this tree.

"Ok boys. Been great knowing you both. Let's go ahead and get to the ground and try to sneak or fight our way out of here. It's pretty much suicide but so is sticking around in this tree. See you both in hell. Hopefully, it's not this hot there." Tom announced and started working his way down the branches towards the deer stand.

Looking below Kyler thought they may have already made it to hell. An eerie red glow flickered around the Zombies. Their demonic screeching rose to a fever pitch when they noticed Tom coming down the tree. Kyler and Pete climbing down after him. They stopped in the branches above Tom as he worked his way onto the deer stand to have a look around. Kyler wasn't sure exactly what Tom could see from his vantage point but from Kyler's vantage point they were pretty much screwed. Zombies faces stared up at them from every direction Kyler looked.

With a loud thump Tom was ripped off the deer stand by one of the adrenalized Zombies. The Zombie and Tom landed hard on the ground a few feet from the base of the deer stand. Pete and Kyler watched helplessly as the Zombies in that immediate area converged on the prone man and began ripping the flesh from his body. The adrenalized Zombie who'd knocked Tom off the platform originally screamed and swiped at the Zombies he deemed to be in his way. That Zombie ripped off one of Toms ears and chewed on it like an appetizer while ripping at Toms throat until his blood started spurting out.

Kyler raised his pistol to shoot Tom. He knew if their situations were reversed, he'd want someone to put a round through his skull. No way would he want to spend the final minutes of his life being eaten alive. Pete reached down and grabbed Kyler's wrist and shook his head side to side to tell Kyler not to do it. Knowing he was going to regret it, feeling like a coward, Kyler didn't take the shot. A minute later the screams from Tom stopped being audible to them over the screeching of the Zombies and the roar of the approaching fire.

Surrounded by the noise of the blaze coming for them and distracted by cannibalizing Tom and all the animals fleeing the fire the Zombies began to wander off. It began to get unbearably hot for Pete and Kyler squatting up in the tree just out of eye sight of the final Zombies streaming away from the fire. A giant glowing ember flew straight into Pete's hair causing him to bash his hands down on his head trying to put it out. He slipped and fell out of the tree. He bounced off the side of the deer stand as he fell to the ground below. He hit and was still.

Kyler scrambled down the tree and flew down the rungs of the old deer stand down to where Pete lie on the ground. He'd been grotesquely saved by landing amidst a pile of the Zombies Tom had shot when they'd first climbed up into the tree. Kyler gently shook him, and Pete looked up with pain glazed eyes. He was admirably able to keep from screaming from the pain he must be experiencing from his left leg being twisted around the way it was.

Kyler ignored the blazing hot ash steadily raining down on them and began trying to extricate Pete from the pile of pungent corpses he'd landed in. When it became too hot to stand it anymore, he grabbed Pete by the arms and started dragging him away from the fire. The man felt excessively heavy, but Kyler just dug in and kept dragging. It was so hot now he had his eyes closed as he trudged backwards through the woods. Once he'd gone about a hundred yards, he collapsed on the ground in a place where they were partially shielded from the heat by two large trees growing next to each other.

He looked down at Pete. Pete was covered in ash and a small dead Zombie was attached to his left foot. Kyler had been dragging along that extra weight as he walked. Sighing and wiping ash off his face to try and keep it out of his eyes Kyler began wrenching and pulling and otherwise working to get the Zombie off Pete's foot. It only took a couple of seconds to figure out the ash covered corpse of a child had a belt on that had managed to get hooked on Pete's foot somehow. Kyler was gratefully for the ash in this case. It kept him from having to look into a kid's dead face as he worked on detaching him.

Pete suddenly shot straight up and began looking around desperately. He spotted Kyler and reached out for him.

"Don't leave me." He sobbed. He was completely terrified. The shock from the fall must've worn off. He'd awakened in the middle of the burning forest in the weird light cast by the fire moving towards them thinking he'd been abandoned. He'd tried to stand up to run but the pain from his twisted leg prevented him from doing that. His first glimpse of Kyler he'd thought he was a Zombie ripping away at the lower part of his body.

"All good brother. I got you." Kyler said shoving the carcass of the Zombie child to the side. He worked on getting Pete to a standing position, but the pain was too much for Pete and he passed back out again. Grateful for his one season of wrestling in High School Kyler threw Pete over his shoulders in a fireman's carry and started moving through the eerily lit woods as fast as he could go without risking a fall.

The problem was that the farther in front of the fire he got the more Zombie's he started to see. He may have been able to blend in with them if he hadn't been carrying Pete. It wasn't like anything was able to see or smell good this close to the blaze. The odd shadow he cast supporting Pete seemed to grab the Zombies attention though. He heard the familiar screech and saw two Zombies running towards him through the undergrowth. Luckily, they were oblivious to the weeds and briars so didn't try to pick an easier path to get at him. Kyler squatted down and let Pete roll off his shoulders onto the ground. Pete let out a muffled moan of pain then lie still on the ground.

Kyler pulled a machete and a hatchet out of Pete's belt. He planned on leaving the hatchet embedded in a Zombie somewhere since the damned thing had been poking him painfully in the back with every step he'd taken since throwing Pete over his shoulders. They had ammunition left but even with the roar of the fire Kyler didn't want to risk attracting more Zombies by shooting at them. He was going to have to kill every Zombie they met by hand. It was going to be a long night.

He walked towards the Zombie closest to them. It'd just beat its way through the bushes and was running towards him with hands stretched out in front of it. The Zombie was a beast. You couldn't really tell the race of Zombies any more under typical circumstances due to the spread of the pus-filled boils across their faces but in the light of the fire with ash covering everything it was completely impossible. Not that race mattered at all in relation to a gigantic Zombie running towards him. Kyler's mind skipped ahead to the fact that equality had finally been achieved. All you had to do was get bitten by a Zombie and you were good.

He realized his brain was latching on to random ideas and thoughts as a coping mechanism. The Zombie coming at him was huge. The whole race thing had popped into his head because his first thought had been this was a Samoan, or a Sumo wrestler turned Zombie. It didn't look the Zombie had missed any meals since being turned. The thing was huge and coming straight for him. Kyler felt like he was standing there with a pair of knitting needles trying to stop a massive bull from running him down. Deciding he'd rather live for a few more minutes than maintain operational silence Kyler dropped the hatchet and machete to the ground.

In the same motion as he dropped the weapons to the ground he reached back over his shoulders and yanked his M-16 around and jammed the stock into his shoulder. Releasing the safety and switching the weapon into full auto came naturally to him at this point. The weapon seeming like an extension of his body. He pulled the trigger and saw red spots flash on the surface of the obese beast bearing down on him. He kept the trigger depressed until the Zombie finally faltered a step. It hit the ground and slid a few more feet forcing Kyler to take a couple of steps back not to come in contact with it.

He kept the M-16 in his hands and waited for the other Zombie coming at him in the weeds to emerge. Once the Zombie had managed to claw its way back up so that its head was visible Kyler put a round right through its forehead. Before that Zombie had even finished falling backwards into the weeds Kyler was picking up the hatchet and machete he'd dropped on the ground. He made his way back over to where Pete was passed out on the ground. Part of his pants had burned away from hot ash falling on them. His exposed skin was also starting to turn a dark shade of red.

Kyler hesitated staring down at the man. Sweat was dragging pieces of ash into Kyler's mouth and eyes. He could barely breathe at this point due to the smoke wafting through the woods. Zombie screeches were echoing all around them as the closer Zombies responded to the sounds of gun fire and began to reverse their course to come back towards the fire to try and locate the source of those noises. Being the source of those noises Kyler knew he needed to do his best to not be here when those Zombies arrived. They were coming from every direction so whichever way he went he was going to have to cut down a few Zombies with the machete or hatchet to make it through. He wasn't going to be able to do that with Pete across his shoulders.

The part of his brain in charge of self-preservation was whispering for him to move out and leave Pete there. Pete was probably going to die anyway and no one would ever know. Pete himself probably wouldn't even wake up. He'd just slip away the victim of smoke inhalation and shock. He didn't even know Pete that well. The guy could be a bit of a blowhard and his stories tended to drag on longer than necessary with punch lines that weren't worth listening to the buildup. From what he did know of Pete, he was pretty sure the man would've left him behind without spending a lot of time thinking about it if the situation had been reversed.

This wasn't really about Pete though. It was about the scouts he hadn't been able to save when he first encountered the Zombies. It was about Mike having thrown him in a boat and allowed him to live while he himself was turning into a Zombie. It was about having to kill Mike so he could sail away free. It was about those people in that condo who he had a nagging feeling hadn't made it out alive even after all his work to help them. He risked his life for people because it was the right thing to do. It's what his dad would've expected of him. It's what he expected of himself.

His hesitation to pick Pete up wasn't based on trying to decide if he was going to leave the man behind or not. It was based on deciding if he wanted to pick him up and try to break through the incoming Zombies or if he should just make a quick stand right there and see what happened. Maybe another opportunity would present itself.

Loud screeches that were danger close solved the problem for him. He wasn't going to be able to pick up Pete and make a run for it before those Zombies were on top of him. The thick smoke from the fire was becoming more prevalent. The sun had sunk below the horizon for good now. If there was a moon Kyler couldn't see it through the thick canopy of pine needles and smoke. He squatted down to get closer to the ground to give himself a rest from the smoke. The closer to the ground he got the cleaner the air was. The less like breathing in fire it was to take deep breaths.

His plan shifted as he breathed in the cleaner air. He'd stay here for a few more seconds and deal with any Zombie's who'd been able to home in on the sound of him firing the M-16. Once he'd done that, he'd pick up Pete and head parallel to the fire and deeper into the woods. He was hoping the bulk of the Zombies were still towards the road since that's where they were coming from. Going away from the road and sticking close to the fire might be their best chance at escape. Especially since he was going to be in full on flight mode with the dead weight of Pete wrapped around his shoulders like a neckerchief. An ungainly two-hundred-pound necklace with weapons sticking out of it that may go crazy when he woke up.

The Zombies he'd heard screeching ran right by in the smoke. Plenty more were screeching in frustration all around him, but visibility was down to about zero. Hoping he didn't walk straight into any of them Kyler hoisted Pete up onto his shoulders and set off at a brisk pace in the direction he hoped was the way he wanted to go. He'd gone about ten feet and was navigating his way over a fallen tree when a Zombie emerged from the smoke right in front of him. Hating himself for doing it Kyler immediately dropped Pete and pulled his machete. The Zombie let out a screech as it realized a real human was standing in front of it. The Zombie moved forward with that horrible screech on its lips. Luckily it was so focused on getting to them it tripped on the log Kyler had been trying to navigate.

Kyler brought the machete down hard on the things head as it struggled back to its feet. The machete hit the top of the things skull and bounced off emitting sparks. Undeterred Kyler swung again. This time he aimed for the other side of the head and hoped whatever steel plate this Zombie had in its head didn't cover the whole skull. The Zombie was thrashing around and the uncertain footing on the side of the downed tree caused Kyler to miss. The machete hit the other side of the things head and slipped off to the side. He lopped off the Zombies ear, but he knew that wouldn't even slow it down.

He pulled the machete back up in the air for another try and felt a hand grab him from behind. He spun around and swung the machete at the Zombie who'd come up out of the smoke behind them. He scored a hard hit across its ribs that made the Zombie stagger back a step. It came at him again immediately though. He kicked it hard and lost his footing in the branches he was standing in. He fell backwards into the side of the log striking his back painfully. The Zombie with the lopped off ear immediately sprang on top of him trying to get its teeth into his shoulder. He'd lost the machete, so he grabbed the disgusting thing by its hair and held it at arm's length while pulling out his knife. Once he had it out, he stabbed upward into the Zombies throat as hard as he could. He was rewarded with a massive spray of blood and the feeling of life leaving the body of his opponent as it slumped down into the branches.

Stumbling backwards out of the pile of bloody branches Kyler looked around for the other Zombie wondering why it hadn't already attacked him. He spotted it lying in the branches on top of Pete chewing on the man's face and neck. Kyler brought the knife down hard into the Zombies back as it ripped a long piece of skin off the side of Pete's face revealing the pink muscle underneath. Kyler kept stabbing until the Zombie stopped moving. He shoved it off of Pete who'd regained consciousness during the ordeal. His eyes blinking as sweat and ash poured into them directly since he was missing his eyelids now.

Pete was screaming in horror and pain. Missing large pieces of his skin. Unable to walk due to the broken leg. He'd been bitten so he was going to turn soon. Rather than forcing him to suffer that final indignity Kyler plunged his knife into Pete's head through the open eye staring at him. He did it over and over again telling Pete how sorry he was the whole time. When Pete finally stopped moving Kyler slowly stood up. He bent down and stripped Pete of his last weapons and the small pack he'd been wearing. It was full of essentials like ammunition and bottles of water. When Kyler opened it later to pull out one of the waters, he also found a few pictures of a pretty woman holding a baby shoved in there as well.

Kyler kept going. There didn't seem to be a tragedy he couldn't survive no matter how many people died around him. The smoke and the fire shielded him from the Zombies. His plan to stick as close to the fire as possible seemed to work. He stuck to that narrow alley in front of the fire where it was horribly uncomfortable and dangerous to be. A shift in the wind would've been the end of him. His luck held and eventually the fire stopped being so intense. He walked until he couldn't walk anymore. His lungs aching from the heavy smoke and ash. He stopped to vomit and drink the last of his water. He kept going until he couldn't anymore. Hoping neither a Zombie nor the fire decided to show up and ruin his beauty sleep he fell to the ground and curled into a ball.

He was too dehydrated to cry real tears. He was too tired and his lungs too damaged to sob for long. He fell quickly into a deep dreamless slumber. Around him the fire raged into the wee hours of the morning. Zombies stumbled around looking for prey. In that tiny copse of trees, he lay undetected with the tight canopy above him keeping out the sunlight the next morning so his exhausted body could keep sleeping.

Chapter 24: The Brotherhood

Randy's hand was turning blue. He was sitting on the floor of a room that'd been retrofitted as a holding room. It looked like it could hold up to about twenty men if needed. There was a metal bar running around the perimeter of the room about a foot off the ground. Randy and Tony were both handcuffed to the bar. They'd been searched and had their weapons and most of their clothes removed. They were both sitting in the room currently wearing only their underwear.

"At least they took the hoods away." Tony said. They'd been handcuffed facing away from each other but quickly repositioned so they could talk.

"I could go for some water though. My hood was all dusty on the inside." Randy replied.

"Yeah. What kind of post-apocalyptic prison are these guys running here anyway? If we can find some living politicians, I have half a mind to write a stern letter."

"As soon as I can get on-line, I'm ripping them apart on Yelp." Randy replied straight faced.

"Can you both please shut up? Can you not read?" The guard sitting at the large wooden desk in the front of the room said in an exasperated voice. He was trying to read a book and their back and forth was annoying him. There were hand written signs on the wall saying to sit silently and wait.

"Hey man. What's your name?" Tony asked.

"My name is you need to shut the hell up or I'm going to beat you with this wooden bat they leave up here for the purpose of beating morons who don't want to pay attention to the damned signs."

"Do you have like a nick name or something you go by? I can't imagine having to say all that every time I need you to hook me up with a trip to the bathroom." Tony said. Randy wondered how long the guard would give Tony to keep up his wise cracks before choosing to whack him a few times with the bat. They'd planned on ingratiating themselves with the guards and doing their best to not have any ulterior motive other than joining up. They were hamming it up a bit at the moment, Randy was just hoping the soldiers here wouldn't see right through it.

The guard didn't bother responding to Tony. Tony got the hint and shut up. Randy took the break to think through what they needed to be doing for this to work. They'd gotten past the first step which was to get captured without being killed. He went ahead and decided they could put a check in that box. They'd talked about trying to capture one of the men and just force the bases location out of them through torture and threats. They'd all really loved that idea compared to the getting captured plan, but it had even more things that could've gone wrong with it. They'd have had to somehow ambush the guys coming for them who had drones and superior firepower. The men they'd be fighting also had ways of communicating to call for reinforcements. Even if they won the fight and captured the prisoners they might not know where the children were being kept. With plenty of time to plan and setup an ambush site it would've probably been possible for them to do it, but as a quick and dirty solution to rescue their daughters it didn't pass the smell test.

Randy was wishing now that Tony hadn't brought up going to the bathroom. That thought kept percolating around in his head until he had to pee so bad it felt like his back teeth were floating. He hated to ask the guard to help them out since he knew the answer was probably going to be negative. Not able to take it anymore he finally asked and was rewarded with a quart container being tossed in his direction. Tony hurriedly moved back as far away from the possible splatter zone as he could. Randy wiggled out of his boxers and carefully started peeing into the container.

At almost the exact same second as his stream of urine hit the bottom of the container the door opened, and three men walked in. They stopped and took in the sight of Randy taking a whiz into the Tupperware. Not the first impression he'd hoped to give. He assumed none of them were going to want to shake hands when they met him. Randy found himself in an extremely awkward position as he knew he wasn't going to be able to stop peeing anytime in the near future. If he tried, he was probably going to end up pissing on himself which he assumed would provide an even worse first impression than the current situation.

"Holy crap dude. How much did you drink? Sorry guys but you may want to step back in case he overflows." Tony chimed in after the awkward silence became too heavy in the room. Randy wanted to crawl under a rock. Especially as the jug was rapidly filling up and he was worried he might actually end up overflowing the container. Whatever bladder pipe is controlled by the bladder faucet finally shut down and Randy was able to stop and seal up the warm jug full of his pee and sit it down on the floor next to him.

"You all done?" One of the men who'd just walked in asked. Randy nodded. His whole face was flushed bright red with embarrassment. Randy sensed Tony behind him getting ready to say something stupid, so he jumped in.

"All done. Sorry about that. When we find water and we can't carry it all we drink as much of it as we can on the spot. Which is normally fine, but this time someone decided to handcuff me to one of these ballerina practice poles after taking me on a scenic tour with a dusty bag over my head."

"You resisted. You were in our territory, using our supplies, and you resisted our soldiers. Everything we did was done with restraint. You're lucky, when people come on our land to steal and attack us, we normally aren't nice enough to let them live. You two are together right?" The man asked. Randy was assuming he was the guy in charge.

"Not like together-together but yeah we've been wandering the roads together for a while." Tony answered.

"Ok. We're going to split you up and ask each of you some questions. That way we can see if your answers line up the same. What's your name?" The man pointed at Tony who said he was Tony. One of the other men came over and took off Randy's handcuff from the rail then had Randy turn around so he could fasten the loose handcuff on to his other hand. Then he was marched out into the hallway to wait while Tony was interrogated. About ten minutes later Tony was brought out the door in cuffs. The guard with Randy marched him back into the room.

Randy sat down on the floor and waited patiently to be handcuffed to the wall. While he was getting handcuffed, he looked up at the man he was assuming was the leader and asked him if it'd be possible to get a pair of pants.

"You're actually better dressed now than you were earlier." The man replied with a smirk referring to them walking in while Randy was in the middle of taking the worlds longest leak. Randy nodded and leaned back ready to answer questions. They'd decided to keep it simple and stick to mostly the truth. They were just going to throw in a little fib about Kelly having died the last time they'd gone into a house looking for the kids. They also weren't going to mention having found Zoey.

"What's your full name?" The man asked as he sat down at the big wooden desk and opened up a worn looking notebook. Randy told him then asked him if he had a name.

"You can call me Captain O'Donnell. Now tell me how you ended up here. Start with where you were at when everyone turned into crazy cannibals. You can speed up through the boring parts. I'll ask if I want you to dive deeper into anything."

Randy told his story. He was completely honest until he got to the very end. That's where he did some acting and told O'Donnell about Kelly dying and how him and Tony had decided to just find the locals they'd run into and join up to try and find his daughters. They thought it was the best way to find his daughters and keep them safe.

"One of my men here tells me you're the guys we took the pilot away from out on the toll road. That right?" O'Donnell asked.

"Yes sir." Randy hadn't hidden that part, but he hadn't really talked a lot about it either. "How's he doing anyway?"

"Better than the rest of us. As long as there's aviation fuel sitting around, he has a very valuable skillset. Him and Amos are busy jetting around the state as we speak. Your friend Tony was in the Coast Guard. We do a lot of work on the coast. The ocean is about the safest way there is to get around now. Especially for Florida. He has useful skills. You have any useful skills?"

"I worked with computers before the power went off. Computers and networking if those things help anyone anymore. I can help setup networks and that sort of thing." Randy answered.

"Ok. Believe it or not that may prove to be useful down the road. Although for now that kind of skill probably gets you a manual labor or sentry job, but we'll see." O'Donnell looked up from his notebook and right at Randy. "Tony already said he was good with signing up with us. Worse case I can hand both of you a gun and have you stand on the walls. Well, I guess worse case for you would be a big step down from that but the lowest level I deal with is guards on the walls. You want to throw your hat in with us too? Once you're in we don't take kindly to people trying to get out. I can tell you that right now."

"I'm in. Like I said I need to find my daughters and I need to give them a safe place to grow up. I'll stand those walls as long as it takes to keep them safe."

"Good man." O' Donnell stood up to leave. "Normally I'd shake your hand but like I said I saw what you were doing earlier. You're going to have to earn it but let me go ahead and extend my congratulations on you joining the brotherhood. It's not an easy path but we're going to blaze our way through this apocalypse and come out stronger on the other side. You're making the right move."

"Can I get some pants now?" Randy asked as O'Donnell stood up to walk out.

"I really hope so."

With a grin and shake of his head O' Donnell walked out, and Tony was escorted back in. They were both handcuffed to the pipe again when someone did come in with a few giant Ross bags. The man with the bags hooked them up with jeans and plain green t-shirts. It made a world of difference not to be chained to the pipe wearing just their boxers. Of course, it'd be even better not to be chained to the pipe at all.

Chapter 25: Good Girls

Mr. Abrams walked Myriah into a room that had a large TV on the wall. There were the desks used in schools scattered around in front of the TV. Caitlyn was sitting at one of the desks with a notebook open in front of her. She looked up as they walked in. Myriah saw the momentary flash of excitement as Caitlyn saw her. Then she turned her attention back to the TV. Myriah got the message. Caitlyn was playing the adults game too.

Myriah sat down and Mr. Abrams went to the front of the room. He fumbled around with the electronics up there until he had the DVD playing that he needed to show them.

"Ok. This will run about an hour then we have several more for you to go through. The lights stay on and you're expected to take notes and be able to pass a test at the end of the day. No talking between the two of you. People will be checking in on you to make sure you're both focused on the videos. Lunch will be dropped off so you can keep watching while you eat. Any questions for me?"

Caitlyn and Myriah both politely said they had no questions. Then they settled in to watch the movie. Mr. Abrams left the room and shut the door behind him. Cailyn stage whispered she was happy to see Myriah and loved her and asked her if she'd seen Doreen and Ali.

"They're both fine. They got beaten because of what I did when they brought us here. That's how they keep us in line here. If we screw up, they'll hurt them instead of us." Myriah whispered back. She wasn't extremely concerned about talking as long as they didn't get too loud. At the end of the day the people in this building had a lot more to worry about than two teen sisters talking to each other during a documentary or whatever this was they had to watch. Myriah opened her notebook to take notes. She didn't think they'd beat Doreen or Ali if she didn't pass this test, but she wasn't ruling it out as a possibility either.

The movie started. It was a tall man with salt and pepper hair sitting at a desk with an American flag and a Georgia state flag behind it. The man began speaking with a cultured down-home southern gentlemen accent. Myriah and Caitlyn began scribbling notes as the man spoke.

"Hello there. I'm Senator Wilcox of the great state of Georgia. If you're watching this then I'm sure you're wondering what's going on. What have you gotten yourself into? I've made these little movies to help you understand. I'm making this one to give you an overview of who we are and what we're trying to accomplish. I also want to share with you my vision for how you fit into this new world. As the young women of this brave new world you serve a greater purpose. You'll be the ones giving birth to and raising the first generations of children to be born into this brave new world. It's a grave and critical responsibility that's been thrust upon you."

"Now to be clear. I'm not just a Senator. I'm also a man of God. I've held multiple titles in my life that've helped prepare me to be your leader in these tumultuous times. I've spent time in the military and the intelligence communities. I've spent time in the business world, and I've answered the call to serve the church. My role as a minister is especially relevant. It gives me insight into what's happening today. God has set a plague loose on the lands to cleanse the earth of sin. The evils that man have perpetuated have caught up to him."

"I believe that while God seeks to cleanse the earth, he does not seek to destroy all mankind. Just like he sent the floods to punish the sinners in biblical times he's sent this plague to remind us of the dangers of sinning. There's going to be a future after this plague. A future that'll be bright and based around the teachings of the bible. Like the proverbial Phoenix arising from the ashes so shall we rise up. We'll rise up better and stronger than ever before. We'll rise up as strong, godly men and women. We'll show God we've learned the errors of our ways. We'll show him how good we can be while understanding why he inflicted his divine justice on us."

"Man is a sinner. We all know that. We all know there's nothing we can do to change that. We can try to lessen our sinning though. We can learn from the lessons of the past and grow in our faith and let it sustain us through the rough times ahead. Let there be no doubt that some of the hardest work is still ahead of us. I know we can walk the path together though since you've shown you have the stuff to have survived until now and kept your decency. You wouldn't be sitting in those chairs watching this video if you didn't show promise."

The senator paused at this point in his narration to stare into the camera. After about ten seconds of staring he started back up again.

"We find ourselves in a world that's ready to be reborn. A world we can shape into the kind of God-fearing community we can all be proud to live in. Let's talk a little bit about how we're going to do that. When this crisis first started brewing the President and the rest of congress all thought activating the military would alert and scare too many people. They shuffled some things around covertly and then trusted in the false god of science to get them out of this mess. None of them were expecting an event that can only be described as the rapture. An event that took ninety nine percent of the people to their final reward leaving nothing but the husks of their bodies to roam the world until they collapsed."

"The final percent left here on this earth must now survive. We must rebuild this world and be ready to welcome Jesus when he comes back down to this planet. We must punish the sinners and make a safe place for those who obey the commandments. We must spread the gospel. First things first though we secure the land we own. When the rest of Congress was trusting in science and trying not to upset the regular folk, we in Georgia called up the national guard. We started insisting on curfews in major cities. We prepared for the day we knew was coming."

"Have no doubt those early days were still utterly horrific. In our big cities like Atlanta there was no end to the suffering. Because we'd prepared though we were able to pull through better than our neighbors to the north and south. Now we've expanded into Florida so that all of Georgia and Florida are part of God's country. We're blowing up bridges and sealing the borders so that we can make our land safe. We'll hunt down those soulless husks who left behind their bodies filled with the evil lust for consuming human flesh. We'll make this land safe then we'll expand into the other states and islands around us."

"Our new militia to enforce God's will is known as the brotherhood. Your responsibility is to support them as they go out to share the word and secure our borders. You are on the journey now to join the sisterhood. Once you're of age and you've proven worthy you will be given in matrimony to one of the brotherhoods to propagate our species. We will be fruitful and multiply. We will fill up these lands once again. Only this time we'll fill it up with people who won't incur the wrath of a vengeful God. Well fill it up with God's chosen and live in paradise on this planet until we're called home to the one and only real paradise."

"Pay attention in your lessons and walk the path of the righteous and you will go far. Do not follow the path of sin. That path was trod before and anyone with eyes can see where it leads. We will rebuild and then we will rejoice. You will be a part of this. I welcome you heartily to your first steps on the journey to sisterhood."

The DVD ended and came up with a few selections you could make. The section they'd just watched was labeled the 'Senators Intro to Sisterhood'. Caitlyn refused to look back at Myriah. She knew there was no way they'd be able to stop from cracking jokes about what they'd just seen. She had a feeling cracking jokes about the senator were probably frowned upon. She had a vague recollection of hearing about the evangelist getting elected to be senator of Georgia and stirring up a bunch of stuff because people thought he was too conservative.

Their family had never been ultra-religious. They'd gone to church most Sundays then gone out for lunch afterwards. They'd done various church events and youth groups and things like that. The church they'd gone to hadn't been that special brand of brimstone and hell fire that it sounded like the senator subscribed to. They were going to need to fake it until they could make it in this new society. Caitlyn hadn't given up completely on escaping, but she saw it as less of a reality every day. With Brenda and Eric both dead she didn't even know where they'd go if they did escape. The hope they may actually find their parents was slowly dying. She was slowly accepting the reality that this was her new life and she'd probably never see her mom or dad again. At this point she just wanted to see her little sisters again and figure out a way to be with them.

That was the other reason she kept from turning around. She didn't want to see the hope she knew would be blazing in Myriah's eyes. Myriah wasn't a practical person. Myriah would never accept their parent's death until she saw the actual corpses. Myriah believed in fairy tales. Caitlyn didn't think she could have the luxury of believing anymore but she didn't want to try and snuff out that flame of hope burning bright in Myriah's heart. It may be the only thing that sustained her in the days ahead.

She stared straight ahead. She ignored the coughs and other noises meant to get her to turn her head to talk to Myriah. She ignored them until Mr. Abrams walked back in and started the next section of the DVD. She leaned back and grabbed her pencil to take notes on how to maintain 'The Hygiene of a Godly Woman'. At least they were getting into some information that was more useful than some old guy rattling on about the end of days.

Chapter 26: To Thine Own Self Be True

He couldn't move. His skin was on fire. Around him a light rain was still drizzling down through what was left of the overhead canopy. He was in a hole that had a few inches of muddy water pooled up in it. He was shivering from the cold while being blistered all over from the heat. He found two water bottles in the bag beside him and slowly drank them both. His lips were cracked, and his face felt like his skin had been pulled hard to stretch over his skull. Every movement brought intense pain. The water burned the whole way down his throat. Every bit of his exposed skin was burnt.

Everything hurt. He thought of how Tom and Pete had both died and he'd made it this far. Their bodies wouldn't have survived the fire. Not that they'd ever be ready for an open casket after having their faces ripped apart by starving Zombies. Kyler put both hands on the ground and pushed himself up to his knees. The pain was intense. His body screamed at him to just lie back down and rest. To slip away into the blackness. What was he trying so hard for anyway?

His body was wracked with coughing. He spit big wads of nasty multicolored bile into the muddy water he was kneeling in. He kept himself from puking by sheer force of will. He didn't have any more water. He knew he couldn't risk puking up the water he'd just finished drinking. He only hoped those two bottles would be enough to see him through. He didn't know how long he was kneeling there staring into the muddy water and occasionally coughing. It crossed his mind that he could either stay there and die or get up and probably die anyway. He didn't think he had it in him to literally die on his knees like that. If he was going to die anyway, he might as well do it wandering around randomly in the burnt-out woods surrounded by the Zombie survivors of the wildfire.

He stood up. New sources of pain reared back and slapped him in the face. A solid wall of darkness descended over him. He wasn't sure if he was standing up or not, but he stayed where he was and just focused on his breathing until his sight gradually returned. He was wicked dizzy, but he was still standing. He took a tentative step. Something felt wrong with his foot, so he sat down on the side of the hole to look. Sitting down felt wonderful but he wasn't sure how he'd be able to summon the energy to stand back up. He forgot for a second why he'd sat down in the first place. Once he remembered he pulled his foot up to take a look.

The soles were missing in a few places where the rubber had melted off. The whole shape of the bottom of his boots was warped. The soles of his feet were burnt and bloody. Not seeing how the boots were helping very much Kyler spent the next twenty minutes hacking them off his feet. They were melted on in some spots and he had to resort to hacking away at the sturdy leather with his Gerber knife. Tears of pain leapt unbidden into his eyes as he pulled off each boot. The rubber of the boot soles had melted to his feet in some places. It was like he was ripping the bottom of his foot off right along with the boots.

He pulled his feet out of the mud after rinsing them around to get the mud off and attempt to cool them down some. He got the medical pack out of his bag and pulled out the one he'd taken from Pete's bag too. He coated the soles of his feet with iodine and then wrapped them with gauze. He finished by taping them up as tightly as he could before sliding on an extra pair of thick socks he found in his pack. He also found another warm bottled water in the pack. He savored it slowly. It was some of the best water he'd ever had in his life. He used it to wash down a generic Oxy and the first two pills of a Z-Pack. The irony of an antibiotic being called a Z-Pack was lost on him in his pained condition.

He gave the Oxy twenty minutes to kick in then stood up to start walking. Whatever little bit of numbness he thought he'd felt from the Oxy went away as soon as he put his weight on his feet. He squealed out in pain and sat back down hard on the ground. He let the rain hit him in the face for a minute. He heard something in the distance. It was a Zombie screech. His squeal of pain must've been louder than he thought. Not having much of a choice he considered the little pill bottle full of Oxy he had in front of him and palmed two more of the little white miracles. He dry-swallowed both of them.

He sat still listening to the sound of the rain hitting the woods all around him. He heard other noises in the woods. There were things moving around out there. None came out directly for him though. The one who'd screeched had sounded within fifty yards, but nothing came of it. Kyler's head was swimming pleasantly. The pain in his feet was forgotten. He'd never been one for drugs. He normally didn't take more than one of the pain killers the dentist would give you for pain after a root canal or getting a wisdom tooth removed. He didn't like the way it made him feel. His body was not ready for three of the strong pain killers he'd dumped into his system.

He stumbled through the woods. Too buzzed to notice the smoldering barbecued bodies he passed. The bodies of the Zombies who'd gotten too close to the fire and been overwhelmed by the smoke and the flames. Covered in mud and stumbling painfully on his bandaged feet through the smoking ruins of the forest with the rain drizzling down he passed by a few Zombies. They didn't even look at him twice. It was a journey he probably wouldn't have survived sober and unhurt. His gait would've given him away as a normal human. At least one of the Zombies would've come at him to investigate and it would've been all over.

He kept walking. He stumbled through the woods until he left behind the fire. He put one foot in front of the other in an extremely drugged state until his exhausted body threatened to give way. He stared at a tree that looked funny until he realized it was a telephone pole. He looked up and followed the wires. A few minutes later he was walking on a paved road. The drugs were wearing off. He felt like every step he took someone was shocking his feet. His pain had reached a level where his brain almost couldn't deal with it anymore. An oversized mailbox with some sort of windmill thing on the top of it was right down the road.

He set his goal as the mailbox. He made it to the mailbox and turned down the winding dirt road beside it. He focused on putting one foot in front of the other. He stared at his legs like they belonged to another person. His force of will the only thing keeping him up and moving. A trailer stood in a clearing with a small driveway branching off to it from the dirt road he was on. Kyler set his eyes on the trailer and kept moving. He somehow made it up the stairs and tried the door. It opened easily. The desiccated corpse of an obese woman was draped across the couch in the single wide's living room.

Kyler barely spared the cadaver a second glance. There was so much death in his world now that it barely even registered with him. A small part of him realized how messed up that was. Mostly he just hoped the bedroom didn't have a dead body in it. He poked around in the kitchen until he found a jug of water. Ignoring the cockroaches and spiders he stumbled past his new roommate on the couch down to a door that opened into a crappy bedroom. The woman could've stared in any of the reality hoarding TV shows.

Ignoring how filthy everything in the room was Kyler crawled into the oversized bed with the broken mattress springs. He opened up the jug of water and drank as much of it as he could stomach. Then he lay down and coughed for a few minutes. When the coughing subsided, he drank some more of the warm water. He knew he should try and change the bandages on his feet, but he didn't have the energy. He put his head back on one of the pillows in the musty bed and fell asleep. His last waking thought being to wonder if he'd ever wake up again or if he was just going to die in his sleep. He figured it was even odds either way.

He woke up. He wished he hadn't. He wanted more than anything to go back to sleep. His skin burned. His lungs ached from the harsh coughing that'd been the reason he ended up awake. It was pitch black in the trailer. The place smelled like mold and death. He couldn't tell if he was covered in bugs or if it was just his skin that felt like he was. He felt around until he found his backpack. He fumbled around with it until he had some pills out. Not entirely sure exactly what he was taking he shoved pills in his mouth then drank as much of the water as he could without puking and lie back down. The Oxy kicked in and he floated off into slumber land again.

He continued that process until he was out of water. He ate the granola bars in his pack. He kept himself comfortably numb with the pill supply he had in the bag. The pill supply was getting close to gone as well. He'd taken the whole Z-pack and started another. He wasn't sure if he'd been in the trailer for one night or a week. He was assuming it'd been about two days based on how much of the water he'd drank. His feet and face were tender to the touch. He lay in the bed killing off the last of the water.

He pondered his next move now that it seemed like he might actually survive. His throat was raw. He kept having to shove his face into a musty pillow every time he had a coughing fit to keep the sound from carrying. He didn't think the noise would carry far enough to be heard by a group of ravenous Zombies but being paranoid was being alive in this new normal. If a gang of ravenous Zombies did show up, he had enough ammunition to take care of the first one or two of them then he'd be Zombie food. His body was in no shape to deal with going toe to toe with any of those insane flesh eaters. He was pretty sure the average seven-year-old girl could kick his ass at this stage.

He rested. He couldn't find any more water in the house, so he made do with a collection of two-liter sodas he found. He named the dead woman on the couch Becky and amused himself coming up with reasons she hadn't ever made it out of the trailer. He marveled at the fact that he was ok with crashing on a dead woman's bed while her corpse decayed away on a couch less than twenty feet away from him. It was the kind of unbelievably traumatic events people used to make horror movies out of. Now it was what you did on a Tuesday.

He gradually got better. His goal had been to survive when he dragged himself into the trailer. Now that it looked like he was going to actually live a little longer he found himself contemplating what he should do next. He guessed he could go back to spying but that'd lost a lot of its luster when he'd found out he wasn't invading the evil empire. It was just another group of survivors trying to survive as far as he could tell. At least that's all it was based on the group he'd been hanging out with so far. He knew it could be a different story in different parts of Georgia or Florida but what was he really going to accomplish by wandering around spying on people? How was that going to help him?

The fact that he'd risked his life to come down and spy on these people based on rumors and hearsay now seemed pretty ridiculous to him. What did he owe the group to the north? He owed them nothing really. They'd taken him in and taught him some valuable skills, but he'd repaid them by scavenging and then fighting for them. He'd done the same thing with this group down here in Georgia. The more he thought about it the less he knew what he wanted to do.

The real problem was all the free time he found himself with to think. It turned out sitting around in a dilapidated singlewide with a rotting corpse in it waiting to see if you lived or died from your extremely painful burns led to a lot of introspection. Up until this point he'd been on the go constantly. He hadn't had a ton of time to spend thinking about his future. He hadn't really thought he had a future. Based on how everyone around him kept dying he'd assumed his card could get punched at any minute. Based on his current situation he still wasn't too sure about lasting out the week.

He needed to make the most of the time he had though. He owed that to his mom and dad and Mike and all the others who'd raised him. He owed it to the millions of infected wandering the land cursed by a disease he'd managed to avoid. He owed it to himself. With those thoughts in his head he grabbed his stuff out of the bedroom and limped down the hallway to scavenge in the kitchen some more. He realized while he was brushing bugs off a bag of hardened sugar that he really didn't even notice the smell of decaying flesh any more. The gelatinous blob of dead femininity draped over the cheap sofa barely even registered with him. She might as well be a lamp that smelled bad.

Opening a pop top of generic canned corn, he sniffed it to make sure it smelled ok. It did so he drank the water out of it then absently chewed on the corn. He'd rummaged through the house looking for shoes he could wear and come up with multiple pairs of oversized socks with the soles of a pair of flip flops taped to the bottom of them. It was a fashion accessory that would've made the most flamboyant hobo snicker at him. It was better than walking around barefoot though. His feet were still extremely tender from the burns he'd gotten on them.

He arranged his pack and his weapons as best he could with his various aches and pains and headed out into the night. His goal was to head south until he hit the road that led back to the base where they'd launched their ill-fated Zombie turning mission from. He was hoping he'd find a vehicle of some sort he could use before then. He didn't think his feet were going to be able to handle a long hike any time soon. If he happened to find a nicer place to hang out for a while with more supplies in it that may become an option as well. For right now he just felt like he should get moving. He was getting nervous being in the same place for so long.

He opened the door and cautiously made his way down the uneven concrete steps leading down to the weed infested brick patio. He was feeling pretty good about his flip flop, duct tape, big sock combo. Not only was it super comfortable it was also super quiet. He just wasn't sure how durable his footwear was going to turn out to be. He hoped they'd last until he was able to find some better shoes in a different house. For such a big woman the lady who'd died on the couch had very petite feet.

By the time Kyler got to the road he knew he was never going to be able to make it as an amateur cobbler. The foot wraps he'd made were no protection against the hard stones he stepped on. The taped together footwear seemed to reach out and grab every briar and weed he walked past. The tape that wasn't trying to fall off his feet was busy grabbing dirt and leaves for him to carry along with him. By the time he made it to the paved road his feet were a huge mess. He stopped to cut some tape off his feet and consider the road in front of him.

If he went left that was north and he'd theoretically end up back with the people from the settlements who'd sent him on this spy mission in the first place. If he went right it'd take him south into the land of the supposed enemy that he'd been sent to spy on. He decided he really didn't have a huge preference between the two sides. He supposed the settlements had been more of a home to him for longer, so he felt like he owed them a higher degree of loyalty than he did the people down here in the south. Which meant he needed to fulfill his obligation to the people in the north by turning south and making sure the people down here weren't up to anything nefarious. He also didn't like the idea of going north and being questioned about why he'd turned around and returned so soon with no useful intel.

Hoping there wasn't any truly useful intel to worry about he turned right and started trudging along the paved road. Every step was a jolt of pain through his body, but the pavement was much better than walking through the dirt and the weeds had been. He kept his machete in his hand. His M-16 hung from a strap around his neck. He was down to half a magazine of bullets even after what he'd scavenged off of Pete. Every part of his body hurt but such was life in the apocalypse. He put one foot in front of the other and hoped that'd be enough to see him through.

Chapter 27: Ain't No Mountain Tall Enough

Tony and Randy sat on the large couch in Captain O'Donnell's office. The couch was a pleather that would've been uncomfortable if the typical Florida humidity had its way. The building they were in was covered in solar panels though. The local government having been the beneficiary of some government grants before the apocalypse to try and ease the global warming crisis. If they'd only known what was coming, they could've installed machine gun nests on every government building instead of solar panels. Although, Randy mused, the apocalypse probably was the best thing to have happened in thousands of years as far as the environment was concerned.

With the factories shut down and the largest cities turned into massive burial sites the amount of pollution humanity typically spewed into the atmosphere had been reduced to pretty much zero. This led to some great star gazing. The air also seemed cleaner everywhere. Randy would've traded in the pollution free air in a heartbeat to go back to the way things were before. Back to the days when the DVR screwing up and missing the show the whole family wanted to watch with their pizza delivery was a major catastrophe. If only they'd known.

They'd been sleeping in houses with no power for so long that they'd gotten out of the habit of flipping on light switches when they walked into rooms. The captain had handed each of them a glass of ice water. Randy let the cold-water trickle down his throat in ecstasy. Looking over at Tony he saw that he seemed mesmerized by the ice cubes clinking around in his glass. The captain cleared his throat to get the two of them to look up at him. He looked bemused by their reaction to the ice water.

"It's amazing how quickly something like ice has become a luxury. This is the only place where we regularly have it. You guys having been out in the field for so long I can only imagine the kinds of things you've seen." The captain stopped to take a long swig of his own water. Having seen the way Randy and Tony were treating their drinks had made the water taste even better to the captain. It reminded him how easy things like that could be lost. "I imagine you're both wondering what's next, right?"

"Yes sir. I'm hoping it includes being reunited with my girls." Randy answered respectfully.

"That'll happen, but not quite yet. We have them in training, and we need to get you enrolled as well. We're going to get you both set on a path to become full-fledged members of the brotherhood. Once you're officially in then you'll get certain perks and benefits which include things like access to your family. Until you've been confirmed as members though you'll be considered candidates which basically puts you at the level of a plebe in college. You can think of the candidate process as kind of an informal boot camp."

"How long does that typically take sir? Becoming a full member?" Tony asked curiously. He was wondering how long the captain was going to continue letting them sit there and ask questions before turning them over to whoever was going to be in charge of training them.

"It varies. There's some testing requirements and some skills you need to learn but the most important task is committing an 'act of valor'. Once you've done that, you're in. An 'act of valor' is showing the brotherhood that you're dedicated to the safety of our land and people. Once your act is communicated up the chain a decision will be made on you to either fully enroll you or wash you out of the program. You can be washed out ahead of that as well, but we normally like to give people a chance if we think they can cut it."

Randy and Tony were lost by the direction the conversation had gone. They nodded along with the captain and tried to follow what he was talking about. They were wondering what some examples of those acts of valor might be. Before either of them could ask that question, another uniformed man showed up in the office and had a brief conversation with the captain. It sounded like a herd might be migrating through the area and coming up the road that went by the facility they were in. Not a big deal as long as the Zombies kept on moving.

"I need to go check on this herd and make sure all's good there. We'll probably be going into a lockdown to avoid them noticing us so be prepared to sit around and stare at the walls for a few days. Stay here. A man will be coming for you soon." With that the captain and the other men left the room leaving Tony and Randy sitting there unguarded and unchained.

They might as well be chained to the radiator naked still though. Randy wasn't about to leave now that he knew his kids were there. Tony wasn't planning on deserting Randy. He also really wanted to reunite the family. He'd traveled down the whole east coast to do that and he wasn't the type to let a mission like that go uncompleted. They were also unfamiliar with the building they were in and it sounded like a mess of Zombies were headed their way. Probably not the best time to try and find the kids and make a break for it.

"Sit here?" Tony asked Randy quietly.

"Yep." Randy agreed.

They didn't have to wait too long. Mr. Abrams showed up about fifteen minutes later. He was a stout man with dark hair and an accent that sounded like he was from everywhere all at once. Tony was thinking the guy must have been a military brat. One of the kids who got dragged all over the world with their dads or moms being in different branches of the military. That'd explain why he grew up and joined the military too. The sons and daughters of most military men feel compelled to serve out at least one tour to feel like they've met their family military obligation.

Randy could care less about anyone's military legacy. All he wanted to do was get his kids and get the hell out of this freakshow. A place where the military was referred to as the brotherhood and you only got freedom by joining them was not a place he wanted to be. The act of valor stuff seemed a bit like gangland material to Randy. Was he going to have to participate in a drive by then get 'jumped in' to the brotherhood? He was starting to freak out about how his daughters may be getting treated here.

"You can both call me Mr. Abrams. When I walk into the room you should both stop what you are doing and come to attention. You should do the same thing for anyone else as long as you are candidates." Mr. Abrams stood there staring at the two of them. Tony popped to his feet and stood at attention. Randy belatedly got to his feet as well.

"Mr. Abrams I was – " Randy started speaking but was cut off by a harsh look from Mr. Abrams.

"You will not speak unless asked to speak. If you have a question you will raise your hand and wait to be addressed. If no one cares to call on you then save your question for later. Is that understood?"

"Yes sir." Tony and Randy barked out.

"The candidate phase ends in one of three ways. You perform well and perform an act of valor that meets everyone's approval at which point you'll be confirmed as a full member of the brotherhood. You don't perform an act of valor or claim something considered unworthy or wash out of the training and become one of the people. Being one of the people you don't have the freedoms the members of the brotherhood enjoy but it's still better than the third option. The third way it ends is you die during training. Is that understood?"

"Yes sir!"

"Do you both still want to follow this path? You can opt out at any time and become one of the people. Not everyone is cutout for the brotherhood. Are you both in?"

"Yes sir!" Randy and Tony echoed again.

Mr. Abrams turned around and told them to follow him. They left the room. Randy awkwardly trying to march along behind Tony until Abrams gave him a weird look. Randy gave up trying to emulate what he'd seen on TV about being in the military. Instead he focused on checking out the interior of the building they were passing through. It was a standard government building. It seemed to be falling apart a little more than most of them, but it was basically a huge expanse of cheap cubicles and long hallways with doors going off in every direction. The main difference between this and most of the buildings he'd been in recently was the fact that there was electricity.

Electricity in Florida made a huge difference. Every house or building they'd been in smelled like mold and rot. Without air conditioning all of the buildings were slowly rotting away. Randy figured a few more years with a couple of decent hurricanes and you'd barely be able to tell people had ever occupied most of the state. The building they were in now didn't smell great either, but it smelled a lot better than most. Based on the areas where the lights weren't working in the building it looked there were some issues with using solar to try and power everything. They must have it hooked up to the most critical areas.

Abrams led them down a long hallway then up a staircase at the end. At the top of the staircase was yet another long hallway with a bunch of doors leading off in either direction. This hallway was lit up like a horror movie as well. Enough light to see by but not enough to feel comfortable in. Randy felt like there could a be a couple of Zombies hanging out on this floor and he might not see them until it was too late. Abrams led them to a door about halfway down the hall and pushed it open. They followed him in.

It was a small room with two bunkbeds in it. None of the beds looked like they'd been used recently. The beds were made. The spartanly furnished space looked like it'd been very well maintained. There was a flat screen TV wall-mounted on one side of the room with a cheap DVD player sitting on a shelf underneath it. There was a small stack of DVDs sitting beside it.

"Ok. I'm going to leave you two here to make your way through that stack of DVDs. It's mostly a high-level overview of how we've structured the brotherhood and the people. I don't know if you guys were religious before but as of now you are. The brotherhood is all kinds of religious tolerant as long as you're Christian. You'll learn more about it in the DVDs. The senator is running everything out of a fortress up in Georgia and he's a very religious man. You'll find that most of what we do is aimed at taming the areas of Florida and Georgia that we're working on rebuilding and repopulating. We're trying to do it better this time. Any questions?" Abrams finished his speech and stood in the doorway looking at them expectantly.

"Do we need to fill out a test or take notes or anything?" Tony asked. He asked mostly to fill up the awkward silence that had descended on them.

"No. No formal written test but you will be asked what you thought of the videos and there may be specific questions as we go through the training. If it's obvious you didn't pay attention or grasp the concepts, then you could get washed out. If you don't have any more questions, go ahead and get settled in and start knocking out the videos. I'll be back or send someone back to take you to the mess for dinner."

Abrams left the room leaving Randy and Tony standing there in their new clothes wondering what to do next. They'd already discussed that there could be listening devices in the rooms. Especially since this place had actual electricity. They didn't think anyone would spend a ton of time listening to them talk but there was no reason to put their plans out there for the world to hear. It wasn't like anything had changed anyway. The plan was actually working out way better than either of them had ever thought it would. This place was oddly accepting of them. As weird as everyone here was and as odd as the experience had been so far it looked like they were on track to blend in soon.

Hoping Kelly and Zoey were doing fine in the house he'd left them in Randy settled back into the bottom bunk as Tony fumbled around with the DVD player trying to figure it out. A distinguished looking man sitting in front of a desk with some flags behind him started talking. Randy steeled himself to sit through endless hours of the indoctrination speeches. Tony mimed putting toothpicks in his eyes then climbed into the top bunk after telling Randy he was up for figuring out what the next DVD in the series was supposed to be.

They'd gotten about an hour into the first DVD when there was a rapping on their door. The rapping was immediately followed by the door being thrown open. A flustered looking man with a beet red face stood in the doorway trying to catch his breath.

"Hey. The commander wants every able body to head over to operations. It looks like we may get swarmed. Grab your junk and let's roll."

Chapter 28: Swarmed

Myriah looked up from the book she was reading on her bunk when the door to the room was flung open. All the other girls had left to go to one of the more advanced classes earlier that morning. Myriah was still considered a newbie. She was currently waiting for the introduction classes to start being taught again. They still had her watching videos and doing workbooks but so far had not moved on to the practical training. From what she could gather the practical training centered around how to establish and run a house hold post-apocalypse. The feminist movement had been put on the back burner for the time being.

One of the girls from her class came into the room and told her to get up and get her stuff ready to go. Myriah started quickly and quietly gathering the few items that could be called hers. Shoving her toiletry items and a change of clothes into her pillowcase then helping gather everyone else's belongings into their pillowcases as well. When they were done, they consolidated everything down to a big pillowcase each then left out the door to go down the hallway towards the auditorium.

All around them other people were quietly making their way down the hallway. No one was talking and whenever Myriah looked up at her guide the girl just put her finger to her lips and kept on moving. When they were halfway down the hall all the regular lights went out and the red emergency lights blinked on. No one was talking but Myriah felt the people in the hallway grow more tense as the lights changed color. Everyone also started moving a little bit faster.

In the auditorium Myriah was told to sit down and keep quiet. She looked around and spotted Caitlyn so went and sat beside her. Caitlyn gave her a half hug then continued scanning the room trying to spot Doreen or Ali. Myriah began looking around as well but didn't spot anyone until a group of kids was brought in by a harried looking grey-haired lady. The apocalypse diet didn't seem to have done her figure any damage as she swept into the room. Her face looked open and kind but there was something about her eyes that had Myriah wondering what the woman was so terrified of. The expression disappeared so quickly from the woman's face that it left Myriah wondering if it'd maybe just been a trick of the light.

Myriah lost track of the woman's face when Caitlyn's hand tightened on her shoulder. Looking at the group of kids being led in she spotted Doreen with Ali. Ali was holding Doreen's hand and looking around the room furtively. She had the look of a dog that'd been recently beaten. Like she was scared to engage fully with the people around her out of fear of being struck. Myriah felt Caitlyn's grip tighten on her shoulder even more and took that to mean Caitlyn had noticed the air of fear surrounding Doreen and Ali as well. A quick glance over her shoulder at the expression on Caitlyn's face confirmed she'd noticed it too. Caitlyn was grinding her teeth together in frustration and anger.

Not knowing or caring if it was allowed Myriah hopped out of her seat and walked quickly towards Doreen and Ali. She remembered what'd happened the last time she tried to talk to the kids so instead of continuing towards them she angled towards the lady leading them instead. She felt Caitlyn's eyes burning into the back of her neck. She knew Caitlyn was thinking of what'd happened to the kids last time as well. A cane pole whipping for Doreen hard enough the marks were still on the little girls' legs. Myriah felt a white-hot flash of anger through her body at the memory.

"Hi. I'm Myriah. Doreen and Ali are my sisters if you'd like me to watch them." Myriah offered. She was smiling and trying to make the offer as casually as she could. She had no idea if what she was asking was the norm or not. The room was starting to get crowded, but it was still quiet as everyone practice the noise discipline so critical to survival in this new normal.

"Oh. Thank you. Yes, that'll be fine. I wasn't even aware Doreen and Ali had sisters here. Please just have them sit over with you and make sure they keep quiet. We're liable to be sitting in here for a while."

Doreen and Ali finally noticed Myriah. They both lit up with excitement and rushed over to join her. Myriah hugged them both and led them back over to where Caitlyn was sitting. As excited as they all were, the habits they'd gotten in staying quiet out in the open held up here and Myriah didn't even have to remind the two young girls to keep quiet. They went over to where Caitlyn was busy finding four chairs all together. She might as well have only gotten three as it was pretty obvious Doreen wasn't planning on getting off Caitlyn's lap anytime soon. Myriah was smiling at the pure love shining from Doreen's face as she wrapped herself around Caitlyn.

"We'll be here awhile." Hissed the principal. She'd wandered up on them from out of nowhere. All of them cringed back a little from the harsh woman. "Be sure you all stay right here unless ordered to leave and not a word out of any of you. You'll be told what to do. When told what to do you need to do it immediately and without a sound. Understand?"

They all nodded at the principal. Happy to be avoiding a beating or any punishment for the crime of being together as a family. Evidently when it was advantageous and convenient for the principal that they all be together then it was ok. They weren't allowed to talk so they sat there in silence. Doreen fell into an exhausted slumber on top of Caitlyn. Ali and Myriah both fidgeted. Neither of them took to sitting idly by for long periods of time. Caitlyn absently combed Doreen's hair with her fingers while her left leg slowly fell asleep from the weight of the young girl awkwardly lying across her lap.

She sat there trying to figure out a way she could get them out of this auditorium and back into the field. She'd had a lot of internal debates on whether they were all better off under the protection of the brotherhood. The terrified demeanor of Doreen and Ali on entering the auditorium had wiped away all of her doubt. Better for them to live alone in a world full of death and Zombies than spend another day in this fake refuge. She didn't want to live a life of servitude. She had more self-respect, more hopes and dreams for her sisters than to allow for that. The videos they'd been watching were all about indoctrinating them into someone else's vision of the future. A vision she didn't want any part of.

It sucked that it took a giant herd of Zombies bearing down on them to get them all back together again. It sucked but they couldn't have tried to escape otherwise because no way would Caitlyn leave anyone behind. Unfortunately, the big mass of Zombies outside didn't lend themselves to an easy escape. Not only would they have to get out of the auditorium where the principal was keeping an eye on them, but the outer guards would all be on high alert too. Of course, those guards would be looking outside the compound, not inside. If they managed to get past the hyper alert guards on the perimeter of the building, then they'd be in the position of having to get past the mob of ravenous Zombies.

Once they made it around the bloodthirsty Zombie mob then they'd still need to find a vehicle to get the hell out of dodge before the brotherhood recaptured them. The brotherhood had drones and outposts and could coordinate a search even in the midst of the Zombie attack if they so desired. The brotherhood had resources. Caitlyn and the girls would have nothing but the clothes on their backs and whatever they could steal from the compound on their way out. It was mission impossible. Caitlyn didn't care. They beat the odds everyday just by being a group of young girls who'd survived this long into the Zombie apocalypse. They just needed to beat the odds a little longer and they'd be free of this prison.

They waited. There was nothing else for it. They'd been told to sit quietly and wait for the orders to get up and move. Caitlyn was beginning to wonder if this was all going to end anticlimactically. If they were just going to end up sitting there until the herd wandered on down the road. If that happened, they'd be separated again, and their chances of an escape would be diminished. As bad as she wanted to get them out of there Caitlyn knew if an opportunity didn't present itself soon, they'd end up separated and sent back to their rooms. She was hoping by being obedient and sitting quietly throughout this event maybe they'd earn a little trust from the principal.

The principal, or warden as Myriah and Caitlyn were both starting to think of her as, was currently up at the front of the auditorium talking to a man dressed from head to boots in camouflage. The soldier was carrying an assault rifle and had other weapons strapped to various parts of his body. The grip of a samurai sword stuck up over the man's shoulder adding a samurai vibe to his get up. The sword made a lot of sense. It was quiet and never ran out of ammunition. Caitlyn mentally added finding a martial arts supply store to loot to her ever growing to do list.

Myriah and Caitlyn had almost given up on getting an opportunity for escape when the muted sounds of automatic gunfire drifted into the hushed auditorium. The hush descended into a dead silence as all the conversations immediately stopped. Everyone seemed to be holding their breaths. They all knew what it meant. The soldiers carried rifles with them but would never use them except as a last resort. Shooting the rifles meant Zombies would be converging on this spot from miles around. Shooting meant that everyone needed to clear this area as quickly as possible if they wanted to live. Shooting that rifle was the desperate act of a man with his back against the wall. That meant the situation outside the building must have turned into a total shit show.

The principal turned and calmly addressed the group in the auditorium.

"The situation outside has obviously gotten pretty bad. You all know with those shots fired we need to get out of here immediately. Follow me out to the south exit and we'll get out of here. We have to hurry. Maintain noise discipline and follow orders and we'll all get out of this alive." Without speaking another word, the principal marched over to the door on the opposite side of the auditorium and disappeared through it.

Doreen yawned and climbed down off Caitlyn's lap. She grabbed Ali's hand and they started following Myriah towards the door leading to the hallway to the south exit with the rest of the group. Caitlyn was thinking fast. She knew they'd just be evacuated to another building similar to this one where they'd be separated once again. If she wanted to get them all out as a group, this might be the only opportunity they got. The swarm slamming into this building may turn out to be a blessing in disguise for them. Or, at least she was thinking they needed to bet on it being a good thing.

Caitlyn reached out and grabbed Ali's hand. She called out quietly for Myriah to stop as well. When she had all their attention, she told them they were going to go the opposite direction. All of them looked like they were going to question her on it, so she just picked Doreen up and spun on her heel to leave. Doreen snuggled into her and Caitlyn told her to just go along with whatever she said if they got stopped. Myriah grabbed Ali's hand and walked up beside Caitlyn. She looked like she wanted to say something but was holding her tongue.

"Hey. You girls need to follow the main group towards the south exit." The guard who'd been with the principal had walked over to them.

"We just need to run back to the room really quick. Our little sister left her picture of our mom and dad on her bed. It's all we have that shows them. It'll only take a us a minute to get there and back. We'll be fast." Cailyn responded. She felt Myriah's appraising eyes on her. The guard seemed to take it in stride.

"Ok. You have a few minutes before everyone makes it to the door anyway. Go now and hurry back. If you don't see the picture as soon as you get there don't waste any time looking for it." The guard looked like he may be thinking of tagging along with them. More gunfire had him turning and running out of the room towards the source of the gunfire though.

Caitlyn led the girls out into the eerily lit hallway and set a fast pace towards the exit on the opposite side of the building from where the principal was headed.

"Are you sure about this Cait? We're basically running towards a mob of Zombies. I want to get the hell out of this freakshow place too, but this may not be the best time to do it." Myriah asked Caitlyn as they walked. The flashing red light given off by the emergency lighting system making this place look like a haunted house. The sounds of screaming and weapons fire was getting louder as they moved towards the north exit adding to the haunted house effect.

"We may not get another chance." Caitlyn replied as they kept moving. Caitlyn's insides were twisting all up. Now that she'd gotten her sisters to follow her out into the hallway, she was second guessing the whole idea. Why had she thought this would be a good idea? Now they'd never get another chance to all be together and make a break for it. She was sure the principal would find out they'd left. Maybe if they turned around right now, they could get back before they were missed too much and in the confusion it might all blow over.

It looked like Myriah was going to say something else when the door at the far end of the long hallway flew open. Sunlight suddenly bathed that end of the hall. The screams of the damned trying to get in and the sounds of the weapons of the defenders rose to a fever pitch. It was impossible to hear anything with those doors open. The silhouettes of men backing into the door were visible from where they stood. The men backing in were firing their weapons as fast as they could to try and hold back the onslaught of the swarming Zombies. In the few seconds Caitlyn stood still taking it in she saw one man get pulled into the mob and disappear. The other two turned and started sprinting in their direction.

A massive flash at the end of the hallway almost blinded her. Luckily, she'd been looking at the opposite wall as she started turning and yelling for Myriah and Ali to start running the other way. She ran along behind Myriah and Ali down the hall. Doreen bouncing on her shoulder. The noise in the hallway had reached a fevered pitch. She couldn't hear anything except gunfire and Zombie screeches. More grenades went off behind them as Myriah began trying the first door to the auditorium. It was locked. Caitlyn hit her in the shoulder to tell her to follow her and ran to the other door that should open into the auditorium.

The second door swung open easily. They all rushed into the large empty room. Without breaking stride, they ran hard for the door that would take them to the south exit. They left the room just as two of the guards came rushing in and locked the second door. The two guards quickly turned and ran in the same direction as the girls towards the south exit. They were stopped when they got in the hallway by the need to turn and fire off some rounds at some Zombies who'd managed to work their way around the building into the south hallway.

Caitlyn and the girls ran out of the south exit right as the guard at the door was shutting it. It was the same guard who'd allowed them to go back to the room to grab the picture Caitlyn had lied about.

"What took you so long? Well. Let me get this shut and try to wedge something into it really quick then I'll take you to the boat." The guard said as he looked around for something to keep the door shut. He spotted a big trashcan and dragged that over to the door. He put it in front of the door then had the girls follow him through an open gate in the chain link fence up a small dirt pile into the brush on the other side of it. He'd taken a few seconds to secure the gate before leading them up the hill.

Caitlyn and the girls scampered up the hill after him. Briars and weeds catching at them and slowing them down. Their long hair was not a benefit when trying to move through weeds that reached easily over their heads. They ended up on a path that took them down to a small clearing. The principal and a few other people were standing around listening to the approaching screeches of the Zombies. A pontoon boat was pulling into the small dock at the edge of the clearing.

"There you guys are! I heard you wandered off and I was hoping you'd make it back ok." The principal knelt down to give Ali and Doreen each a hug. Then she gave a wary looking Myriah a hug as well before pulling an asp out of her belt and facing a panting, sweaty Caitlyn. She flicked her wrist and the metal rod extended to its full length. Caitlyn saw what she was doing but was too slow to react as the principal swung the asp and connected with a solid blow to Caitlyn's arm.

Caitlyn winced in pain and launched herself at the principal. She didn't have any weapons but if she could get close enough, she was going to rip the bitches eyes out of her sockets. The principal swung the asp again and connected with the side of Caitlyn's head. Caitlyn went to her knees in pain. Her ear split open and bleeding. She could feel the blood running down the side of her head.

Myriah jumped in to help her sister and was slammed to the ground by the guard. He kicked her in the stomach hard and she doubled up in pain. Caitlyn looked up as the principal pulled a pistol and aimed it at her head. Ignoring the pain in her head Caitlyn snarled out a challenge and threw herself at the principal.

Shots rang out. Myriah tried to sit up but the pain in her stomach was too much for her. Tears leaked out of her eyes as she gasped for breath. Tears of sorrow for her sister. Tears for herself now that she'd be alone in this world. A man in camouflage came over and picked her up. The man threw her across his shoulder then stooped down and grabbed Doreen. Myriah watched while the other guard flung Caitlyn across his shoulders and then started running into the weeds away from the pontoon boat.

Ali jogged along with the two men carrying her adopted sisters. She ignored the dead and bloody bodies lying all around them in the clearing. The principals dead eyes stared sightlessly into the sun peeking down through the foliage above her. The driver of the pontoon boat slumped lifelessly over the steering wheel. The brief firefight had attracted the attention of the Zombie mob swarming the base. A large group of the Zombies broke off and started heading that way along the outside of the fence.

Chapter 29: Trailer Trash

He couldn't find a car that'd run. The numbness from his very last pain pill was wearing off. Every step he took it felt like someone was jamming hundreds of red-hot needles into his feet. He was dying of thirst, but his throat hurt so bad he could barely drink. He needed to find a place to crash. He needed help getting better. Kyler knew his best chance was to make it back to the base where trained medical personnel could take care of him. Assuming the base had survived the massive Zombie train he'd lured by it.

He was feverish. He thought he could see the asphalt coming up out of the road and buckling in little waves. He had enough of himself left in his head to understand that he needed help, or he was going to die. He stopped walking and looked around. There was nothing. He was in the middle of a road surrounded by a million trees. A small road through the backcountry like any of a thousand other small roads scattered across the state. The kind of road you drove mindlessly down in the old days with one hand fiddling with the radio dial as you searched for something to take your mind off how boring the drive was.

Kyler reflected on his situation as he trudged down the middle of the road. He decided he'd take boredom over excitement any day in this new normal. Excitement typically meant someone, or something was trying to kill you. Normal humans had been replaced at the top of the food chain by their infected brothers and sisters. The strap of his rifle was heavy. It rubbed on the red, blistered, angry looking skin on the back of his neck. If Kyler had bothered to look in a mirror, he'd have been shocked at just how bad he looked.

His skin was covered in little blisters everywhere that'd been exposed when he was in the woods by the fire. His clothes were hanging off of him. His feet were covered in the ridiculous flip flop sock covering he'd made for himself. This covering had now been augmented with all kinds of briars, leaves and dirt. He couldn't remember the last time he'd shaved or brushed his teeth or put on deodorant. The rough beard that was growing in on his face was patchy due to the burns he was covered in.

He kept walking. Every step wracking his body with pain. He wanted to just lie down in the road and die but his pride wouldn't let him. An hour later he spotted a turnoff coming up. Without giving it a ton of thought he took the small road that branched off into the woods when he got to it. The road led to the 'Happy Springs Trailer Park'. Kyler wasn't sure if the place was truly happy or not, but he figured the more trailers the more likely he'd be able to find one with supplies he could use. What he needed was rest, a few gallons of water and then to find a working car he could drive out of here. This walking crap had to go.

The first trailer door he opened hit him with a stench so putrid he fell off the stairs trying to back away from it. He lay on his back in a weed covered gravel driveway vomiting. He hadn't eaten or drank anything in a while, so he was pretty surprised at how much he was able to puke up. He lay in the driveway for what seemed like forever. His own vomit slowly drying on his shirt. He heard some large rodents or cats or something shuffling around under the car in the driveway. He hadn't even bothered trying to see if the car would run. It looked like it'd been out of commission before the apocalypse had ever even become a thing. A lime green Sentra sitting on four flat tires. It was the perfect complement to any trailers gravel driveway. He wondered why it wasn't up on blocks sitting in the front yard yet.

He painfully got to his feet and limped around to the front yard then back out to the road that wound its way through the trailer park. Everything was overgrown and dilapidated looking. Some of the trailer homes had been tipped over by some storm at some point and now they just leaned precariously over or were actually laying on their sides. Whatever state mandated tornado wind straps or whatever they were supposed to have obviously not standing the test of time against mother nature. He limped past a couple of trailers that looked pretty beat down. Passing them up he headed towards a double wide that looked like it might actually have kept the rain on the outside of it.

He hobbled up the cobble stone path from the driveway to the front porch of the double-wide. The stairs leading up to the door were made of concrete blocks. They may have been neat and orderly at some point but now they were crooked and covered in weeds. It looked like there was a pretty decent gap between the top step and the door itself. He figured he would deal with that once he got to the top of the stairs. Slowly and carefully he walked up to the top of the stairs. He reached out and turned the knob, but the door was locked. Of course, he thought. He'd hate for anything to be easy.

He took out his knife and jammed it in the side of the door moving it down until he popped the lock and the door opened up a few inches. It stopped abruptly when he tried to push it farther and he realized it must be stuck on a chain lock on the inside. Most chain locks he'd found out didn't stand up to a solid kick on the door. The screws that held them in were typically short little screws. They'd rip out as soon as a decent amount of pressure was placed on them. Balancing on the rickety top step he realized there was no way he was going to be able to actually kick the door given the state of his feet.

With the door kicking option out he settled for pummeling the door with his fists and cussing. The cussing wasn't all that poetic sounding since his throat still hadn't healed from sucking down all the smoke in the forest fire he'd barely survived. All he wanted to do was find a bottled water and a couch to crash on. He didn't think that was too much to ask. After all he'd been through, he really felt the cosmos could give him that gift. Getting more and more pissed at the door he started hitting it harder and harder. He was thinking about putting a few rounds into it when the chain lock finally gave. He heard a zing noise as it pulled loose from the door jam.

Feeling like he'd finally gotten a win he took a step into the trailer to check it out. He'd made so much noise beating his way in that he knew any Zombies inside would've already made their presence known trying to get at him. All the physical exertion on top of his weakened state had also made him extremely dizzy. He knew he should clear the place better but settled for just stepping in and hoping for the best.

The baseball bat hit him right in the nose sending him stumbling painfully backwards out of the house. His foot got caught on the door jamb and he tumbled backwards down the hard-concrete stairs. His body exploded with new levels of pain. His face was covered in his own blood. His burnt skin was protesting painfully about being stretched so much again. He'd just fallen out of the last trailer less than twenty minutes ago. Looking up he saw a dark-skinned woman come out the door holding an aluminum baseball bat in her hands. Behind her another woman was staring down at him.

"Finish it off! Before it gets back up." The woman in the shadows of the trailer was saying excitedly to the dark-skinned woman holding the baseball bat. The woman walked carefully down the stairs holding the bat over her head. She looked like she was ready to land the killing blow. What part of Kyler holding an M-16 did she not understand? He had a pistol belted right to his side as well. Fighting back the urge to puke he worked the M-16 around to aim at the woman.

She stared at him in shock as he tried to get words out.

"Are you infected? You look infected?" She asked him.

Kyler slid backwards away from her carefully keeping the gun pointed at her. He slowly and carefully spoke to the two trying his best to enunciate every word.

"I'm alive. Not infected. Was in a forest fire and got hurt. I'm not infected. Do you have water?" He asked this last part a little desperately. His throat was on fire. He needed to quench it now.

The two women whispered to one another then the one came out with a gallon jug of water. She handed it to the dark-skinned woman who walked it down the stairs and handed it to Kyler. Making the decision to trust them Kyler let the M-16 dangle off its strap while he took a big swig of the water out of the jug. While he was drinking the woman swung her bat one handed right into the side of his head putting him down on the ground.

He woke up on a couch. He remembered wishing for water and a couch and thinking the cosmos owed him at least that much. He laughed out loud thinking the cosmos must've decided to teach him a lesson. He'd gotten his couch and he vaguely remembered getting some water as well but at what cost? He'd reached a level of pain in his head that he wouldn't have thought possible if someone had tried describing it to him.

"Good. You're awake." One of the women said to him.

"Yeah. Great." Kyler mumbled back. Even the act of mumbling hurt.

"We've got pills. We can help you out with the pain you're in. Tell us who you are and what you're doing out here first though." The blond woman said. Kyler stared at her dazedly. What she was asking may seem straightforward enough but the two words he'd mumbled earlier seemed to have sapped all his strength. No way was he getting out the dissertation they were demanding.

"Are you of the people?" the dark-skinned woman asked.

Kyler shook his head no then decided it actually hurt less just to say no. He had no idea what the woman was talking about.

"Are you of the brotherhood?" She asked him next. This one was a little harder for him to answer. He knew he was getting setup to be in the brotherhood but as of now he was in more of an intern stage. He had to attend some more training and accomplish some sort of good deed or something to be admitted. It was all a little fuzzy in his head. There was also the issue that these two women may hate the brotherhood. He had no way of knowing. He decided to just go for it.

"Initiate. Plebe. Uhm. Intern for it." He stuttered out feeling like an idiot. He'd been told the correct information, but he couldn't seem to remember any of that right now. Something he said seemed to relax the two women though.

"I'm Kia and this young lady over here is Diamond." The dark-skinned woman had identified herself as Kia and the blond as Diamond. "Before you make any stupid jokes about stage names those are our scavenger names."

Kyler nodded as little as he could to avoid the pain. He had no idea what she was referring to or why he'd make fun of their names.

"I'm Kyler." He managed to say finally.

"Ok Kyler. What are you doing out here? You're not making a run for it are you?" Kia asked. She was staring at his eyes trying to catch him in a lie.

"I turned the Zombies on the road to the north." Kyler choked out. That seemed to impress both the women.

"Alright then Kyler the intern. Assuming you are who you say you are, and you did what you just said you did you're ok in our books. Luckily for you we happen to be out here on a scavenging mission for opiates. The preferred drug to keep the people in their place. It also happens to be the drug you look like you are going to need a bunch of to get through what must be some really bad pain."

"Yeah, his face must really hurt since it's killing me." Diamond said as she came back with some crushed-up pills in a glass of water for him. She tilted the glass and helped him drink it. Within a few minutes he was passed back out. Diamond soaked a t-shirt she found in one of the drawers in the trailer in some cool water and used it to dab at the blisters covering Kyler's exposed skin.

"You think he's really an initiate?" Kia asked while Diamond worked to try and clean up Kyler as much as she could.

"I don't see why he would've made all that up or even known that term if he was lying. The mission seems to jive with the fire and all the Zombies and everything too. We've collected enough pills to buy us some family time back on base anyway. We drop him off at the outpost on our way home and if he is who he says he is we'll get even more of a bump. If he's lying, then they'll deal with him and we'll still get a bump."

"Works for me." Diamond said and went back to dabbing Kyler's head with the wet shirt. Her mind already calculating how much family time she'd be able to negotiate with the pills they'd already collected and the possible initiate they'd rescued. More than anything in this world she lived for the time she could spend playing with her baby sister between scavenging missions. Knowing that the bigger the haul she brought back the better her sisters life and the more time she'd be allowed to see her. If she failed to bring back what was requested, then the pills they'd stockpiled would be used to addict her sister. That was the way the brotherhood had figured out to compel her and the other scavengers to work harder to bring back what was needed.

Chapter 30: Ohana

Randy jogged along behind Tony and the out of breath guard who'd come to get them. The guard led them into a room at the end of the hall that served as the armory. A couple of frazzled looking older men were handing out kits to the soldiers rolling into the room.

"You both know how to handle M-16s and Glocks?" One of the men behind the counter asked.

"Yes sir." Randy answered. He nodded again when asked if they'd ever used grenades or flash bangs before.

"What's a flash bang do?" Randy asked Tony as they were putting on their gear on the opposite side of the room.

"Based on the SWAT movies I've seen they flash followed by a loud bang." Tony answered. He was loading up the two spare magazines he'd been handed wondering why they didn't just go ahead and make sure all the magazines were loaded all the time. When you needed a loaded magazine, you needed it right then. He shook his head at the imagined military logic behind not having this chore completed already.

"When you guys are ready head to the north entrance. The north entrance guards will show you where to go. You'll need to follow orders and maintain operational silence as much as you can for as long as you can." The guard who'd brought them there disappeared out the door. That left them both sitting there loaded up with weapons and faced with a dilemma.

They walked out of the armory and headed towards the north entrance at a fast walk.

"We trying to die defending this place?" Tony asked.

"I could care less about this place." Randy answered. "What I care about is my kids who are somewhere in here. If we need to risk our lives defending this place so they can escape or be safe, then I'm down. We see a way to get out of here and take them with us then the rest of this place can go to hell."

"Cool. Here we go then. Get your game face on and don't die." Tony replied as he slowly pushed on the bar on the door at the north entrance to exit the building. The door let them out into a concrete stairwell that had another door leading to the outside. The little room had a few men standing around in it. They were gearing up and looking like they were ready to go mix it up with the Zombies outside. One of the men was holding a small walkie talkie with an earpiece and seemed to be intently listening to something.

"Ok men. You two new guys listen up." The man waited until he had everyone's attention before laying out the plan.

The plan sucked.

"You want us to open the door and run out into a Zombie mob and try to distract them so everyone else can sneak out the other exit?" Randy asked out loud. Everyone stared at him. He realized he'd said it out loud in a tone of voice that didn't lend itself to the type of proper military respect he should probably be showing up the chain of command.

"Yes, I do. This building has plenty of windows and the lookouts we have on the roof already verified the Zombies are starting to break through them. Somehow the infected bastards know there's a lot of snack sized humans inside and they're not going to stop until they get in. So, we're going to distract them. Let's not spend a lot of time thinking about this. Let's open the door and do some killing."

Then the guy pushed the door open and ran out of it with everyone following him. Tony and Randy stared at each other for a second before exiting the space much more carefully than the other men had. Outside the staircase the world had gone insane. The rest of the guards had formed a skirmish line and were sweeping in towards the Zombies.

An attack formation like that was intended to break the enemy mentally and send them scurrying away in all directions. Mindless Zombies didn't react the way normal people would to the same tactics. Mindless Zombies just saw humans and heard noise and ran towards it to rip and consume. The Zombies ran teeth first into a hail storm of bullets. The pile of bodies quickly growing to a height that was making it very difficult for more Zombies to get at the humans attacking them. Tony and Randy joined the line taking shots at the charging Zombies.

Despite not having any knowledge of military tactics the Zombies had perfected the flanking and encircling maneuvers. They had these down mostly because there were so many of them that this is how they always ended up winning against military might. Tony bumped Randy in the shoulder and pointed behind them. A massive force of Zombies was emerging from the woods where they'd broken through the lowest bidder provided chain link fence that separated them from the road. The Zombies were screeching in anger as they charged the human battle line. There was no way the small group of men were going to be able to hold the position and get out of there alive.

They tried to move back towards the stairwell in an orderly fashion. That lasted for about ten seconds before the men noticed the Zombies seemed to be getting closer to them than the stairwell was getting at which point, they all broke and ran for it. The man who'd led them into his mess tried to assemble a couple of guys to hold the line while the others retreated. He physically gabbed one guy and tried to make him stand in the rear and guard the retreat. Tony saw the man punch the other one and then he lost sight of them as a couple of Zombies sprang on top of both of the fighting men.

Tony and Randy made it to the door simply because they'd been the last to come out the doors. Since they'd been the last to come out the doors and because they'd tried hard to make their shots count, they still had full magazines left for the retreating portion of the ill-fated attempt to distract the Zombies. Of the patrol that'd gone out only one man made it back into the stairwell with Tony and Randy. He came in the door right after Randy and then got pulled right back out by a massive Zombie. Tony shot that Zombie in the head but another one jumped in and bit into the screaming man's stomach while others started biting any other exposed flesh they could find.

Tony and Randy found themselves staring in a daze at the fellow guard having his skin ripped off his body right in front of them. They snapped out of it when the Zombies decided to notice they were standing there as well. The Zombies charged in while Tony and Randy opened fire. They burned through a magazine apiece backing their way into the door to the main building. Tony fumbled with a flash bang and tossed it into the stairwell. They tried to use the confusion to get the door to the stairwell shut.

It turned out they'd mostly confused themselves with the flashbang. The noise and bright light attracted even more Zombies. They both had to let up on their triggers since their eye sockets seemed to have been burned out of their skulls. Flashbangs were no joke. Especially in an enclosed space like that. Ears ringing and eyes burning they stumbled down the hall away from the Zombies. They took turns being in the rear shooting at the approaching Zombies.

Ahead of them a group of kids pulled open the door into the auditorium on the first floor. Vision slowly returning they rushed into the room behind the kids and immediately began looking for some way to block the doors. They'd locked them when they pulled them closed. After a quick search turned up nothing better to secure the doors with, they turned to follow the other small group out of the exit heading towards the south exit from the building.

They ran out into the hallway and immediately heard screeching from down the hall. Neither Tony nor Randy were going to race past a group of kids and let Zombies take them out. They opened fire on the Zombies running in ones and twos down the hallway towards them. After a minute of shooting Tony figured the other group should be almost out the south entrance by now. He punched Randy in the arm, and they turned and sprinted for the exit from the warehouse.

Someone had blocked the door with a heavy barrel of some sort. It took Randy and Tony a minute to get around that including having to turn and shoot a few more Zombies who'd gotten way too close for comfort. They finally got it open enough they could squeeze through. Once they were through, they turned and focused on getting the door shut again as Zombies slammed into it from the other side. Zombie arms and fingers were sticking out the crack in the door as they tried wedging the barrel back in front to hold it.

Randy tried bashing the fingers sticking out but since the Zombies could care less about getting their fingers broken it did no good. Not seeing where the rest of the people had gone after they came out this south exit Randy motioned to Tony to let go of the door and they'd haul ass to climb the fence and get over the little weed covered dirt mound on the other side of it. Tony nodded and Randy held up three fingers and did a countdown. When the last finger went down, they dropped everything and ran for the fence. If the Zombies pouring out saw them, they'd be overtaken and eaten within minutes.

Not wanting to stick around to find out if they'd been discovered or not after hurdling the fence, they started moving through the weeds away from the building. They went down a narrow well used path for about forty feet before they heard voices up ahead. They carefully moved forward on the trail listening to the voices in front of them. It sounded like someone welcoming someone back then there was some grunts and the sound of someone crying out in pain.

Exiting the trail into the edge of a clearing Tony saw a pontoon boat pulling in, a girl being pinned to the ground by a guard, and an older girl fixing to be shot in the head by the principal. The next thing he saw was the principals head explode as Randy emptied a magazine worth of ammunition into the clearing. Tony joined in as well. He helped kill everyone in the clearing who wasn't a child. When everyone looked dead, he helped Randy throw the kids on their backs so they could get them out of there before either the Zombies or more guards showed up.

Randy was completely shell shocked. He'd gone through more emotions in the past two minutes than he'd have even thought possible if you asked him. He could hear the Zombies screeching in the distance and knew they'd be pounding into this clearing in minutes. He had to get his girls out of there. He still couldn't believe he'd found them. When he'd walked into the clearing and seen Doreen standing there his heart had almost burst with love and happiness. He'd wanted to pick her up and hold her so much that he almost missed the rest of the drama taking place in the small open space beside the lake.

Glancing to the side he'd seen Myriah spread out on the ground getting kicked hard in the stomach by some guy who was going to die for that kick. Then he saw the woman aiming a pistol at Caitlyn's face. His brain was cutoff at that point and his red-hot rage took over as he blew that bitches head off before working the stream of lead through every other person in the clearing. Some distant part of his brain in that moment knew that Tony was standing with him and shooting as well.

The screeches were getting way too close. He worked with Tony to get the girls out of there. He assumed the extra kid they'd picked up was the Ali that Zoey had told him about. She seemed to be the only one able to walk so he had her follow them as he led the group out of the clearing and into the dense brush hoping to lose any pursuers. His mind was whirling as well calculating the odds that they wouldn't even be missed. Especially if the Zombies got to the clearing and did some snacking before anyone showed up from the main boat to see what was going on with the pontoon boat that should've returned with passengers form the clearing.

For right now they needed to get far enough from the Zombie mob and the clearing to be out of danger. He didn't want to go so far that they got spotted though. There was still a lot of the brotherhood around here and everything could go to hell in a heartbeat. He was mindful they could have drones flying or men standing on buildings to monitor everything around here. He wanted to find somewhere to relax and lick their wounds until nightfall then move under cover of darkness. It was killing him not to just take off sprinting right now to try and get the whole family reunited. He was terrified something would happen to Kelly and Zoey while they were away. He couldn't wait to see the look on Kelly's face when they came waltzing in with the girls in tow.

Chapter 31: Honey I'm Home

Kelly rolled the dice and moved her character around the board again. Her character was a red checker and the board was drawn on the floor of the kitchen in red sharpie. Zoey still giggled incessantly every time she landed on the slide that was connected to the drawing of a toilet. Kelly loved to hear that laughter. She'd gone too long without the laughter of her girls in her life. The long journey down from Rhode Island had taken a toll on her and Zoey's laughter was just the medicine she needed to feel like her old self again.

Zoey laughing buoyed her spirits, but it also threatened to pull her back into her despair. She had three other daughters and a husband that were still missing. She'd hated the plan that Tony and Randy had come up with right from the beginning. She hated even calling it a plan. It had been more like a hail Mary last resort. She'd only supported it because she knew at this point in the game a Hail Mary was needed. If the girls disappeared now, they may never find them again.

Kelly hadn't really been tracking the days on a calendar but now that Randy was gone, she found herself obsessed with it. The red sharpie she'd used to draw the faux chutes and ladders game on the kitchen floor for her and Zoey was also used to track the days Tony and Randy had been gone. She lay awake at night trying to work out how many days it would take for those two to get captured and then somehow work their way into the standing guard at the facility then get the girls and escape. There were so many moving pieces and so much that could go wrong that she kicked herself for ever agreeing to let them go in the first place.

The one thing she found solitude in was that she still hadn't been able to come up with a better plan. When you have no real intel then you have to go with the best plan you can come up with. She figured they must've gotten captured at least or they'd have come back by now. So that part of the plan should be in motion. She drove herself crazy trying to estimate how many days it'd take to go from prisoner to worker to escapee. All assuming the girls were even in the same facility and assuming they kept all the girls together.

She tried hard not to think of the massively obese elephant in the room. What did she do if they never came back? She couldn't just sit in this moldy house playing fake chutes and ladders until the world finally collapsed around them. They were rationing food and water but at some point, they'd need to leave to gather more supplies if they were going to stay. She was thinking she'd need to go on a scavenging trip within the next day or two. She was paranoid about leaving the house though. If something happened to her while she was out who'd take care of Zoey? What if a Zombie got in the house while she was out and went after Zoey? What if she attracted the Zombies back to the house and they ended up having to abandon the house? How would Tony and Randy find them then when they finally escaped and came back with the rest of the girls?

How long should she wait here with Zoey before giving up and leaving? That was the question weighing heaviest on her mind. She couldn't stay here too long scavenging, or the brotherhood would end up spotting them and they'd become prisoners too. They had enough food for another day at least so she decided to just bask in the joy that was Zoey playing the game they'd made up together and worry about it the next night.

They were on the fourth game of the day and Zoey was telling Kelly all about how Eric had helped save their lives when there was a tapping at the window. Kelly immediately put the glowstick they'd been using to play the Chutes and Ladders game with into her pocket and grabbed her nine-millimeter handgun off the counter. She motioned for Zoey to stay behind the counter as she moved towards the window.

Her heart was beating fast with worry and anticipation. To avoid getting shot in the face by knocking on the front door or the sliding glass door they'd come up with a system when returning to one of the houses after being gone for whatever reason. They'd knock lightly on one window then do exactly five taps on another window. Kelly knew it must be either Tony or Randy outside. She'd grabbed the gun because you could never be too careful. They'd come up with rules and those rules had kept them alive when everyone around them kept dying. Her heart beating out of her chest was because she didn't know who to expect to see on the other side of the window.

Not bothering to try peeling back the curtains she'd taped to the window frame she opened the front door instead. She stuck her head out and saw a shadowy figure coming around the hedge towards her. Her heart dropped only seeing one person. That must mean either Tony or Randy hadn't made it back. Then another figure emerged from around the hedge carrying a childlike figure. He put the little girl down that he was carrying, and she immediately made a bee line for the front door.

"Mommy!" Doreen yelled completely forgetting about keeping quiet outside at the sight of her mom. Kelly scooped up her little love and carried her in the house so any more noises out of her wouldn't bring every Zombie in town to their family reunion.

One by one the others stomped in. Zoey came out from around the counter astounding a shocked Myriah and Caitlyn. Caitlyn lost it and fell to her knees sobbing with joy and relief. Tony stood off to the side taking it all in. He was proud to have been a part of all this. Zoey whispered something to Kelly and Tony watched as Kelly went to the girl standing shyly off to the side.

"Hi Ali. Zoey's told us all about you and your brave uncle Eric." Kelly said squatting down in front of the girl. Ali just nodded shyly looking lost and alone. Randy walked over to join them.

"We know you've lost a lot since this all started. We wanted to let you know for everything you've done to be a friend to Zoey and the other girls and for everything your uncle did to help we want you to consider yourself one of our daughters. If you'd like that?" Randy said and held out his arms to the young girl. She sprang into his arms knocking him over backwards and buried her face in his neck crying with the surge of emotions she wasn't able to handle.

Tony walked over and hugged each of the girls as well. After everyone had hugged and cried and been checked over for injuries it was dawn and time to go to bed.

"Alright, everyone needs to try and get some sleep. Once the sun goes down, we're going to work on getting out of Florida and away from the crazies running this place. I want everyone to keep quiet today and be ready to move out at first night." Kelly rolled her eyes at his play on words, but she couldn't keep the grin off her face. Randy wondered if any of them were actually going to be able to sleep enough to move out that night. He didn't think they had much choice though. They wouldn't get another chance if the brotherhood located them. They'd be taken out in the street and shot gangland style. As far as Randy was concerned it was time to find out how California had made it through this whole Zombie thing.

Epilogue

Amos pulled the sheet back from the half-eaten face of Senator Wilcox's older sister. He'd landed at the Sanford airport the same morning as the swarm had hit the building. The swarm had killed way too many of his brotherhood guards. Way worse was the loss of the sister though. Her body had been gnawed on by the Zombies, but the actual cause of death didn't require a coroner with a doctorate degree in pathology to figure out. The big hole in the back of her head lined up well with the smaller entry hole in her cheek.

Amos had his men working on figuring out who'd died during the swarming and who was missing. So far, he knew the girls they'd picked up most recently for the bride program were missing and he knew that their father and another man had been given weapons and asked to help defend the facility against the swarm. He remembered the two men from their run in on the toll road. It looked like he should've shot them down right then and there instead of assuming the Zombies would do the job for him.

He gave orders to get the drones up and send out patrols. He gave orders to alert the other regional commanders. The senator was going to want pay back for the death of his sister. Amos knew since the principal had died in his region the senator would hold him responsible. He either needed to find the people who'd actually done it or he'd be the one left to bleed out in a pen full of hungry Zombies.

Authors Notes

Thank you so much for joining me on this journey through the apocalypse with Randy and crew. I'm watching the movie of their adventures in my head and trying to capture as much of it as I can in these books. People ask me what is going to happen to them next and I honestly know about as much as you do until the story actually unfolds in my mind's eye. As I type and picture what's going on in that world things can change in a heartbeat. People die that I don't want to see go but if it's true to the story then it needs to happen that way. The characters take on a life of their own and each one does things their own way.

I come from a long line of men serving in the military. My grandfather was a Naval Gunner's Mate at D-Day. My dad was a force recon scout sniper in the USMC before getting out and serving in the USCG for 20 years. My brother served as an enlisted 'grunt' then as an officer in the USMC after attending college. I did my time haze grey and underway on a Nuclear Cruiser. People in the military definitely have a different mindset and bring different skills to the table that I think would better enable them to survive in a world like this one. I also think that same mentality could be abused by superiors to make them look down on the very people they should be protecting.

"The only thing needed for evil to win is for good men to stand by and do nothing."

I'm looking forward to the next novel in this series. Seeing how Kyler copes with learning the truths about the brotherhood he's joining. Seeing how far Randy can get his family from the craziness of that same brotherhood. Thank you again for reading this far and I hope to see you again in the next book!

Ready to keep reading? Click here for the next book in the Zombies! series!

Other Books by R S Merritt

If you are enjoying the Zombies! Series please check out some of these other books by R S Merritt:

The Zournal Series!

Steve wakes up one morning after a horrible couple of weeks in which he's lost his girlfriend, his job, his savings and the majority of his self-respect. Dragging himself out of bed he sleepily wanders over to the window with a warm bottled water and a handful of Advil. Looking out of his apartment window he sees people running around crazily and a bunch of burning shrubbery. He decides to go back to sleep and see if it all goes away. When he wakes up the next time it turns out the view from his fourth-floor apartment wasn't a nightmare. Armed with a blunt samurai sword and some stolen steak knives he ventures out into the fray.

These aren't your standard Zombies, but Steve isn't your standard Zombie fighter either. Join him in book 1 as he heads out to check on his parents and try to survive in a world that's gone crazy...

Book 1 - "It all started"

Book 2 - "Cruising The 'Poc"

Book 3 - "Scorched Earth"

Book 4 - "Reap What You Sow"

Book 5 - "Feeling Lucky?"

Book 6 - "The Final Countdown"

Over 2,000 years ago the Xandians were forced to flee their world by a horde made up of dark forces that had spread throughout the universes like a plague. The Xandian king and a handful of nobles stood alone on the wall against wave after wave of the horde forces as the last remnants of the Xandian people fled through a portal to the planet of earth. They've been fighting and protecting this planet from being overrun by evil ever since.

The horde continues to grow stronger as the Xandians have gradually had their forces diminished. When their queen is killed their last hope switches to the potential powers of an eleven-year-old boy whom no one has told may be the greatest magical force of all time. The day comes quickly for him to embrace his birth right and fight to save not only his own people but all of the people of earth and ultimately of the universe itself.

Son of the Keeper: Book 1: "The Principles of Magic"

Son of the Keeper: Book 2: "The Weight of the Crown"

Son of the Keeper: Book 3: "The Fate of the World"

Made in United States
Orlando, FL
24 June 2022

19117459R00207